PICTURE THIS

MARRY THE SCOT, #4

JOLIE VINES

WWW.JOLIEVINES.COM/NEWSLETTER

PRAISE FOR THE MARRY THE SCOT SERIES

Paula - "I loved this book! It had all that I would expect with **hot Scots and rambling castles.** I had to giggle when I discovered that I was reading this book with my own manufactured Scottish brogue! Can't wait for more."

J. Saman, Bestselling author - "Jolie Vines has fast become a **one-click author** for me!"

Zoe Ashwood, author - "I'm impatiently waiting for the next book - I just know it'll be **another sizzling story** from Jolie Vines."

Viper Spaulding - "(Hero) is an amazing work of art, highly recommended for anyone looking for a **modern-day Highlander to swoon over.**"

Chikap09 - "I swear, every time I pick up a Jolie Vines book I think: this is him, **my favorite hero**, no one will be able to top him. And then I read the next book and the process begins again."

Pam Graber - "If you haven't read the other books in the series Marry the Scot, you should really start with Storm the Castle, then move on to Love Most, Say Least before diving into Hero. **I cannot wait to see what Ally and Wasp get up** to in their stories! I've enjoyed the first three books immensely!"

Carmen Davis - "Jolie Vines is an amazingly talented writer. I am so **completely obsessed with this series** and so madly in love with the characters. Each book gets better than the last and when you start off with a 5 star? There just aren't enough stars. I can't wait for the next book in this series and anything else Jolie Vines writes."

Editing by Emmy at Studio ENP

Proofreading by Zoe Ashwood

Cover design by Natasha Snow www.natashasnowdesigns.com

❀ Created with Vellum

To my husband. The best photographer around, and my best friend

BLURB

Picture This (Marry the Scot, #4)

The only man she loves is the one she can't have.

Taylor has lived with threats and blackmail her entire life. Either she behaves like the perfect, dutiful daughter, or gives up her most desperate wish. With her father's election on the horizon, the pressure is on to appear as the all-American family, including her marrying the son of the next president. Her final month of freedom could be her last chance of happiness.

Wasp has worked hard, building his name as a photographer, but he's never forgotten the woman who first stole his heart. At a red-carpet photo shoot, his heart races when he sees Taylor. No way does he expect her to be naked in his room within the hour.

One hot kiss leads to an indecent proposal and a cross-European bucket list tour. But Wasp is no longer the boy

Taylor once knew. The clock might be ticking, but her hot Scot has his own plans. Even if he has to choose between love and his career.

The heat between them is enough to set the world alight, or burn everything they care about.

If you adore second chance love stories with sensuous chemistry and a gorgeous backdrop, *Picture This* is perfect to sweep you away.

1
———

THE QUIET ONE

*W*asp

The security team swarmed, ushering us through a side door into the Metropolitan Museum of Art. Away from the red-carpeted celebrity entrance at the front of the building.

Josie, my mentor, and the thorn in my side, heaved a sigh. "When this job is done, I'm drowning myself in a Mojito then going to bed for a week."

I was with her on that—the going home part. Tonight was my last assignment in the US, and tomorrow, I'd fly to Scotland. As great an opportunity as the past couple of months had been, my heart hurt every time I thought of seeing my family again.

Yet there was one specific draw that this final job had on me. A name I'd spotted on the guest list of actors and politicians. A lass I hadn't seen in years.

One who made me catch my breath at the memories alone.

A uniformed man, bigger than most but an inch shy of

my height, pointed to my camera bag. "Sir, I need you to open that for inspection."

"Aye, but watch what you poke with that stick," I grouched, exposing the lenses and camera bodies, frowning deeper when the guard jostled my kit. Decent photographic equipment cost a fortune, and most of mine was borrowed.

Cleared, we entered a corridor that led to a cavernous, pillar-lined hall—the staging ground for tonight's glittering charity gala. Artwork adorned the walls, interspersed with elaborate floral decorations and a blue lighting scheme.

Automatically, I scanned the faces, searching for *her*.

For Taylor. The woman who'd taken my virginity five years ago, when I'd been a lad, and who I kept sleeping with, somehow, on the rare occasions we saw each other.

Even thinking her name had my groin tightening.

"I'm going to mingle." Josie brought her camera back to rest on her shoulder. "Work through your list then shoot what you like, but be bold. Particularly when Senator Miller arrives. If you believe the polls, he's going to be our next president. If you can, get his son and his date. The kid's meant to have a new girlfriend. His running mate's daughter. Do you know who I mean? Irene someone..." She paused, tapping her lip.

A sense of unease had me shifting my weight. I knew an Irene. That was Taylor's first name. Irene Taylor Vandenberg.

Like she'd read my mind, Josie clicked her fingers. "Vandenberg. That's it. Fucking nepotism. My little bird tells me they'll be onstage together later. Maybe they'll even make the big engagement announcement here. Be front and centre for that."

My stomach dropped. "Engagement?"

"Wasp, seriously? If you don't keep up with this kind of

news you won't make it as a celebrity photog. Look them up. Then go do your job."

"Got it." I offered Josie a ghost of a smile and peeled away into the crowded room.

Waiters circled with trays of champagne, dodging me as I stomped off to a corner by myself. Then I paged through my phone, searching as commanded.

I didn't read celebrity gossip—that wasn't the field I wanted to work in—but multiple sites spewed the news that the son of the hugely popular presidential candidate might soon be settling down. There were no pictures of Taylor, just of the guy with his famous father, but her name was there in black and white.

Christ on a bike.

The lass I'd held in my arms and fallen asleep on when I'd been seventeen, who I'd fucked against a wall in my brother's castle after a party at nineteen, and who I inexplicably missed, though we'd barely been in each other's lives, was going to make headlines in American politics, marrying into the first family.

I palmed my bearded cheek and sighed. I might be all man now compared with the boy she knew, but the idea of her marriage punched me in the gut. Yet I hadn't seen her in two years. The disappointment had no merit.

I buried my shock and threw myself into my work. Over the next hour, I racked up shots of socialites in incredible outfits, wealthy old guys in suits a thousand times nicer than my hired one, film stars I recognised and ones I guessed were important from their entourage, and members of the political scene. Josie's contacts landed her—and me—the insider scoop, numbering us among the few photographers permitted inside the building to document the night.

The opportunity to expand my portfolio and make

money was immense, and I uploaded the shots as I went, operating on autopilot where my concentration was fucked.

"Lads." I raised my camera to three men standing together. Dressed in edgy, distressed suits and with punky hair, they were familiar. A band, probably. "Can I take a shot?"

The first man, about my age, so early twenties, and with a strip of blue hair, broke into a smile. He threw his arms around the other two. "Nice to hear a familiar accent. You're a Scot. Highlands?"

"Aye." I ducked, lining up the photo to get the charity banner in the background. Blue Hair nudged the other two to grin.

"Where are you from? South?" I asked.

Though Scots, too, their accents were smarter than my soft brogue.

"You don't recognise us?"

I pulled a face. "Sorry. I'm new at this."

"Kick in the teeth, man. We're Viking Blue. From Edinburgh."

"Viking?" I couldn't help my smirk at the name.

"Aye. Women love it. Wait a sec, Highlander. We'll give you a good shot."

The first guy broke his hold on his bandmates then leapt, forcing the two men to catch him. He lay in their arms and stuck his hands behind his head. "I'm Rex, singer and songwriter."

"Wasp," I introduced myself, snapping the ridiculous pose. People often did daft stuff when the camera was on them. Rex's behaviour reminded me of Ally, my twin. A painful pang of missing him rose.

Rex's bandmates dropped him, and he clambered to his feet, taking a bow for the people watching. He lifted his chin at me. "Got a card? I'll hit you up if we're ever in need of a cameraman. We're new to this, too."

I produced one and handed it over, and the guy slipped it into his pocket. Then his gaze found a target over my shoulder.

"Whoa," Rex said. "The evening just got more interesting. Check out Miss USA."

I twisted, following his gaze.

Oh boy.

Like a vision, Taylor stepped into the room. She shimmered, her sheet of blonde hair pinned up in a fancy style, and her floor-length blue dress accentuating her hourglass form. My camera would never pick up that detail.

Besides, I'd frozen solid.

Ingrid Bergman. Lauren Bacall. They could eat their hearts out. Hollywood's Golden Age had nothing on Taylor.

Alone, she paused for a moment then raised a hand, presumably spotting a friend. Another lass swept over, and they embraced without touching, gesturing at each other's dresses.

Taylor glanced again over the crowd. Her eyes found mine. Locked on.

Christ.

A surge of fierce emotion hit me, and I opened my mouth. *Engaged. Almost.* I ought to congratulate her.

But we both just stared.

"You know her?" Rex asked.

"Who's that?" Taylor's friend asked simultaneously, her words just audible from my position across the hall.

Taylor's eyes widened for a moment, but then she looked away. "No one I know. Let's get a drink, I have a feeling I'm going to need it tonight."

No one?

I was no one. Ouch.

That punch in the gut I'd felt? It had barely been a tap. I'd grown up with three brothers and an abusive da—I could take a hit. But the lass's dismissal knocked the wind out of me. I pressed a hand to my chest, stifling the ache.

She'd recognised me. She'd chosen to blank me. Aye, it stung and then some.

"I guess not," I told the band, suddenly needing to get away. "Thanks for the photos."

The men bid me farewell, and I strode off.

"Wasp?" Near the back of the hall, Josie found me, her short, stylish grey hair damp with sweat. "In twenty minutes, Senator Miller arrives. I'll cover the front, so back me up then take stage left and remain there through the speeches. After, you can go. Our contract is covered, and I'll only be staying to drum up more business. Your flight is in the morning?"

"Aye. Four AM."

"Get the best shots uploaded before. Drop me a line if you need a reference or if you're in town and need to borrow a spare body."

She meant a camera body, but in the six weeks I'd been on assignment at her New York studio, this was the kindest the surly photographer to the stars had ever been.

"Thank ye."

I wanted to say more, about how I'd learned a lot from her, and how I appreciated her advice and guidance, but Josie already had her viewfinder to her eye, and she strolled away, snapping new arrivals.

If I'd wanted to leave before, I was dying to now. But I had an hour of speeches to capture. I spun on my heel and marched down the corridor, heading away from the throng, needing a minute alone.

Security guards dotted every corner. They eyed me as I passed. I guessed with my height and brawn, I could be considered a threat. Maybe I should be the worried one—the sheer number of them was alarming—but I kept going until I was in a quieter part of the museum.

For a moment, I just stood there in the cool, darkened corridor. Artwork watched me.

I was homesick. That was all. Seeing Taylor's name on the list had made me think of Scotland. With her being friends with my brother's wife, it was where I'd seen her most.

In a couple of days, this would pass.

This fucking ache would dissipate.

I'd be back at the castle, throwing myself into the hard, physical work of restoring the crofthouse with my brothers. No moments to wallow in the meaningless rejection of a lass I barely knew anymore.

A door closed inside my head. A violent *slam* that cut off the what-ifs and maybes that came with long blonde hair and a bonnie smile.

"William?" a voice rang out, breaking the silence.

Holy fuck.

Even if I didn't know Taylor's clear tones, no one else here used my real name.

I rotated slowly, flinching at the sight of her gorgeous face close up. "Taylor. You did recognise me, then."

She wrinkled her nose and took a step closer, clutching a glass of wine and a small purse that matched her outfit. "Sorry about that. You took me by surprise. I didn't expect to see you here, especially tonight..." Her gaze flitted over my features, lingering on my beard. Then she cleared her throat. "I mean, how are you?"

"Grand."

"Are you working here?"

I raised my camera by way of answer, my tongue thick in my mouth. God, this was awkward. If only I had the natural chatter of my twin. But no, I was always the quiet one.

"Dumb question." With a rough laugh, she raised her drink, downed the wine, then placed the glass on the floor.

"How are ye?" I repeated her question, wincing at how I sounded. Then I continued, because it was good to see her, even if she'd originally cut me. Whether she had on a bombshell dress or a t-shirt, I could never resist her draw. "I'm glad you found me."

"You are? Even if I acted like a bitch?"

I tilted my head, inviting elaboration. She wasn't a bitch. Not her.

Taylor took a deep inhale. "Let me explain. I guess you heard—"

A *boom* interrupted us. An explosion, with the tinkle of broken glass, reverberated down the hall, coming from the direction of the party.

On instinct, I grabbed Taylor's arm and pulled her against my body, spinning her away from the sound.

"Shit!" she squeaked, huddling into my chest. "What was that?"

"I have no idea." I snapped a look down the corridor.

An alarm blared, a rising din that sped up my heart.

Cries echoed. Footsteps drummed. People emerged into the dark corridor. Two security guards ran towards the main hall.

Taylor gaped. "Was it a bomb? Is that a bomb alarm? Oh God. We need to get out of here!"

"Aye, we do." The entrance Josie and I had used was close. "Come on."

With practiced ease, I manhandled my camera into its space in the bag then grabbed Taylor's hand and jogged.

Taylor flew alongside me, agile in her heels.

We joined a group heading for the same exit. One man yelled into his phone a frantic message about terrorists. Another stumbled, pinwheeling. I thrust out an arm to right him, losing no pace.

At the closed door, a security guard waited, pressing his earpiece into his ear.

"Open up!" I roared.

The man gaped but flung open the exit, positioning himself outside. "Keep moving. Leave the building immediately and convene on the sidewalk."

"What's happening?" Taylor demanded as we passed.

"That is not yet clear, ma'am. Move on."

Outside, rain splattered us, instantly soaking and plastering my hair to my forehead. Sirens from emergency services vehicles filled the night, the approaching lights reflecting in the puddles at our feet.

Traffic stopped where attendees in evening wear spilled into the wet street. Scared people huddled behind a hastily erected police cordon while passersby got caught in the drama, drawing closer to gawk.

Panic built in the air. We couldn't wait around here.

Shite. Josie. The guys in the band. Already moving Taylor away, I peered over the heads of the crowd and spotted the small woman, her camera in action, ignoring the police officer trying to move her on. At least she was safe. Behind her, the three band members spilled down the steps, an older man ushering them on.

"This is chaos," Taylor said. "They'll start grabbing people to search and interview any second. What should we do?"

"It isn't safe to hang around. My digs are close." For weeks, I'd bunked on Josie's photography studio's sofa. The place was empty at night and affordable, unlike anywhere else in Manhattan.

A loudspeaker whined with feedback before a stark voice ordered us to move into the police cordon.

The crowd shifted. People jostled.

"Keep close," I uttered, and we fled, diving into the crowd and the rain.

A river of people flooded in the opposite direction. Taylor blindly let me lead, and we kept on track. As we moved, I slipped off my jacket, placing it over her shoulders then put a protective arm around her.

At the junction of East 82nd Street and Park Avenue, I produced a set of keys from my bag and opened the door at the top of the steps, under a covered porch.

We climbed four flights of stairs and entered the studio. In the darkened space, Taylor headed straight for the window, peering out at the city and the route we'd just come. More flashing lights streamed towards the museum.

No more explosions had followed, but still my heart pounded.

If I'd stayed, I could've taken the pictures of my career— a first-hand account of a terrorist attack. But no, keeping Taylor safe had been the only thought in my head.

I deposited my camera equipment on the small table that acted as the reception desk then stooped and unzipped my sports bag that was stashed on the floor. From amid my packed possessions, I pulled a soft fluffy towel to offer my poor cold, wet lass.

Then I gazed at her for a second, silhouetted in the window, her hands grasping her elbows.

Every time we'd found ourselves like this before—alone,

a dimly lit room, limited time—we'd torn each other's clothes off. Clawed at flesh to burn up our passion on the other's body.

I could never explain it, the sheer thirst I had for this woman. I'd had girlfriends, a few one-night stands. Nothing came close to what I felt around Taylor.

What was worse? It hadn't gone away.

Despite her news. Despite the man in her life.

The man she's about to marry.

That last thought had me clamping down on the inappropriate lust, and I crossed to stand next to her and held out the towel. Being the good guy, not a dick. "Here, bundle up. You must be freezing."

But to my horror, as Taylor peeked up at me, tears filled her eyes. Then the lass, the happy, joyful force of personality I had always been drawn towards, drew a shaking breath, flung her arms around me, and crushed her lips onto mine.

HEAT FLARED

*T*aylor
Kissing William McRae was a bad move, guaranteed to hurt more than just seeing him and walking away. But I never claimed to be smart. Only desperate.

And this man never failed to make me feel...everything.

Shock from the kiss zinged through my body, and my mind instantly went to my happy place. Somewhere dark. Hot. With this huge Scotsman using his powerful body on mine.

I hugged William like my life depended on it. Our lips moved together, his new scruff scratching my skin, and I gave a moan of pleasure.

This. Home.

William dropped the towel he'd brought, bracketed me with his strong arms, and returned my kiss. I melted onto him. No one else could do this—hold me up. Keep me safe. He couldn't either, no matter what my body told me.

Then his tongue touched mine, and we both gasped.

"Wait. Fuck." William reared back. He breathed in through his nose, and his muscles flexed under my grip.

Then he closed his eyes and rested his forehead on mine. "I shouldnae have done that. This is wrong."

Ever the gentleman—taking the blame for my lips on his.

"Probably. But I needed it." Embarrassingly, my eyes were wet, and I wiped them, not wanting him to see. The pressure from the evening had already been immense, pre-explosion, but I'd owned it. I'd been in control. Seeing William had knocked my resolve.

"Your boyfriend..." William started.

"Don't have one." We were still hugging. My heavy, soggy dress pasted to his suit. I'd barely noticed the room we were in, save for the fact it was a workplace. A studio with rigging for lights.

No bed.

William's shoulders lowered an inch, shadows deepening the furrow of his brow. He studied my face. "I read that ye were engaged. That it would be announced tonight."

"Oh, that." He was right. Didn't that throw the mother of all wrenches into the works. "It might have happened. If someone hadn't tried to blow up the Met."

"Right." He released me from his warm hold and moved away. "I'll... Fuck."

I gripped my fingers together, suddenly compelled to explain what I'd told no one.

My bag buzzed—a phone call.

William's gaze shot to the clutch. "Go ahead, take it. Someone needs to know you're safe. I'll make coffee, then we'll check out the news."

He disappeared through a doorway, and I sagged gracelessly to the floor to collect my phone. Dad's name screamed from the screen. I had him by his job title: *Governor to the State of New York.*

"Irene? Where the fuck are you?" he barked.

I winced, pulling the device from my ear. "I'm at a friend's place. There was an explosion. We ran. Did you hear about it?"

"I heard. I've not been told what happened yet, but I'll find out. Luckily I've only just landed so I wasn't in the building." The line went muffled, and he barked at someone. Probably his driver.

It didn't bother me that he hadn't worried for my safety. I knew my father's priorities.

He came back. "Tonight's plans obviously have to change. We'll meet Linc and Theo at their hotel instead. I'll be there in twenty, then I'll send my car for you. Give me the address."

I paused. For months now, Dad had been constructing this plan. A match between me and Theo Miller, twenty-six-year-old beloved son of the next president. Tonight would have put our name on the front pages. No wonder my father was pissed.

Through the doorway, soft light glowed, and a coffee machine whirred into life. William moved, collecting mugs, and I got caught up, staring at the broadness of his shoulders under his clinging, damp white shirt.

"Address," Dad ordered.

"I'm soaked through," I spluttered. I didn't want to go. I'd never wanted this. Any of it. I needed to stall. "The road is closed off. Even if I could dry off, I'm only going to get drenched again."

Dad paused. "You mean you look like shit?" He wasn't wrong, but the insult stung. "Tomorrow, then. Brunch at the Four Seasons at eleven. Don't be late." Then he hung up.

William returned, placing a steaming mug in front of me. I clambered to my feet and landed on the couch, tracking him as he collected a laptop from what looked like luggage.

"Going somewhere?" I tipped my head at his bag.

William sat beside me and opened the machine. "Home. I fly in a few hours."

He brought up a news site and, side by side, we gazed at the silent pictures. A scrolling banner told us what we already knew. The explosion. The mass panic. No reports of serious injuries, though. No arrests.

"I heard ye say on the phone that the street was locked down." William pushed the laptop away and interlaced his hands, watching me. "Fifth Avenue might be, but this road isn't."

"That was my dad. We've been lying to each other since I could talk." I picked up my coffee and took a swig. William had sweetened it, just like I preferred. Had he ever made me coffee? My brain fixated on the question, just as much as my skin fixated on the inches of distance between us.

Then I shivered. Hard. The hot drink sank into my chilled flesh.

"Christ, woman," William said, his voice low. "You must be freezing."

My teeth chattered. "For such flimsy material, this dress holds a lot of water. Do you have anything I can change into?"

"Aye. Hang on." He leapt up and returned with his bag, pulling out a neat stack of clothes. "Long-sleeved t-shirt." He handed me the item. "I don't have any drawstring trousers. My jeans would dwarf you. Maybe keep your underwear then use the towel as a blanket for now."

My mouth twitched. "I'm not wearing underwear." At his outraged look, a shaky laugh burst from my chest. "What?

You don't with dresses like this." I plucked at the ruined gown.

"Don't tell me any more. Christ, lass. You'll give me a heart attack."

I grinned then unclipped the buckles from my heels and let them drop to the floor. Then I stood in front of William, bundling the borrowed shirt and the towel in my arms. He'd always towered over me but he was bigger still; the last few years had added muscle weight to his height.

I liked it, the brawn. The sheer masculinity of this mountain man.

William McRae, all grown up. How about that.

"When we met, there wasn't such a height difference between us," I murmured, stifling a full body shiver.

William's green-eyed gaze held mine. "There's a lot that's different between then and now."

Wasn't that the truth? I left him and padded on bare feet to the room where he'd made the coffee. I closed myself in and commenced the wrestling match that was removing my dress. Couture was not meant to be soaked. It clung like it had been glued on, and I wanted to call for help, but William would blow a fuse at the sight of my boobs popping free.

I had nice boobs, but I didn't want to inflict an injury on the man.

A *rip* came as I tugged the frock over one shoulder. I blew a damp tendril of hair from my eyes and tried not to think about the cost.

Finally, I was free. In William's soft t-shirt, which fell to my mid-thigh, I returned to the studio floor.

"I have a small problem. The dress is dead. I don't think I'll be wearing it home."

William had changed clothes himself, out of his suit and

into jeans and a dry shirt, instantly appearing younger and sweeter.

"I'm sorry about the dress. It looked incredible on you."

What a nice way of putting it—not that I had been enhanced by the dress, but the other way around. What was strange was that, when I'd chosen the dress, William had been on my mind. He had a thing for old movies, and it had reminded me of him. Once, we'd been on the same flight together, and the airline had been showing *Casablanca*. I'd watched it with him. And, alone, I'd watched other movies from the thirties and forties since.

"We'll work something out," he continued. "Where are you staying?"

"A hotel downtown. Later, when we're sure nothing else is going to blow up, I'll get a cab. There's nothing unusual about a woman skipping around New York City dressed in oversized clothes and a towel."

He pursed his lips but made no further comment.

Taking care not to flash him, I lowered myself to the couch and wrapped my legs with the towel. Nothing new had popped up on the news report. If the all clear was announced, I'd have no reason to stay.

A not-so-small part of me wanted the police to delay as long as they could.

"I just sent a message to my family to let them know I'm safe. Is there anyone else ye need to call?"

"No." Mom wouldn't have a clue where I was supposed to be. "The acquaintance you saw me with left with her date. They were outside."

"Maybe we should report ourselves as safe to the organiser. Our names would be listed as attending." He took up the laptop and typed something into a new search.

Idly, I raised my hands to my hair, sorting through for

the pins that were tangled in the mess. "I must look like a drowned rat. I'm glad you got to see me at the beginning of the night."

William frowned, his face illuminated by the screen. "Don't be daft. If anything, I like you better now."

"You're kidding?"

"I'm not. You look more like the lass I remember."

I giggled—God, when had I last laughed?—and extracted the last of the pins, freeing my hair.

William stared now.

"You always had a thing about my hair," I said without thinking.

He rumbled a laugh. "Aye. And every other part of you."

Another guy, and that would've come off as creepy. Not him. William was good. Good in bed, sure, but a good man, too. He loved his brothers, cared for his friends. I trusted him more than most people I knew, and I barely knew him.

"How long have you been in the States?" I asked, pushing past the unnerving thought.

He finished his message then sat back. "Six weeks. This was the final placement in my degree. I've been doing all the grunt work for Josie Addlestein but I've learned a ton."

"I've heard of her. Is this her place?"

"Aye. I've slept on this couch every night."

I scrunched my nose. It was a plush couch, but nowhere near long enough for William's big body. "You must be killing it to get a job here."

"Mathilda name-dropped a few times and got me the gig. I'm hoping it has given me enough of a profile for an agency to take me on."

Mathilda was his oldest brother's wife. His second brother, Gordain, married my best friend, Ella. I visited her whenever I could, but I'd made a point of avoiding William on the past few trips to Scotland. I knew where my path in life was taking me, and getting more hooked on him wasn't going to do me any favours.

"And the beard, is that mandatory wear for a photographer?" I smiled, but it was weak.

His gaze took me to pieces. "If we're doing question and answer, want to tell me how a single lass is expecting a proposal?"

"Do you really want to know?"

"Aye. I really do."

"It's an arrangement my father is making."

William froze. "Arrangement?"

I sighed, switching my gaze to the rain-splattered window. The first time I'd met William had been after my original attempt at an arranged marriage. One I'd organised to get away from my dad and obtain something else I badly wanted. I'd been eighteen then and reeling from news I'd had. That plan had fallen through, and since then, the situation had only gotten worse. It made this second attempt even more important. "I know what you're thinking—"

He gave a short bark of a laugh. "I'm not thinking anything. Other than how different my world is to yours."

I felt it, then. The chasm between my life and that of this good, kind man, who came from a happy, boisterous family of brothers, who had nieces and nephews to spoil, a wild Scottish estate to roam. Who had love pouring at him from every side.

Utterly unlike being raised in a boarding school because my parents' acrimonious divorce meant they couldn't share me. Not that they'd wanted to.

I curled in on myself, suddenly unable to speak.

"Hey." William lightly jostled me. "Come back. I'm not passing judgment. It's none of my business."

It wasn't. It wasn't anyone's.

My gaze landed on the laptop again. New words appeared. "There's an update."

We both leaned in to view the screen.

The catering company's use of pressurised gas canisters had not been sanctioned by the museum, and an investigation will look at the process that led to this chain of events. To recap, the explosion that caused the panicked evacuation of a red-carpet event, moments before the arrival of Senator Miller and Governor Vanderbilt, caused no injuries but damaged a number of works of art...

I stopped reading and blinked at William. "It wasn't a bomb, then."

"Christ." He palmed his neck. Amusement danced in his eyes when he brought his attention back to me. "I'm not sorry, though. Seeing you has been the highlight of my trip."

My laugh came unbidden. "You're joking, aren't you? All the people you must have photographed. All the places you must have been."

His lips quirked, but he just watched me.

I knew he was being sweet, but I'd store those words away and keep them as comfort for the hard times to come.

Pressure ate at me. I stood and looked out at the flashing lights that still lit the night in the distance. There were fewer now.

It was time for me to leave.

"Wait," William said. Like he knew I was about to bolt. "Sit down again, will ye?"

I hesitated. If I did, I'd probably do something stupid like throw myself at him again.

"In a few hours, I need to get a taxi to the airport. Stay here until then. I can drop you at your hotel on the way."

"You don't need to do that."

His gaze caressed me. "I want to. That way I'll know you got back safe."

"What shall we do until then?" Heat flared, blazing along my nerves.

Everything was about to change. As soon as the announcement was made, my low profile as the little-photographed daughter of a politician would be obliterated. The press would expose every secret that hadn't already been buried, and my private life wouldn't exist anymore.

I had one chance left to do something for me alone.

William rested back on the couch, his arms behind his head making his biceps pop. "Get your thoughts out of the gutter. We can chat. Catch up."

"Or," I dropped the towel and advanced, straddling him with one bold swing, "we can do something more fun instead. Just like old times."

3

HUNGER

W *asp*

Ah fuck. This was wrong. I told myself to stop, yet my lips moved with hunger, and I gripped two handfuls of Taylor's bare backside.

Our tongues met in a battle, warring for dominance, sliding in and out with slick heat. Taylor tasted of wine and heaven, and I couldn't get enough.

On my lap, she pressed into me, the shirt I'd given her riding up around her middle.

In the dark of the room, I was right back in a place I'd dreamed about far too often. The lass was a year older than me. When we'd met, she'd been the experienced one. Every time since then, I'd wanted to show her what I'd learned. To prove to her that I could match her.

Please her.

Best her.

She moaned and broke our lips apart. We both breathed heavily, staring at each other.

Then, she grabbed the hem of her shirt and started to lift it.

I hated myself. I hated the values I had instilled in my blood.

I fucking hated being the good guy.

"Stop," I ground out. Gently, I took her fingers and held them, forcing myself not to look down at the soft skin revealed.

"Why?" Taylor's blonde eyebrows pinched in.

"Ask me again in a minute when my cock isn't battling for ownership of my thoughts."

She gave a sparkling laugh. "I've missed your cock. Let me say hi."

"Ah, stop." I closed my eyes and rested my head back on the couch, my lips pulling in a grin.

"You want me."

"I always have," I murmured to the ceiling.

"Are you seriously turning me down?"

"Aye."

"Did you get hit on the head since the last time I saw you?"

I burst out laughing now and grabbed her, swinging us around so she was on her back on the couch and I was on top of her. Then I rubbed the tip of my nose against hers, because if I didn't make this cute, I'd lose my willpower. "You make me crazy. You always had the knack." I kissed her softly then reached for the towel she'd dropped, covering her up. "But this will only make things harder next time we see each other."

"Huh?"

"You'll visit Ella. Bring your new husband. Arranged or not, you'll be part of a couple." One that didn't involve me. My chest ached again, and I shifted away. "We can't keep doing this. If we stop now, we can learn to be friends instead."

Taylor made a noise of frustration. "This might be my last chance of good sex. I might be a bitch but I'd never cheat. Even stuck in a marriage I hated."

Argh. "Sorry." Then my brain caught up. "You're not a bitch."

"I am. I've never been a nice person."

"I disagree. I like ye." I spared her a look.

She gazed back, wide-eyed and fucking gorgeous. Blonde hair spilling over the midnight-blue couch. "Including if we're not sleeping together anymore?"

"Do ye think that's the only reason I like ye?"

She blinked, appearing to consider the answer. "Yes. No. I don't know."

Granted, we hadn't spent much time together just talking, but her visits had usually been short and time with me limited. I gave her an outraged glare, and she giggled.

"So..." She put her feet on my lap. I took them in my hands, resisting massaging her. This was already hard enough. Quite literally. "We're friends?" she continued. "What does that mean?"

"We see each other without wanting to have sex."

Taylor blew out a breath. "I don't think that's ever going to happen. But if you want it, I'll give it a go. What do we do now?"

"Fill me in on the past couple of years?"

"You start. Your Highlands life has always been more interesting than mine."

For the next couple of hours, we talked. While my photos uploaded for Josie to sell, I told Taylor about my family and home, about university, my last girlfriend who'd suggested for my career I move to the city permanently— something I wasn't prepared to do—and Taylor gave me a few small details of her life. Her dad's political aspirations, her strained relationship with her mother. The university degree she'd taken and aced but wasn't using.

Then she fell silent, and I glanced over to find her head dropped to the side, and her breathing gentle in sleep. We had to leave in forty minutes, but I didn't move. The chest pain I had worsened. I'd never told her, but years ago, when sex had been a mystery to which she'd given me the answers, I'd thought myself in love with her. It had been puppy love, but powerful all the same.

I'd never felt anything like it since. I doubted I ever would again.

But Taylor wasn't for me. Until the last possible moment, I just sat with her, letting her rest. Then I gently shook her awake, collected my bags, and straightened up the studio, leaving my hired suit and lenses for Josie's assistant to return. Then I took Taylor to her hotel. Red-eyed, she didn't speak, but before she got out of the cab, she leaned over and kissed me. Soft, now. None of the urgency of earlier.

She walked away in my shirt and bundled in my towel.

"It's hard saying goodbye," the cabbie told me, idling the car and letting me have my moment, staring across the grey pavement.

Strange. It felt like a sort of heartbreak, though that couldn't be right. I needed to board a plane and go home. Get back to my life and put Taylor behind me.

"You have no idea," I replied, and the cabbie drove me away.

4

MAKE IT COUNT

Taylor

"Fuck," I said to my reflection in the lobby's mirrored door. "Fuck, fuck, fuck."

In his cab, William couldn't see me now, but I watched him until the last second. His car drove away, and a kind of angst rose in me. A desperation to run, to do something crazy like follow him. A feeling not dissimilar to when I'd first found out about Charity's illness.

Some things you couldn't fix.

Some people you couldn't have.

Some lives weren't meant to be lived like others.

In my hotel room, I curled up in the centre of the bed, inhaling the scent of William from his borrowed shirt. From my skin.

I breathed in and out and thought of nothing.

Then, at nine-thirty, I showered, dressed carefully in a respectable but attractive skirt and blouse, pinned up my hair—it looked best when down, but for some reason, I associated that with William, and wanted to keep it as his—and got in my father's car.

"Were you near to the blast last night, miss?" Terence, Dad's driver, asked me, taking the car out into the busy Midtown street.

"Luckily not. But it scared the heck out of me."

"I bet. We heard about it on the radio just after we left La Guardia. I can't tell you how relieved I was to hear you answer your father's call."

I didn't ask if Dad had worried for my safety. After all, he'd called only after remaking his plans for the evening. But it was nice to know that Terence cared. I changed the subject and asked about his new grandson, and we settled in for the short journey.

Outside the Four Seasons, I took a second and prepared my face. In my compact mirror, I looked the part, my makeup covering the dark rings under my eyes, but no amount of makeup could conceal the odd sense of grief that swamped me.

"I'll keep your luggage. Where am I taking you after the meeting?" Terence enquired, holding my door.

A cold breeze wrapped around my legs—spring had not yet warmed Manhattan.

Dad would tell me where to go. After the formalities were done, I was a possession once again. Just like being a child at boarding school. Waiting to be told my next move. "I'm not sure yet."

"Just give me a call when you're done."

I thanked him and entered the interior of the hotel. Dad's assistant, Pippa, leapt up from a chair and bounced over to greet me. Her blonde bob—so similar to the style Mom used to wear—swung with her enthusiastic moves.

"Good morning! Governor Vandenberg has asked me to step in this morning. He's tied up at present so won't be available to see you."

"Hey." I gave her a short smile. It wasn't her fault Dad was an asshole. "Is the meeting still on?"

"Yes, indeed! You are to see Theodore Miller in his room. I'll take you there now."

In his room? Like a brood mare to be inspected? I masked my surprise and trailed Pippa to the elevators.

"Your father and Senator Miller had a late meeting last night and came to a decision. You kids can make your plans yourselves. They both feel you're more than capable of arriving at a sensible arrangement."

"Uh-huh." This didn't sound like Dad. He needed control. The senator had made that decision, I was certain. "Am I to call Dad the minute it's done to check my sensible decision is right?"

"Of course!" She happily tapped in a code, and the elevator rose.

At the penthouse, the doors slid open, revealing a corridor. Two men stepped towards us and did their duty with brief questions and bag searches. Seemed the Millers were fancy. Once married, this would be my life. Security. No freedom.

I'd never felt safe. Never been safe. Now I never would.

No, my brain whispered. Because I had felt safe with William. Except that had been a temporary sensation. No doubt brought by the blissed-out post-sex haze we usually had going on.

I blanked out the thought that the same feeling had happened last night, yet we hadn't slept together. Not in the sense I'd wanted to, anyway. Maybe safety was a kind of muscle memory or a learned response. That was why I'd felt it with William.

"Irene, come on through. I'm on a call," Theo's tones found me, and I followed his voice.

I rounded the corner to find him arguing into his phone. He paced away from me, his other hand pulling at the knot on his tie. I swept my gaze over the living room.

Dad liked fancy hotels, but this place took posh to another level.

An assortment of white couches and glass coffee tables sat in little clusters in front of a sweeping view of the city. The floor-to-ceiling windows let in the morning light and, to the right, a man and a woman sat at a table, typing into a laptop. Both glanced up, but only the man smiled.

Theo walked the floor. On his return circuit, he raised a hand to me and gestured for me to sit.

I perched on a chair at the dining table at the other end of the long room, under an enormous teardrop-shaped chandelier. Pippa hovered at my elbow.

I smiled politely at her. "I'll call you if I need anything."

"Oh, but your father said—"

"That Theo and I were permitted to make our own plans. You told me so."

Dad's assistant opened and closed her pink mouth. Then she formed a smile, dipped her head, and left.

Along the skyline, a bird dove from a rooftop, speeding, chasing something down the staggering fall. Some kind of hawk maybe? Who'd have thought they could survive here in the city.

"I apologise for that. Busy morning. Now, let's talk." Theo took a seat opposite me and turned on his tablet. He paged through a diary, every date stacked with lists of meetings and activities.

We'd met a handful of times, even danced together once at a country club. With his neatly combed mid-brown hair, super-white teeth, and all-year tan, he was handsome enough, but we didn't know one another. He muttered to the device, and I stared at him, trying to imagine him being my husband.

We'd probably go well together. Maybe that was why his dad had agreed to my dad's proposal. My looks really were my only appealing feature.

"Here it is. My assistant made a list of possible engagement dates and then wedding dates. Dad's election manoeuvrings have mostly dictated the wedding date, but the engagement date is up to us. We can also put forward a limited number of names to be considered for the invite list."

Finally, he glanced my way. Brown eyes, inoffensive and utterly unremarkable, blinked at me.

Panic struck me. For Charity's sake, I had to do this. For my own sake, I wished I'd been born into any other family than mine.

"I need time," I blurted, finding my voice.

"Time to...?" Theo rolled his hands, prompting me to continue.

"I have a friend who is overdue a visit, and a couple of places I want to go."

He mock-wiped his shiny brow. "I thought you were going to say you needed to spend time with me."

I spluttered a laugh. So did he.

Theo put the tablet down. "I launched into that, didn't I? I apologise for being insensitive. I've been in meetings since five this morning, and this is a business deal after all, so excuse my lack of feelings over it."

"Feelings aren't a problem," I said. "I'm not all that sensitive. It's just..."

How the hell did I explain what I didn't understand?

"You need some space before being dragged into the mad house?"

I exhaled, some small relief filtering through my layers of armour. "Something like that."

"It actually suits me to have more time to tie off...a few loose ends." He glanced across the room to the people sitting behind me. A fleeting glimpse, but I noticed all the same. "How about a month? If we both tell our dads that the other needs the time, we'll be in the clear for a little breathing space. Dad will be winding up to announcing his bid for the presidency and your dad as his running mate, so it'll be a nice boost for their campaigns." He went back to his calendar. "May twenty-third is the last date on the list. Dad is in California for a trade deal, and there's a party planned for the evening. There will be a lot of big names there, and the traditional press will be present. We can tip off the others. Sound good?"

A month. There was a lot I could do in a month. I dipped my head, my mind filling with possibilities.

"Done. We'll say I did the whole down-on-one-knee thing earlier in the evening and Dad had time to organise the band to play our favourite song, the flowers for you etcetera etcetera. Send my assistant your ring size. He can pick up something of the right value."

"What's our favourite song?" I felt like laughing again, but this really wasn't funny.

Theo flipped a hand, no longer looking at me. "Someone will choose it for us. Now, I'm free for a phone meeting on the twentieth at four PM. We can make any last-minute arrangements then. Is there anything you need to cover now?"

I felt like a pleasant, preppy boy-shaped steamroller had flattened me. Why, I had no idea. I'd been preparing for this role for years. "Nothing."

"Wonderful. My assistant will give you my office number. Carl?" he called.

The waiting man appeared beside us at the table.

"See Miss Vandenberg to the elevator." Theo came back to me. "Irene, it was lovely seeing you again. Until next time."

With that, my engagement was arranged.

In the airy lobby, after dispatching a far too nosy Pippa, I called Dad. He blustered about the date but settled when I explained that Theo needed the time. I guessed the senator's son could do no wrong in Dad's eyes.

"Now this has been organised, I would like the money for Charity to be put into a trust," I said carefully. I never made direct demands of my father.

"After the wedding," he replied.

"But that could take a year. I'd be much more comfortable if I knew she was taken care of." Then I took a risk. "A happy bride makes for a happy husband." What bullshit, but my meaning behind it was clear.

There was a pause. "Her next year will be paid for upfront. After the engagement is announced. The trust will be established after the wedding. Will that please the bride?" Sarcasm leaked into his tone, but I didn't care.

"The year now. Then the trust after." I held my breath at my recklessness. But Dad had everything to gain from this, and I had nothing left to lose. This was his blackmail. Caused and delivered. I had only ever tried to find the best path.

"Fine."

He'd agreed? Inwardly, I cheered. "I'm going to the UK to visit Mom," I added before he could give me a new instruction. Another day, another lie.

Dad snorted. "Give her my best, won't you? See you in a month."

I hung up the call and wrapped my arms around myself.

"Miss?" Terence approached, two coffee cups in his hands. He passed one to me.

"Life saver." I grinned at him then took a sip.

"Have you eaten?"

"Um…" I hadn't eaten since mid-afternoon yesterday.

Terence rolled his eyes and turned, heading back to the restaurant. Unlike Dad, I never sent him to fetch and carry things for me, but he'd always looked out for me. Far more than my actual parents ever had.

I trailed after him and finished my drink. The much-needed caffeine fuelled an instant and wild plan. I had a bag of clothes. I had an excuse to put a plane ticket or two on Dad's credit card.

Terence reappeared with a sandwich bag and a smile. Together, we left the hotel and emerged into the daylight.

"Where would you like to go?" Terence guided me by my elbow, and I grinned up at the white-haired man I'd known since I was a little girl.

If I had only a month left, I was going to make it count.

5

WE'RE HERE FOR YE

*W*asp
Sweat stung my eyes, and my arms shook with the effort of holding aloft the newly hewn timber support beam. I'd been home for four days and was well into my aim of killing myself with physical work. The croft-house's decaying roof had to be replaced, and my brothers and I had thrown our backs into it.

I needed the distraction. The hard, exhausting work kept my mind off other things.

Sexy, blonde, half-naked things.

But at night, though my aching muscles screamed for rest, I lay awake, wondering if I should've done something different with Taylor.

That whole evening had messed with my head.

"Is she level?" Ally called.

"Left," I yelled back across the shell of a house. "Another inch."

"Good my end. Slide her in, baby." Ally catcalled as the beam fitted snugly into its setting.

"We have a frame!" I whooped and leapt down from my

makeshift scaffold, landing on the broken floor tiles in the interior. Wrenching my gloves from my hands, I tossed them aside and grabbed my twin into a hard hug.

It was only the two of us here this morning. We slapped each other's backs then gazed up at the new framework.

"Gordain's due any minute with the crossbeams. We'll have a roof in no time."

Ally kept his gaze on the grey sky beyond the roof. "You will."

This again? "You've worked as hard as I have on this place. I can't live in a four-bed house on my own."

"Aye. I owe you the labour. But I'm nae moving in." My twin stuck his hands into the front pocket of his hoodie.

For almost a year, since I'd asked Callum, our oldest brother, if I could buy the derelict building from him, Ally had matched my efforts in rebuilding it. Yet he refused to consider it his or contemplate moving in when it was done. He had this daft idea that he owed me for shite that had happened when we were kids.

It was ridiculous, but he hadn't changed his mind.

"Shut up," I said maturely.

"You shut up." Ally withdrew a hand from his pocket and shoved me.

"Fucker." I punched his shoulder.

He ducked into a fighter's pose, a smirk on his face. I followed suit, the change from full-grown man to idiotic boy as natural as breathing. We charged and clashed, grappling, trying to force the other to the ground. Our scuffles always went the same way, us being identical in strength and size. Only luck—or cheating—gave the other an advantage.

"Six weeks in America, and you've gone soft." He tried a knee to my balls.

I dodged. "Mind your pretty face. I wouldnae want to lose you money."

Ally modelled, his extrovert nature and swagger making him a perfect fit for runways. Luckily, he had us to keep him grounded so he hadn't got vain. Yet.

He ducked to shoulder barge me. I grasped his forearms and dropped to the floor, taking him with me. Dust flew.

"Cheat!" Ally gasped, the wind knocked out of him.

"Who's the soft one now?" I pinned him. Victory was mine. Almost.

A shadow fell over us from the doorframe.

"What the hell? Ye pair of flipping kids."

We paused and raised our heads, breathing hard.

Gordain, our second-oldest brother, planted his hands on his hips, a quizzical brow raised. "You'd think with all this hard work, ye wouldnae have the energy to fight."

I grunted and rolled away, edges of broken tiles digging into my back.

Ally loomed over me, his blond hair falling in his eyes. "What's with ye? I don't mind a scrap, but you've been burning up like no one's business since you've been back."

Sitting up, I hooked my arms around my knees. It was bothering me, everything that had happened that night. My brothers knew about the explosion and evacuation of the gala, but not about who I was with.

"Maybe it's about a lass."

Ally and Gordain exchanged a look.

"I wish I'd made a bet on that." Ally sighed dramatically.

Gordain kept his gaze on me. "Go on."

"Have ye ever turned a woman down? Ye know, one who was eager."

"Aye," Gordain said.

At the same time, Ally replied, "No. Are ye mad?"

Gordain pocketed his car keys and joined me on the floor, crossing his legs beneath him. "Who was the lass? Because there's something I need to tell ye. Ella had a call from Taylor a couple of days ago."

My phone blared and I jumped. I'd been expecting a call from a photographic agency I'd signed with; one I hoped would give me regular work.

"She did?" I replied to my brother, staring. My phone kept ringing. "Shite. Hold that thought. I need to get this. Hang on a sec." Clambering up, I exited the crofthouse. Ahead, cool sunlight flickered over the glen and shone off the loch.

The remote spot, perched on the rise of Mhic Raith, the mountain in my brothers' backyards, had the best views in the whole of the McRae lands. Both Castle McRae, Callum's home, and Castle Braithar, Gordain's place, were visible. I was surrounded by family but in my own space, too.

Even here I couldn't get away from the lass's name.

I faced the stiff breeze and answered the call. "Wasp McRae."

"Wasp. This is Claire from Reportage One. I'm just processing your sign-up papers and, by strange coincidence, I have a job for you."

"Already?"

"Have you heard of Viking Blue?"

They were the band I'd photographed at the Met. "Sure."

She rattled on. "They came into the office we share with our sister company, PR One, and I happened to comment on your nickname, it being unusual. The singer overheard. He said he knew you. He booked you there and then."

"He did?"

"You said you were available for international travel, correct? The tour starts in three days, but get to Paris at the latest by tomorrow evening because they need promo shots stat. Book yourself a flight to France, then you'll drive between the rest of the European locations. There'll be space for you on one of the tour buses and a bed each night in a shared hotel room. After that, you'll need to be on a plane to the States. They are playing six dates there."

I blinked, trying to catch up. Paris and the States. This was huge. "They're on tour?"

"It was last minute. They're supporting Hedonist. The original support band that had been booked pulled out."

I'd heard of Hedonist. They were a huge US rock band. Go Viking Blue. What a turn up for them.

And for me.

A smile broke across my face. I'd expected to be home for longer, not jetting off to photograph rock stars, but this sounded like a lark.

Apart from one small aspect I wasn't about to explain to them—no one wanted to hear about my screwed-up head. I took a breath and made a necessary request. "I'll be there, but I'd prefer to drive myself between the gigs. Would that work?"

Claire paused. "I don't see why not. You'll need to make the arrangements, but it'll be covered by expenses."

"Book it in."

"Details coming your way by email." The agent hung up, and I pocketed my phone, still grinning.

In order to be free for any work that came my way, I'd submitted my final portfolio to the university and wrapped up my formal education yesterday. This new job was a surprise but a welcome one. On the road, I'd be too busy to keep up my obsession. I'd be in places that had never heard of Taylor Vandenberg so there would be no reminders. Not like here.

I was almost afraid to ask Gordain to finish his sentence.

Back inside the shell of the crofthouse, I grinned at my brothers. "Guess who's going on tour with a rock band tomorrow?"

Ally gave me his typical wide-mouthed grin, but his eyebrows dug in, and the smile was short-lived. "Nice. But I thought you'd be home for longer."

"I did, too." As boys, we'd always been together. As men, our lives took us apart more often than not. He'd likely be away on Fashion Week auditions when I returned. We kept missing each other.

I blew out a breath. "We'll have to work our arses off to get this roof on."

The two men grunted agreement, eyeing the frame.

"Ella will be busy for the next couple of days, so I'll help. We'll pull Cal in, too, and between us, we'll get this place watertight," Gordain said. Then he fixed me with his gaze. "Ella's gone to the airport."

"Aye?"

"That phone call was her friend coming to stay."

I dragged my thoughts back from planning the roof battens and driving across Europe and stared. Still, I didn't ask.

"Was it Taylor you saw in the US? The woman you turned down?" he asked.

A groan left me, acceptance dawning. "Yeah. Ah, fuck. She's here?"

He inclined his head, his grey eyes keen.

"She didn't call me. Or text," I thought aloud.

"Probably because you turned her down," Ally informed me. "You must've offended her."

"It wasn't like that." There had been more involved than just our bodies. When I'd known her before, she'd been resilient and so determined. Nothing could hurt her. She'd been a bright spark, fun and dangerously attractive.

This time, I'd felt the attraction, but her spark had dimmed. "I would have been taking advantage. She's got... life-changing stuff going on."

Fuck it. I planted my arse against a low window, the stonework neat and intact—probably the only thing in the house that was. "It's a good thing I'm leaving. I'll stay out of her way until then."

But I didn't want to. I eyed my Land Rover parked outside and imagined the journey to Braithar, Gordain and Ella's home. I pictured welcoming Taylor with open fucking arms, begging forgiveness for acting like I had and resuming our old habit by taking her to a room with a locked door and giving her what she'd asked for.

Would one more time hurt?

She knew herself best. She'd wanted me. Needed comfort before she got herself tangled in whatever insane deal her father had strong-armed her into.

My brothers were both staring when I turned back around. My inner turmoil probably showed on my face because I already knew what I was going to do.

The good guy won out.

Every fucking time.

"Fuck!" I groaned. "Fuck, fuck, and fuck it. If ye see me heading her way, stop me, aye? She's got plans that don't involve me, and I'm going to end up..." What, heartbroken? Surely not. She'd loved and left me a number of times before.

Maybe she wasn't the only one who had changed. Maybe I had, too.

"We're here for ye." Gordain took out his phone. "We've

got everything we need for the roof. Ye can work through your angst."

I grunted agreement, banging my head on the stone behind me for good measure.

"Cal?" Gordain said, making his call to our oldest brother. "We need you. We're going to get the roof on the crofthouse today and we're going to stop Wasp making a fool of himself with a lass. Ye with us?"

He listened then ended the call, a smirk on his lips. "He's on his way. Consider yourself under guard."

* * *

*F*or the rest of the afternoon and well into the evening, we were on the scaffold, fitting cross-beams and nailing battens onto roof felt.

Mathilda, our sister-in-law, took a break from work and brought us sandwiches, her two kids scaling the building like little monkeys. I received hugs, sustenance, the love of a tight-knit family, but still no peace of mind.

I worked until my muscles burned and my arms quaked.

By nightfall, I still had the urge to run to Braithar, but with my three brothers around me, shielding me without question and without unnecessary chat, I wouldn't make it down the track. I didn't try, though my mind made the journey over and over.

When the last batten was nailed into place, we cheered, toasting our efforts with warm beer.

Callum and Gordain left, but Ally stayed, bunking down with me on the newly roofed-in upstairs floor. The crofthouse had no power yet, so Ally and I rigged up a lamp and huddled into sleeping bags for warmth.

With the last dregs of battery on my phone, I read over

the contract Reportage One had sent, then booked my flight and car hire.

"Where are the gigs?" Ally asked.

"The first is Paris, then over to Milan, and after that up to Berlin. Then they're flying me to the States for a couple of weeks." With the first American date in New York City, I'd be right back where I'd just come from, but I could handle it.

Tomorrow, I'd be gone. Taylor could enjoy her visit with Ella, and I wouldn't be haunted by her presence.

Or she by mine.

My brother traced the route with a finger in the air. Then he blinked. "I'll be in Milan next week. What day are you there?"

I read out the date, and he pulled a thinking face. "My audition is right before your gig. Same day."

"I'm only there a day, then I'm driving to Germany." An idea struck me. "Join me. I'll be bored as fuck driving between cities on my own. We can have a laugh."

"A road trip? I'm in. Anything to put off flying again so soon."

We grinned at each other, and I lay back beside my brother, gazing through the gap left for skylights. Purple night crept over the land. Endless stars popped up, spreading over us.

"It's so quiet here," Ally said. "We already live miles from anywhere. But the castle has life and noise, where this place is a work in sensory deprivation."

"I need that. It's like I need isolation to breathe. You got all the extrovert genes and me the introvert."

He blew out a breath. "How are ye going to handle the crowds? It'll be nonstop."

I loved my job, but spending time around people exhausted me. "I have no idea."

"Ye know the question you asked earlier?" Ally said into the gathering dusk.

"Which one?"

"Had I ever turned down a lass. There was one time I should've. I didn't, and it's been bothering me."

My twin carried an air of not giving a shite about anything. I, more than anyone, knew that to be untrue. He cared, and deeply. "Who?"

"Remember Kaylee?"

The name was familiar. "She was your fan?"

"Aye. And my first."

Ah. The first girl he'd slept with, back when we'd regularly post videos online of us messing around on the estate. It had been the same weekend I'd lost my virginity to Taylor. Oh boy, now I was remembering that night...

I shook it off and focused on my brother. "I thought you never slept with the same lass twice."

"I don't. Except for her. She came to see me a few months ago and she was upset. We'd always chatted, and I didnae like to see her unhappy."

"So you slept with her?"

"Don't judge."

"I'm not. I almost wish I'd done the same with Taylor." Except that was my hormones talking.

"No ye don't." Ally propped himself up on an elbow. "I didn't plan to sleep with Kaylee, but she'd had all this shite happen in her life and she told me the one good thing, the only thing that kept her going, was her memories of us."

I grimaced. "Poor her."

He made a sound that was half laughter and half frustration. "Aye, I pitied her and then didn't stop her when she pounced on me. In fact, once we got started, I did everything I could to make her happy."

"Stop. If ye try and give me a single detail, I'm throwing you out the window."

He reached over and shoved me then buried his face in his sleeping bag. "I wasn't going to. I just wanted to talk about it."

"Are ye still in contact?"

"No. I drove her home and I've sent her a couple of messages, but she hasn't replied."

"I'm not sure what else ye can do."

The battery-powered lamp flickered, dimming.

The inexplicable hurt of missing Taylor rose again. "If Taylor asked me again, I don't think I could turn her down."

"That's because you're in love with her," Ally replied, muffled.

"I'm not."

"Ye would be if she stayed around long enough."

Fucking hell. At least I was leaving her this time. Not that she'd been in contact. Despite the fact that she was on my family estate, thousands of miles from her home, she hadn't even sent a one-word *Hi*.

Which told me all I needed to know.

It was a messed-up kind of torture, having something, someone, I badly wanted so close but so far.

The want would fade with the distance. It had to. One more day, and I'd be gone.

6

WHAT WE'VE ALWAYS DONE

Taylor

  In my teenage years, stuck in boarding school, I'd been an impulsive girl. Leaping from grand idea to new plan. Chasing boys. Pushing the limits of the school's rules. Always craving the things I couldn't have and imagining the time when I'd be able to tear the world apart to get them.

I'd been so close to freedom.

Then Charity's illness had struck.

Everything had changed. At eighteen, I had been poised to take over the world, finally out of my parents' control, then *bam*. The news hit me like a missile, exploding my dreams.

I'd made bad choices then, that was for sure.

I'd nearly lost the friendship of the woman sitting opposite me now, Ella, my best friend, but we'd healed. She knew everything. I'd told her years ago, and she understood. Ella's own family had been torn apart by tragedy, and she knew the importance of making good what you had.

Tonight, after she'd waited hours for my delayed flight, I'd told her about my engagement.

She'd simply hugged me. And this time I'd resisted the urge to burst into tears.

With Terence driving, I'd visited the Hamptons care home where Charity, my aunt, lived. I'd spent three days at her side, learning about her routine, meeting her carers and seeing the changes from my last visit.

I'd had to do it.

To remind myself why I had put myself forward as a human sacrifice. To remind myself why I wouldn't consider other options. Then I'd travelled to Scotland with Charity's words in my head, needing the hug of a friend.

It was evening by the time we'd got back to the Cairngorms and the castle Ella owned with her husband. He'd eaten with us but had otherwise left us to catch up.

I liked Gordain, but I didn't think he thought much of me. He'd certainly looked at me oddly before he'd left.

"I told Charity about getting engaged," I said to Ella.

"What did she think? I assume you didn't tell her you were doing it for her."

I shuddered. "God, no. I can't even imagine what she'd do if she knew. No, she had another idea. Do you remember when she last came to visit? We were about fourteen."

Ella pushed her fingers into her hair, shaking out her black curls from a clip. "I do. She took us out. It's hard to forget days like that when we were the only girls who no one came to see."

A painful pressure built in my chest. "She knew she was ill then. But she never told me. She made a decision to travel as much as she could, and visiting England was part of it. Visiting me because she knew she'd never be able to again."

My friend picked up the wine bottle and waggled it. I held out my glass, and she topped me up.

"I want to follow in her steps. She gifted me her diary, so I'm going to make a bucket list. Then I'm going to do all of those things before I get engaged. After that, I won't be able to use the bathroom without an interested party attending."

Ella raised her eyebrows. "I'm flattered to be first on your list." Then she paused. "Or maybe I'm second. Do you plan on seeing Wasp?"

"Yes." The word dropped out of my mouth and hung in the air. "I've told myself that it's to apologise for throwing myself at him—"

"But it isn't," Ella finished for me then flexed a toe towards the musical-note-patterned rug in front of the couch. Her study was set up as a musician's Aladdin's Cave, with bookshelves lined with music, her precious violin that her husband bought for her on a stand. Then on the walls were family pictures; her brother, James, and his wife, Beth, plus their son and daughter. Then Gordain with his brothers.

I stared at William in the frame. In the picture, all four men wore kilts. Kilts! Dressed for a wedding. The effect was devastating. "I want a night with him. Or a few days. Or a week. I want to bury myself in someone good and honest and just forget."

"You'll end up hurt."

"I know."

"Both of you."

I opened and closed my mouth. "Not if we are upfront. He knows about the arrangement with Theo. If he's up for this then we'll set boundaries. We've been doing this for years and we've both walked away unscathed in the past."

Whether my friend agreed with this or not, she didn't

say. Instead, she moved to her desk and woke her laptop, gazing at the screen. "I'm waiting on an email, sorry. There's a posse of musicians staying here over the next week. We're recording a piece for a film score. It'll be noisy, and I'll be distracted. You're more than welcome to listen in, but it'll get boring after a while."

"Then if I disappear off with William you won't mind?"

She shook her head, her attention still on the screen. "I'd expect it. You know, it's so weird to hear you call him William. Nobody else does."

"Force of habit." I cast my mind back to when I'd first heard of William McRae. "You told me your brother had met this family. These Highlanders who lived in this incredible place. You called him William then, before you knew his nickname."

"That's James's influence. He doesn't use nicknames."

Inwardly, I winced. Ella's brother was a no-go territory for me. And the rest of the McRae family. Ella and the twins were the only members who didn't judge me.

My best friend fitted in here in a way I never could.

She tapped away at her laptop, making her arrangements for her busy and fulfilling life. Her career had taken off, and she produced music for movies and video games. I envied her that. I envied her everything.

"Can I borrow your car?" I leapt to my feet, energy flooding me.

Ella blinked. "Are you going to see Wasp? He isn't at the castle."

Right! He'd mentioned a house he was renovating. "Then can I borrow you, too? Can you take me to wherever he is?"

After a childhood of deprivation, Ella and I never said

no to the other. I knew that, and I abused our history all the same.

She slipped off her chair and grabbed her keys. "Let's go."

* * *

*W*e exited Braithar Castle and climbed into Ella's 4x4. She drove us into the night, plunging us into darkness. Before, when I'd visited her here, I'd always found the absolute blackness intimidating.

I didn't now.

Everywhere else felt threatening, but the Highlands enveloped us like a blanket, soft and protective.

After twenty minutes of bumpy lanes and a climb over an open hillside, a long, stone building appeared in the headlights. A single window let out orange lamp light, immediately obscured by two bodies jostling to see who was coming.

My throat constricted.

A raucous laugh echoed as we neared.

"Ally stayed with Wasp. He knew you were here," Ella explained.

"I should've called him. I don't know what I'm doing."

"You'll work it out." She brought the car to a halt and paused. "What else is on your bucket list? Had you thought past getting here and seeing us?"

"Not really."

In the house, the lamplight moved, appearing again in a downstairs window.

"After Charity visited us at school, she went to see the Eiffel Tower in Paris, then the Leaning Tower in Pisa. She ticked off a whole host of amazing sites. Once William gets fed up with me, I make a start on her list."

Ahead, the door to the house flung open. Two tall, almost identical men appeared in the frame, shielding their eyes from the headlights. William frowned, but his twin wore his typical wide grin.

A shiver took me. "What if this is a terrible idea?"

"What if it's not?" Ella killed the headlights and opened her door, the car's interior lights putting us on display.

"I knew it!" Ally howled, slapping his brother on the chest.

William didn't say a word, but he approached the car, his twin disappearing inside the house. I hopped down, my legs suddenly wobbly, the cool night air slipping under my skirt.

"Hi," I said as soon as he was close.

"Hello," he replied.

"I..." No more words came.

We stood there, gazing at each other.

"Not like you to be tongue-tied," he murmured.

That was a fact. The first time we met, I'd practically jumped on him, ordering him around, instantly attracted to the lanky teenager and needing the sort of comfort that could only be found in strong, eager male arms.

But this was so different.

He wasn't a stranger, and he wasn't quite a friend. I had no idea where to place William in my life.

At William's back, Ally bounded from the house, shrugging a jacket onto his shoulders. "Els, drop me home, will ye?"

He slipped past his brother and lifted me from my feet, embracing me in a hard hug. "How ye doing, Tay? Nice of you to stop by."

"All the better for being here," I said into his shoulder. I loved Ally, I really did, but the wrong twin was holding me.

"Put her down," William groused to his brother. "And go away."

Ally laughed and set me back on my feet. "I knew this would all be for naught. See ye in the morning. We'll be here early to get the roof on before ye leave. Don't make us wait while ye find your clothes."

"Goodnight, Ally," William and I both said in unison.

"See you tomorrow, Ella. I won't get in the way if you're working," I said to my friend.

She gave me a quick grin then swapped a meaningful glance with William. Ella loved her family deeply, including her brothers-in-law. But she loved me, too. Otherwise I had the feeling she wouldn't have brought me here at all.

Then they were gone, leaving us alone in the dark.

"Are you going somewhere tomorrow?" I asked. Ally had said he was leaving.

William gestured to the house, and I followed him inside. By the light of the single lamp—I guessed he hadn't yet got power—I took in the open space. Stone walls. Big rooms. Irregular window and door openings. Charmingly rustic.

Under my feet, crumbling tiles made up the floor, and to my right, a new wooden staircase led up to a second floor. The left side was wide open and airy. I could imagine it being gorgeous when fitted out as a lounge, with tall windows giving views back down the hillside.

How like William, to be able to take something broken down and see past the decay to picture it as a thing of beauty.

"This place is incredible."

"It's cold. Come." He started up the stairs, and I traipsed after him.

Like downstairs, the next floor hadn't been divided up into rooms yet. In one corner, a little camp had been made with sleeping bags and a few beer bottles. I hadn't noticed the chill until now, but I shivered.

William sat on one bag so I took the other. Warmth spread through my limbs, and my shiver turned bone deep.

"That one's mine, but I'd rather I took Ally's than you." He raised a hand as if to touch me but dropped it again. "Why did ye come here?"

"I have a month of freedom."

Emotion flickered in his otherwise carefully neutral expression. "You're not engaged?"

"Not yet."

Before, when William and I had found ourselves in each other's company, one shared look would have been enough to have us sneaking away. Lust turned William into a different man, giving him a kind of dominance that weakened my knees. His usual calm exterior rippled, and raw energy flooded my way.

After he'd turned me down in New York, I wasn't sure if I'd ever see that same expression on his face again.

He raised his gaze, and his eyes flashed with heat. "Ye came here for me? To do what we've always done?"

It wasn't quite the truth, but I dipped my head. Please, please let him not turn me down again.

"Then get on your feet and get downstairs, lass. If this is going to be our last time, we're going to make it good."

Thank God for that.

7

CLASH AND CLAW

W *asp*

Heat and lust had my muscles tight, and I leapt up, prowling after Taylor. She descended to the ground floor, peeking over her shoulder at me, eyes wide and bright and fucking gorgeous.

How I'd said no to her in New York was beyond me.

Now, I was a slave to the age-old attraction I had for the lass.

As she moved, she slipped off her coat and left it where it fell. I stepped over it, dragging my work-roughened hoodie over my head, tossing it to the floor.

Taylor stopped in the centre of the room, gazing up at me.

With menace in my moves, I slipped my belt from my jeans. It always went this way, my alpha male side taking over. She brought it out in me. Only her.

"Kiss me," she whispered.

"No. On your knees."

She complied instantly, and a chill ran down my spine.

"Slip your dress straps down your arms."

One after the other, the straps fell. Then, without my asking, she unclipped her bra and discarded it, palming her breasts, exposing herself to me.

My blood flooded south, hardening my dick and leaving me lightheaded. Her tits had the power to drive me insane. A perfect handful. Fucking mouthwatering.

And she knew it.

She massaged herself, keeping her gaze fixed on mine. "I hated you telling me no."

"I hated telling you no."

"But you're saying yes now."

"Stop talking. My house, I'm in control."

She gave an excited grin. "Then tell me what to do."

I took a seat on the wide slate windowsill. The lamp remained upstairs, so only a dim glow lit the room. "Undo my jeans."

Taylor shifted over to me, topless and so sexy. She palmed my thighs and tossed her untied hair over her shoulder, working my button and zipper. My dick sprang free, and she instantly caught hold. Then she put her mouth over the end.

Christ.

Heat enveloped me. She moved on my cock, giving me my first blow job in forever. A groan escaped my throat, and I dug my fingers into her hair, slowing her down.

"I love your cock. It's thick, and you taste amazing," she said, easing up.

"Hush your mouth."

Reaching out, I took two handfuls of her irresistible round tits. Taylor moaned and worked me harder. Then I had an idea.

I wanted to get her out of my system. I'd told myself if

she came for me again, I wouldn't turn her away. Maybe the two could be combined. There were so many things we hadn't done together. Our trysts had always been fast and hard.

Fuck. No. There wasn't time to start that list. We only had tonight.

Her hand snaked between my legs, and she took hold of my balls, returning to her job of blowing me. I gritted my teeth and took it for as long as I could, all my nerve endings alight with sheer fucking pleasure.

All of a sudden, it was too much.

"Stand up," I barked, my head in a whirl.

She did, and I clambered to my feet. Then I switched our positions and bent her over the windowsill.

Sinking to my knees behind her, I lifted her skirt, exposing her pert backside in a barely there thong.

Oh *fuck*.

"Legs apart. Wider," I ordered, my voice hoarse now.

Taylor complied, exposing her crotch to me. In a second, I had her underwear aside and my tongue giving her a nice long lick.

"God!" she yelled.

I used my thumbs to open her to me and set about licking the soaking wet pussy I'd dreamed about.

Taylor swore, pushing against my mouth. Under my tongue, she grew swollen and even wetter. The distance between her inviting centre and my hard, waiting dick tantalised me.

I needed her to come quickly so I could slam inside her.

Angling my head, I licked her clit then slid two fingers inside her, pulling back to watch my work. She clenched hard on me, and her noises of pleasure got louder.

This, I loved. This game of getting her off. Gliding into

her tight heat and hitting the spot that made her moan. Whatever we were or weren't to each other, sex came as natural as breathing.

"Please, William. Fuck me. I need you. I want to come on your cock."

Yes. In my wallet, I had condoms. But that meant running back upstairs.

Then a dawning realisation had me losing my rhythm. Confusion overrode my horny state. In the same way I'd refused to kiss Taylor, I knew I shouldn't—couldn't—fuck her. Not if I wasn't sure where my head was at.

She wanted satisfaction.

We both did.

That I could do.

Ramping up the pressure, I crooked my fingers, using my other hand to work her clit. I made fast circles, guided by her reactions. She groaned helplessly, and I laid my head on her arse and bit down on her cheek, no small amount of frustration in my act.

"Oh fuck. You're going to make me come. Fuck!" She yelped, then her muscles tightened on my hand, her moans turning long and undulating. Taylor collapsed onto the windowsill, breathing hard and spent.

I reared up, blood surging. Taking my neglected dick in my hand, I pumped my shaft. What a sight, her body ready and waiting for me to fuck.

It would be the easiest thing in the world to push inside her now. Use the last throbs of her orgasm to fuel my own. She'd howl. She would feel like heaven.

I let the thought push me to the edge and concentrated my efforts on the end of my sensitive dick, frantic in my moves.

With my free hand, I splayed my fingers across Taylor's lower back, then, with a roar, I came, hard, splashing come onto her pert, round backside.

My balls emptied, and my head swam in dizzy release, and I gripped her hip, digging my fingers in to keep me steady. But as I came back to earth, calming from the lush high, intense dissatisfaction replaced my happiness.

What the fuck was that?

Taylor chuckled. "Um, did you just come all over my ass? Maybe a little help on clean up?"

I muttered an apology, stumbling as I sought a roll of kitchen paper I knew had been left down here.

Locating it, I cleaned her up, and silently, we set about righting our clothes.

Awkwardness fell over us.

We didn't make eye contact.

This was new, too. Sex had always been fun. We'd clash and claw at each other then hug it out after, satisfied and joyful.

Unhappiness dogged my movements, and I had no fucking clue what to do.

"If you want, I can run you back to Braithar now," I muttered, not looking at her.

"I don't mind bunking here. I never went camping. It'll be fun."

I raised my chin in agreement, and we returned upstairs. A sort of flatness had come over me. I'd never felt like that before and couldn't clear my head.

Taylor crawled into my sleeping bag, and I took the other. Then I killed the lamp.

For two people who'd known each other as long as we had, we could've been strangers.

"Thank you for letting me come here. I mean stay here." Taylor gave a short laugh that was anything but humorous.

"Night," I managed in return, then I lay on my back and listened to her breathe while I didn't sleep a wink.

THAT KISS

Taylor

After an hour or so of unsuccessfully trying to sleep, I rolled over to find William's eyes open. In the starlight, he watched me, his head on his hand.

"Can I ask you something?" I said. A number of things were bothering me. I wouldn't give air to most of them, but a sense dogged me, an insidious voice in my head that told me bad things. It had always been there, but I'd learned to ignore it.

Mostly.

It said I was ugly inside. It said I was unlovable. It said I wasn't good enough.

Maybe on some level I believed that voice; after all, my parents hadn't kept me around. But being with William had always silenced it. Every time.

Tonight had been the first time I'd heard it in his presence.

"Anything, lass."

"Why did we go downstairs to have sex?"

He drew a breath. "That was to do with this house."

"How?"

"I had my eye on this place since Ally and I discovered it when we were about six. It has stood here for three hundred years but been empty for God knows how long. Even as a boy, I wanted to strip it to its bones and make a home of it." His voice grew earnest. "It would be my space. Maybe living here first with my brother but then, eventually, I'd raise a family, ye ken. With my lass."

I blinked, not quite understanding.

"It felt wrong having sex where I'd be sleeping with the woman I loved," he finished.

Oh.

Right.

The picture became crystal clear. In a rush of mortification, I rolled to my back, feeling cheap. The second time I'd become emotional in his presence. Why did I care? What the fuck was wrong with me?

But wasn't that the point he was trying to make?

William was a good man. He'd be an excellent husband and father, when he was ready. He even paid respect to that imaginary family long before they existed.

Then there was me.

Pretty enough to mess around with, but even my presence put a stain on a happy future. I could be a trophy wife, valued only in how much I'd been bought for. Not beloved or cherished or enough to build a life around.

Breathtaking, really, in how different the two roles were.

A startled laugh left me, like a small animal scared from its hiding place.

"Ah fuck. I just realised how that sounded. I didn't mean it like that." A rustling of sleeping bag came, and William bundled me into his arms. "That came out wrong, I hear it now."

He tucked his head down against mine, aligning our bodies. Where my sleeping bag was zipped up, cocooning me, his had been open, acting as a blanket. It allowed him now to throw his knee over my hip and pull me into his space.

We lay together for a minute, just breathing. Him holding me tight.

He spoke in a whisper. "For a long time, I had you in my head when I thought of living here. You were my bride."

"You did not imagine me here," I disagreed, my voice shaky in a way I hated.

"Fact. It only changed when you stopped seeing me on your visits to Ella. I figured you'd moved on so I had to as well."

"What does your wife look like now in your vision?" I managed.

"I'm not answering that." His voice dipped lower still.

Soft lips landed on my hairline.

I tipped my head up, and William's hot mouth carefully took mine. It was an apology kiss, I guessed, but in the dark, with the warmth of his body finding its way to mine, it became the most sensual kiss I'd ever had.

We moved together, mouths fused, keeping it slow but oh so tender.

I stretched out against him, and he held me close, but this wasn't about sex or our bodies. It was something else I couldn't name.

God, I envied that future wife, getting this kiss every night. To have his full care and attention; even the friendly edge I'd had filled me up to overflowing.

If I'd been the type of person who could love, I'd have fallen head over heels for that kiss. I think I even whispered the words to William, earning a fresh surge and a harder hold.

But I wasn't a normal woman and I wasn't made for anything good.

At some point, wrapped up in William, I fell asleep, dreaming of a sweet and happy life I could never have.

* * *

"*U*h, guys?" Ally's voice woke me with a start.

I opened my eyes to William blinking back at me, inches from my face.

"Yeah?" He raised his head and called to his twin.

"What did I say about picking up your clothes?" Ally said from downstairs, laughter in his tone.

"Oh shit. My bra. Your sweater and belt," I squeaked.

Not that I was bothered about Ally seeing my underwear, but I suspected William might be.

He kissed me on the nose then pushed up to sitting, grumbling as he found his feet.

My gaze locked onto his crotch, and I stifled a laugh. "You might want to wait a second before you go down." I pointed at his prominent bulge.

William glanced down then snorted. "I grew up with three brothers and, after Ma left, no women around for most of it. Dicks do this in the morning. None of us care." He trod into his workman boots and strode down the stairs.

A laugh bubbled up. Unwittingly, he'd painted a picture of four men in the castle, all with erections, bleary eyed and ignoring the others while they made their morning coffee.

I added kilts to the image and cracked up.

"You sound chirpy, Tay," Ally hollered from the bottom of the stairs. "Good night, was it?"

"Wouldn't you like to know?" I replied.

"Aye. Give me details. I'm sex-starved."

"I find that hard to believe."

William returned, our clothes clutched over his middle and a flask of coffee in his hand. "Shite, Ella's down there. Lucky she wasn't looking." He politely turned away, and I reinstated my bra while he poured a cup.

"Nectar of the gods," I muttered, taking the offered coffee and burning my lips in my eagerness.

"Morning, Ella. Hi, everyone," I called to the newcomers.

"Hey, Tay," Ella yelled back. "I'll give you a lift if you're coming back to Braithar."

"I will, give me a minute."

A variety of *Morning, Taylor* and *Hey, lass* floated up from William's brothers. I grinned, for the first time feeling that they didn't all hate me.

William took a deep pull of coffee, and I admired the line of his throat under the overlong scruff.

"We're putting the tiles on today," he said, pointing at the open framework of the roof above our heads, daylight highlighting the carefully made structure.

Following his gesture, I gazed up with interest. "I can't believe you've done all this."

"Fits and starts. I've been away a lot so it's only now that it's house-shaped again."

"You never did say where you're going next. Or when." If we could have a few more nights like this, I'd be in Heaven.

He passed back our shared coffee. "I leave tonight for work. I'm away for a few weeks."

Oh. I took a drink, concealing my disappointment by twisting to disentangle myself from the sleeping bag. Well, what had I expected? He wasn't mine to follow around.

Ella was busy recording for the next week. I could stay with her but I'd be in the way.

I'd have to ramp up my ideas and start my bucket list. Today, even.

"What are your plans?" William asked.

"Is it safe to go up on the roof? We don't want to accidentally see anything we shouldnae through the skylights," one of William's older brothers called.

"Go for it, G. We're decent," he shouted.

"I'm going to Europe. I have some travelling to do." I put the cup on the floorboards and slipped on my shoes. With the crofthouse having old windows and gaps in the roof, the cold of the morning enveloped me. I shivered and took up my jacket.

William watched me. "Alone?"

"Yep. But I've been catching flights alone since I was eleven. It's no biggie. I'm happy on my own."

Overhead, bootsteps clopped on the roof. Male voices called instructions, and I took my cue to leave.

Fifty different ways of saying goodbye passed through my mind. I wouldn't see William again now until after I was engaged. He had work booked in for the entirety of my month of freedom. Maybe it would be better this way, but that didn't explain the strange pang in my chest or my entire inability to put voice to my farewells.

So, instead, I leaned in and kissed him.

His lips took mine, hunger and a new kind of possessiveness in his move. "Talk to me later. Don't go anywhere without speaking with me first."

I should nod and leave but I paused, desperate for crumbs. "Why?"

"What is the first stop on your travels?"

I plucked a location from Charity's itinerary. I could go

anywhere, in any order, but I opened my mouth and said, "Paris."

William's dark-blond eyebrows drew together in a deep frown. Someone shouted for him again from the roof, but he ignored them. "I am, too. Tonight. Same place."

He dragged his fingers through his hair and took a step back. "I need to finish this roof today, but wait for me, aye? Travel with me. Like we did before."

The day after we'd first met, after I'd taken his virginity, we'd flown to the US together, separate destinations but together through the flight across the Atlantic. He'd held my hand, chatted happily, this fresh-faced tall teenager. He'd changed so much, whereas I was the same selfish, awful creature I'd always been.

Still, his orders... I could never ignore them.

The relief of having more time with him washed over me like a gentle wave on a beach. "I'll wait."

William kissed me square on the mouth. "Book your ticket or change it to match mine. I'll text you the details." His eyes lit, and he shone, effortlessly handsome and good. He bounced over to the nearest skylight, boosted himself on the windowsill, and peered up. "Cal. Give me hand. Let's get a roof on my house."

A thick arm descended and hauled my laughing High-lander through the gap. I gaped at his disappearance then descended the wooden stairs to where Ella waited.

For the first time in forever, my smile was genuine and my step buoyant. If I had a heart, it would be hopeful.

If I was anyone other than myself, tonight could be the making of something wonderful.

* * *

*F*or the rest of the morning, I mingled with Ella's musician friends, some of whom I'd met when I'd visited her at university a few years back. They got down to the business of chopping up the track they were recording, and I watched for a little while before making myself scarce.

A woman swept into Braithar's great hall, two blond children at her heels, entering through the front door while I emerged from the dining room. It was Mathilda, Ella's sister-in-law.

Also best friend to Beth, James's wife.

In the same way I'd avoided William on my few visits to the Highlands, I'd also avoided his extended family, knowing they'd think badly of me.

I'd been the alternate bride for James, causing strife in his family, though he and I had nothing to do with each other, other than by the arrangement. Beth would certainly dislike me. Her closest friend would be with her in solidarity.

I wouldn't blame them one bit.

"Hey, if you're looking for Ella, she's just started recording. She might be a while." I plastered on a smile and hid my nerves.

Mathilda gave me a curious look, her gaze flicking over me subtly. "We popped by so Lennox could pick up a sketchpad he left here." She gave a nod to the two pretty children, and the boy and girl vanished down a corridor. "But I need a second pair of eyes on a contract I've been offered. I was going to ask Ella's opinion."

I knew Mathilda ran a wedding business. I also knew a decent amount about contracts. Not that I thought she'd accept my help. Still, I opened my mouth. "I have a business degree. If you like, I could...?"

The older woman blinked then tilted her head, blonde spiral curls bobbing with the movement. "That's kind of you to offer. Yes, I'd appreciate that."

At my gesture, we moved to a table under a window. Mathilda brought out a tablet from her bag and found the document from a food supply business. In a few minutes, I'd read over the salient parts and understood the issue.

"This isn't a strict supply arrangement. The offer they are making is to share the management of this whole function. Fifty-fifty ownership of a segmented part of their company. Is that what you wanted?"

She shook her head. "Not at all. I said I could maybe provide staff—we have several casual workers who help with the weddings. Teenagers mostly. I didn't want to do them out of a job by hiring this company. But I don't need the headache of having another part of this business to run. My office manager quit a couple of weeks ago, so it's all on me right now."

I skimmed the next set of paragraphs. "I don't think you should sign this. Go back to them and explain your offer— to hire them to provide the full service as you described, using your pool of staff at their discretion. Otherwise you take on liability and all kinds of trouble." I checked the dates. "This is for the autumn? You've got time."

She sighed, her gaze tracking the children as they returned, the boy scowling at a pad of paper in his hands. "Time maybe, but there's not enough of me to go around. I knew this was too good to be true. Thank you. You've saved me."

I went to reply, but my words got stuck. My degree, my whole education, had languished, unused, and I hadn't really cared. But this buzz from helping out, from spotting a potential problem... I felt smart.

"Let me give you my email," I blurted. "Forward me the next version. Or I can write back to them. If you want."

Mathilda's eyes widened. "Really? That would be incredibly helpful. Are you sure?"

We exchanged details, and I promised to help however I could. She left, and I sank back into my seat, a little freaked out.

Other than Ella, I had few female friends. More acquaintances who associated with me because of my name. I didn't know how to act around women. At least, I didn't think I did before that conversation.

Buoyed, I took out Charity's diary from my purse and, for the first time, read it through from end to end. Against each of the entries, she'd added notes in an untidy scrawl, like a tick list of goals or achievements. Perhaps aiming to follow everything she did would be stretching my time, but not all were location-based. As I worked my way through the list, only half were tied to actual places. Like, *Stand under the Eiffel Tower and look up.*

Some were so way out there, they made me snicker out loud.

Scream into a storm on the edge of a cliff.

Laugh until I pee myself.

Where others had sadness rearing its head once more.

Make love to someone I'm in love with.

She'd crossed them all off, adding details but omitting others, and I wondered who her beau had been on the latter point. She'd never married, so it clearly hadn't worked out.

I wouldn't make it to the end of the list, but I'd make every effort to see the world through her eyes. If William could be by my side for the beginning, I'd have a good time, too.

Which made me consider an idea. A proposal for the Highlander. I wanted more than the flight together. After last night, maybe he'd thawed to spending more time with me.

I just had to think of a way to convince him.

INDECENT PROPOSAL

W *asp* The crofthouse had been my passion forever. Completing the roof and making it watertight, working alongside my brothers plus the glazers who'd already installed the skylights and were now at the other end of the building putting in huge folding doors, should've been a dream.

In the winter, I'd be able to watch the Cairngorms wildlife from the snug lounge. Golden eagles soaring over the glen. Pine martens and grouse stepping over the snow drifts. I'd underplayed the importance of quiet and isolation when I'd spoken to Ally. My brain didn't work well without it.

But right now, my mind was otherwise engaged.

Off down the rutted track, over heather-strewn Glen Durie, following the loch's river all the way to Braithar. Right to the feet of a yellow-haired lass.

Lord, I was fucked.

It was the words Taylor had muttered while we'd kissed that had me distracted.

"If I could love..."

Why couldn't she love? What was stopping her?

Down the roof, Callum handed off a stack of tiles to Gordain, my two older, *married* brothers working in comfortable silence. Ally had gone to fetch lunch. Gordain turned and descended the ladder once more, and I moved over to squat on the roof ridge, adjacent to Callum.

The man, ten years older than me, had practically raised me. He knew all my secrets, and I'd never hidden a thing from him. I found the question coming out of my mouth before I realised I wanted to ask it.

"When did ye know that ye wanted to be married?"

Callum raised his head, his forehead lined in consternation. To strangers, he looked fearsome, but we were used to his stern expression. "About the first moment I saw Mathilda across a crowded hall. Why?"

Callum's wife had been engaged to someone else when they'd met. Or that someone else had announced their engagement before Mathilda had actually agreed to it. I'd been with her when it had happened. My brother was fiercely protective of his wife, so I wasn't about to raise that fact, but the parallels were there.

I placed a hand on a tile, securely fixed. "Because in my head, this place is my family home, but the only woman I ever pictured marrying is Taylor. A woman I've barely spent a day with at any one time. One who once told me she didn't like the outdoors or hiking. Who couldnae be less suited to me."

Callum tilted his head. Concern filled his expression. "Gordain said that your lass is getting engaged next month. She asked Ella if the two of them would go to the engagement party. She said she'd need the moral support."

Well, fuck. "Aye. She might. It's a political match. An arrangement."

Marriage and fatherhood had mellowed Callum. He used to shout before he thought. Now, he pondered for a minute, setting a neatly cut tile in place around a skylight before answering. "What does she get out of it?"

This was the bit I wasn't clear about. I shrugged, fixing my gaze down the glen to the loch. "I'm not sure."

Callum rose, carefully easing over the roof to sit next to me on the apex. The man was huge, several inches taller than my six-three height. "The lass showed up here last night, looking for ye."

"Aye. For sex."

Callum winced. I did, too, because it sounded so tawdry. Plus, in his eyes, I was no doubt still a wee lad needing his care and protection.

I continued, "I think seeing her again is why marriage is on my mind. It's not like I'm ready. I don't have a steady income or even savings now. I've blown all the money I made in New York on tiles and windows." Until I got my first pay cheque from Reportage One, I was broke, using the remainders of my cash to cover the expenses of my next job.

"And then there's the other issue. With me."

My brother drew back, a silent question in his quizzical look.

"I mean how I get."

"There's nothing wrong with you."

"That's not true." Our father had been the first to call me on my weird behaviour, masked though it was by Ally's more exuberant, attention-seeking ways. I had times where my brain maxed out and couldn't take any more. An extreme form of introversion caused by overwhelm. My career would strip me to the bone but, if I was careful, I hoped I could manage it. Maybe I could do the same with Taylor. Have the sex-fuelled fling she wanted then return home.

Callum shook his head. "So you need quiet sometimes? Everyone does to a greater or lesser extent."

"Not everyone. Not Taylor. She's like Ally, happy to be in the middle of things. Even if she wasn't getting engaged, she couldn't be happy living here with me."

"I thought you weren't ready to settle down?" My brother threw my own words back at me.

That was the true issue at stake. No matter how much fun Taylor and I had, we just weren't compatible. The fling was really my only option.

I gave a frustrated laugh. "I'm not. If all this goes wrong, if I crash and burn, at least I can come back here and hide in my cave. I want to do well at my job. I want to be a friend to Taylor but I know we'll end up sleeping together. Should I save myself the heartache and walk away now?"

Callum pulled an unamused expression. "That's the sort of question only you can answer, and ye most likely already have. You're leaving together tonight, aye?"

I nodded, needing him to give me the modicum of hope in what felt like a hopeless situation. Callum stretched out a long arm and hauled me into a side hug. We braced ourselves against the tiles, and I braced my heart for what was to come.

"I want ye to put yourself first. I also want ye to be a good friend to those you care about. The best plan is to find out what exactly her problem is and why she feels she needs to fix it with a wedding. There's always more than one way to a solution. That might not be easy for her to see, so help her, if ye can."

He'd said what I needed to hear. But he wasn't done.

"And at the end of it, we'll be here regardless. If ye come home and don't want to talk? Just tell us what work needs doing, and we'll follow your lead. We're here for ye, aye?"

I wanted to work out my head. One way or another, I'd get Taylor—the woman who couldn't love—out of my system. Even if it cost me my precious peace of mind.

* * *

A couple of hours later, with all four of us brothers toasting another completed job, rows of shining dark grey tiles at our feet, my oldest brother called our attention.

"I have news for ye." He stood on the scaffold and made eye contact with us each in turn, telling me that this was important. "Before ye all disappear off on travels and with work, I'm glad to tell ye that Mathilda and I are expecting again."

"Ah!" Gordain yelped and slid down the roof to embrace Callum. "Congratulations! Ye always wanted a big family."

Ally and I joined them, taking care at the edge of the roof but hugging our brother with rough thumps to his back.

Callum beamed. "Aye, well, it took a few years, but we're finally there. A single bairn this time, due in the autumn."

We celebrated with another beer, and I was so thrilled for them. Psyched that I'd get to be an uncle again.

But deep down, a wee unexpected hurt made itself known. Here we all were, working on my family home, but what plans did I have for a family?

Maybe I was more ready than I thought.

* * *

"*I* have a proposal for you," Taylor announced. She sat on her hands on the airport seat, her knees jiggling under a flowing skirt. I'd never seen her in trousers, or anything very casual. "A couple of days of doing what we do best. Sex. My schedule is flexible, so after Paris, I'll go where you go and be waiting when you finish work."

Despite the area around us being mostly vacant, my cheeks still heated with the idea of being overheard. "You're making me an indecent proposal?"

"I am. But not indecent. Very, very decent. Satisfying for both of us."

She didn't need to add the end to the sentence. *Unlike last night.* If anything, our clinch had only made me hornier for her. All day, through the repetitive hard work of carrying tile stacks up ladders, scratching my hands to hell even with heavy-duty gloves, I'd pictured her body.

Those gorgeous weighty breasts in my hands.

That wet, sweet centre waiting for me to bury myself.

Her smile, her lips, the way she made me fucking happy.

"Last night could've been better," I admitted.

"It was perfect."

"Nah. It wasn't."

"Then take my proposal. When you get bored of me, I'll go, but until then, we'll have a good time."

I gaped at her. "Bored of you? How could that ever happen?"

Her smile fixed, and she glanced away, her gaze skirting the line of passengers boarding another flight. "It's okay. I know what I am and what I'm not. Plus, you'll be working, so I'll take what I can get."

"No," I barked, annoyed, and annoyed at myself for letting it show. "I happen to be a great fan of spending time with ye. And I don't want ye travelling alone. Tell me your plans, and we'll see how we can go on after tonight."

She bit her glossy bottom lip. "I'm following a diary. Visiting the places in it."

"Whose?"

"A relative of mine." Taylor curled up in the chair. "When I was at boarding school, she came to England and visited me. That was kind of a big deal. I didn't get many visitors."

I leaned in, listening closely. I knew from Ella a little about their horrible time at school but never from Taylor.

"After that, she went on and did all of these exciting things, and I want to follow in her footsteps."

I raised my chin, fishing for more details. "Maybe I can document some of it for ye. It'll be fun for her to see how ye get on. Is visiting her on your list?"

"I just saw her before coming here. I'll go visit her again when I get back to the States." Her gaze clouded, but she drew a breath and squared her shoulders. "Now, tell me where your work is going to take you."

"On tour with a rock band. First, a few cities in Europe, then over to the US." I read out the places and dates.

She raised her eyebrows. "I know we found each other again in the middle of a gala, but following a rock band around is not what I expected you to say."

I hid my reaction. I had no idea how she saw me but maybe I should find out. Tell her about myself. Maybe that could be an aim of the couple of days we had together— truly get to know each other.

Taylor continued, "I can work around that plan."

My traitorous heart leapt. "For how long?"

"We'll see. Let's get there and make up our minds after we've burned up some of this heat." She gestured between her body and mine, zero embarrassment in her hopeful expression.

"I have to work tonight. I can't fucking believe it but I'll be going straight into a shoot with the band."

She raised an easy shoulder. "Like I said, I'll wait around. Do you know why?"

Taylor shifted onto her knees on her seat. She leaned on me, and her lips found mine in a slow, achingly sexual kiss.

Totally inappropriate for where we were. Clearly, neither of us cared.

Automatically, my eyes had closed, but I opened them again as she pulled back an inch, her fingers sliding through my beard.

"Because of that. Your kiss on its own is worth the wait."

Then she hopped off her chair, leaving me hot and hard, and staring after her.

"Come back," I said, helpless.

"Nope." Taylor cocked her head to listen to the Tannoy system. "They are calling our flight. We've got a plane to catch."

Where we weren't even sitting together. A groan left me as I rolled to my feet. "This is going to be the longest flight ever. Followed by the longest shift ever."

In response, I got a laugh, then we joined the queue of passengers at the gate. Taylor slipped her hand into mine and, though I was a head taller and twice as broad as most of the crowd, pride filled me at having her by my side.

We inched forward in the line and, near the front, Taylor pushed up onto her tiptoes and laid a sweet kiss on my cheek. To an onlooker, it might appear innocent, but the surge of pressure and the long, lasting look she gave me had me staring while she sauntered on ahead to book in.

Then the true torture began.

Just before I took my seat, half a plane away from Taylor, my pocket vibrated. Several times. I squeezed past the guy in the aisle and extracted my phone, sitting in the narrow chair.

Seven messages from the lass waited.

Do you remember the first time we met? I've been thinking about it.

I pretty much pounced on you, but you didn't say yes right away. I'd never met anyone who made me wait.

Then you fucked me like a machine. All power, and this pure kind of focus. You've said to me more than once that you felt conscious of your inexperience, but I never did.

I had no idea you were a virgin. I don't know if I ever told you that.

You're naturally an amazing lover, so giving and instinctive. We fit perfectly together.

It was always you I thought about, when I was alone and needing to get off. Your hands, your tongue, your heavy cock.

Christ, she was trying to kill me. I pulled at my collar and sank deeper into my seat, glancing around to ensure no one was peeking at my screen.

Another message landed.

Want to play a game? It involves trust.

My mind boggled, but still I responded quickly. *Yes.*

No reply appeared. I craned my neck to spot her in the cabin. Then I spied her blonde hair, braided down the centre of her head, as she stood from her seat. The plane had mostly filled, overhead compartments being slammed. Taylor slipped past fussing travellers and appeared at the end of my row.

"Sweetie, I think you have my phone by mistake." She held hers out to me, over the aisle guy, unlocked, and with her classy black-and-white case removed.

She might've tried to make her phone appear less feminine, but mine certainly looked masculine. For one thing, it was much bigger.

Still, I wanted to play.

I produced the device, raising an eyebrow in question as I offered it out.

"Unlocked," she mouthed, and I complied, a wariness descending.

Taylor journeyed back up the centre of the plane, and the stewards ushered the remaining passengers to their seats before locking the doors. In my hand, Taylor's phone lit with a message. From me.

I snorted a laugh and read it.

Now for the trust thing—your phone in my hands and mine in yours. All the opportunity to delve into each other's secrets. Or not. We'll swap back in thirty mins. Use that time to write in my notes a top fantasy you have for me. As dirty as you like, and as detailed as you like. I'm starting yours now, and oh boy, wait until you read it. Once we've read each other's, we can write a new one and swap back. By the end of the flight, we'll have a list to work through in the next couple of days.

The flight was under two hours. I was already sporting a semi under my thankfully thick jeans. This lass would be the death of me.

The flight mode sign pinged on the plane's seat controls, and the engines powered up, the stewards concluding their takeoff routine. I opened Taylor's notes app and stared. She'd already typed a header. *Yours, however you want me.*

Blowing out a breath, I tapped my head on the seat back. If only her statement were true. But what the hell. The game sounded a lot of fun.

I was in.

For thirty minutes, I sorted through a variety of fantasies

I'd had of her—yeah, there were many—before picking my favourite and typing it out.

When Taylor rose again from her seat, I did the same, squeezing back into the aisle before meeting her halfway.

We traded phones with shared, secret grins.

"I badly want to kiss you right now," I murmured in her ear.

The aircraft dipped, and she stumbled, clutching on to me.

There was no chance, not a tiny iota of an opportunity, to get away with the mile-high club. The plane was too small and far too busy, but still I placed a hand to her lower back and pressed her against me, showing her how she'd made me rock-hard with her game.

A person coming the other way down the plane forced us apart, but not before Taylor squeezed my fingers in her hand and whispered, "Round two, now."

Game on, lass.

10

PICTURE THIS

T̶aylor

I hurried back to my seat and opened the notes app on my phone, eager to read William's fantasy. From the first line, it didn't disappoint.

I'll take ye anyway I can have ye, but picture this: it's a Saturday afternoon. I get back from the castle gym, and you come in from a run. We arrive at the crofthouse door at the same moment. Before we've even stumbled inside the hall, I have my hands inside your running shorts, dragging them down your long legs. You get caught up trying to strip off your sports bra so I have unrestricted access to bury my face in your pussy.

I eat you out on the stone floor.

You're screaming in minutes. We're sweaty already but we get so hot, then you pull me up for a kiss, and I slide inside you, then we're fucking right there, like we can't keep our hands off each other to even make it to a soft surface.

God! My thighs clenched. I wanted that scene, and I made a mental note to find a hotel room with a stone floor to reenact it properly.

There was more.

After, I carry you up to our bedroom, and we take a hot shower. You go down on me, and I hold your gorgeous head, controlling the most incredible blow job. But I don't come. I save that until I'm inside ye again, bending you over under the hot water. Maybe using the powerful showerhead on your clit while I fuck you from behind.

There's a cheeky last line which has me smiling through my blushes.

After that, we have dinner and watch an old film. I might even let you choose.

Ah, William. He delivered on the sexual part of his dirty dream, but he'd also made it into a date. How wonderful was that?

My own fantasy had been for him to surprise me at work —which patently put it into fantasy land as I'd never have a proper job—then drag me away into an empty office and bend me over, too urgent to even undress me. Funny how we both liked that idea.

The flight tracker put us at halfway to Paris, and I needed a second to cool off before I jumped back into round two.

Instead, I considered my options for my bucket list. I'd visit the Eiffel Tower, sure, but maybe William could help me out with one or two more. Maybe the laughing until I cried one. Or perhaps the tears could wait until we had to part.

Would I cry for William McRae? This newfound emotion I had would guarantee a little heartache. How strange to be so sure of something I hadn't experienced yet.

How miserable, too. Not that I'd tell him. No need for both of us to mope.

I drummed my fingers on the phone then typed up another of the endless sexy times I wanted with this man.

We switched phones again. As we did, he kissed me right there in the aisle. It only lasted a second but contained a none too subtle message. He'd wavered over how much he wanted me, but the animal inside had won.

William was mine, for a little while, at least.

And I was his.

By the time it came to disembark, I was wet and more than willing, but there was no time to rest. After a ride in a high-smelling taxi from Charles de Gaul to the centre of the city, we came to a halt, the streetlight-illuminated road blocked by a chanting crowd.

"Christ. Look at this. They found the bands, then." William peered out of the window and enclosed me with one strong arm, but I could tell he was itching to start shooting.

Our fantasies would have to wait. Paris had plunged William right into his first job.

11

PANDEMONIUM

*W*asp

On the roadside, I kept Taylor in front of me, shouldering our luggage so the cab could drive away. The pavement heaved with people clamouring to get close to the front of the hotel Reportage One had directed me to.

Taylor gave a little hop and pointed up the building. On a brightly lit balcony, the lead singer of Hedonist stood with Rex, Viking Blue's vocalist.

"Hey, y'all!" Hedonist's singer howled. She shook out a mane of black-and-white hair. "What the fuck are you doing down there in the streets? Get your asses to the ticket office and buy up the last tickets for Saturday night. We have Viking Blue on our tour. How do you feel about that?"

The crowd roared, surging to get closer.

"That's Effie from Hedonist! Oh my God!" Taylor whooped.

For a second, I was torn. I should be pushing forwards to get into the thick of it and document the moment. This was what I was being paid for. But I couldn't take Taylor with me. Which meant leaving her here.

"Get your camera out!" Taylor whipped around and grabbed the bags at my shoulder. "This is huge! Effie never talks to the public. I'll carry these. Get the shot!"

With our sports bags braced in front of her like a battering ram, she thrust her way into the crowd. I hustled, keeping a gap around her as best I could while sliding my camera from its cushioned compartment. I snapped a burst of photos, instantly knowing that I had a cracking shot of Rex and Effie, the two lead singers, smirking at each other.

But the swell of people thickened. At the edges, French police barked orders. Taylor ducked to avoid a rowdy bunch of tourists caught in the mix.

"Want a sneak preview?" Rex shouted, riling the crowd further. "What do ye want to hear?"

On the balcony beside him, a uniformed guard appeared, his face apologetic but stern. They were being pulled back.

That one good shot would have to be enough.

"Let's get inside," I directed.

With a determined expression, Taylor shoved her way to the hotel's entrance. I produced a digital ID I had on my phone, and the wide-eyed doorman let us through, blocking attempts for others to follow. Then at the desk, I had them dial Viking Blue's publicity manager.

In a few minutes, Taylor and I were in an elevator heading upstairs.

"I'm crashing your gig." She gave me an apologetic shrug. "I would've gone off on my own but I kinda got swept up with it."

"I had no idea this was going to happen. Sorry," I replied, but we both grinned all the same. It was a rush, being in the centre of things.

On the tenth floor, we were met by security guards and

ushered into an overcrowded room. The place was in pande-monium, people everywhere. Reporters, lackeys, band members draped over furniture, everyone yelling at Rex and Effie as they returned from the balcony. I couldn't spot the manager so I started capturing the fuss.

"This is Mr McRae, official band photographer," Taylor said, talking to someone behind me.

I didn't look around, keeping my focus on getting the pictures.

"Ah right. And you are...?"

"His girlfriend and assistant, Taylor," she declared, effortlessly lying.

I guessed to make sure she wasn't thrown out, but it had my gut clenching all the same.

"Hey, it's the Highlander!" Rex spotted me and charged over. "You made it. Just in time, too."

I dropped my camera to my shoulder and raised my chin at him. "Nice gig you found for yourself."

He lifted his eyebrows into his blue punky hair. "Luck of the Scottish."

"Isn't that Luck of the Irish?" I snapped a shot of his delighted face.

"Not the way I'm looking at it." He smirked back. "We fell on our feet getting these nights. I can hardly believe it, but it's true. And I want the whole thing documented so we can prove to everyone that we hit the big time."

He ran through a list of events he wanted me to capture, all of which I'd already had from Reportage One. Then something caught his attention, and he stared over my shoulder. I glanced around to find Taylor chatting with a couple of people. She caught my eye. And blew me a kiss.

Fuck. That woman...

When I turned back to Rex, he had that same look in his

eye as when he'd first seen Taylor at the Met gala. Of hunger and want.

I knew that look. I wore it whenever she was around, too.

"Taylor. My lass," I announced, justifying the claiming because she'd done it first. Besides, fuck buddy didn't have the same ring.

And I really wanted that look off his face.

If Rex remembered her as the woman who'd blanked me a week ago, he didn't say, and the greedy lust melted from his expression. He gestured for me to follow him then introduced me to the band's publicist and a myriad of other faces. Then he and Effie posed for photos at the doorway of the balcony, the police presence now stopping them from whipping up the crowd any further.

I snapped into the zone and tamped down the buzzing in my head that came from being in such a busy place.

It was a good couple of hours before the meet up calmed and the group dispersed. The tour staff and managers had made their plans, and I hunched over my camera and laptop, getting the first batch of photos sent to the PR company. Within minutes, they'd been posted on various sites.

I never failed to get a kick out of seeing my photos out in the wild. I'd also never stop agonising over any perceived imperfections with white balance or lighting, but nobody complained, so I figured they were good enough.

"Wasp! Nine tomorrow at the tower?" The publicist, a neat, permanently smiling man named Freddie, waved.

"Aye. See ye there." My phone showed me it was after one in the morning, and I scoured the space for Taylor.

I couldn't see her, and there was no message, so I packed up my kit in a rush. Did I have the right to call her up and go to her? She could've found a room in the hotel.

She could've got bored waiting.

My mind slid to a darker place, where Taylor's wants might be fulfilled by someone other than me. We might be friends, but I had no claim over her. Rex wanted her, that was plain; hell, half the guys she walked past openly gawked.

If she'd wanted, she could've entertained herself in any number of ways.

I shook off the unwarranted jealousy, powering down my laptop and sliding it into the compartment in my camera bag. I shoved my kit about a little too hard.

Yeah, Taylor and I needed to talk about what this fling looked like or I'd go nuts by day two.

Then warm hands slid around my waist from behind. Taylor whispered in my ear, "Why the frown? Didn't your evening go well?"

Actually, it had gone really well. At least I hoped so. "Just had some miserable thoughts in my head," I grumped.

"Maybe I can help with that." She winked, and I brought her into my arms, abandoning my bag to the hotel room's coffee table.

Taylor dug her fingers into my hair and raked her nails over my scalp. I shivered, hopelessly turned on already. Like at the airport, this wasn't exactly the time, but at least here there was already an atmosphere of sex, drugs, and rock and roll. We didn't stand out.

"If you're done, can we take a walk and tick off my first item?"

"You haven't been out?"

She shook her head. "No. I socialised, drank a couple of glasses of free wine, and watched you. Not a bad night."

I ran a possessive hand up her spine. There were a few

people still milling around the space, so I resisted bringing her mouth to mine for a kiss. "We need a hotel room."

Taylor's eyes sparkled. "Ain't that the truth. But I already tried, and we're out of luck. Paris is crazy expensive, and it was too late to book into the cheapo places. The band's tour manager block booked rooms here for people to share. You have a bed in with two guys, and I bummed a day bed in with two sound technicians."

My mouth dropped open, and Taylor grinned. "Female ones. Chill, oh fearsome Highlander."

"Fearsome?"

She gazed at me then traced a finger over my furrowed brow. "You used to always be happy. Now, you have this stern look in place half the time. Nearly always when your attention is on me."

"Sorry, lass."

She heaved a sigh. "Call me lass again and you can stare at me with whatever expression you like."

A familiar Taylor-shaped bolt of happiness lifted me. "Right, *lass*. Let's find our rooms then go for a nighttime explore. If we can't sleep together then we'll walk around until we're tired."

She led the way, and I dropped off my kit. Taylor had already left our bags to claim our beds. She'd given herself the title of Photography Assistant, and no one had blinked. The woman could charm a grumpy troll.

Then we were outside the hotel and walking into the Parisian night. We picked our way down the pretty cobbled street in the 8th arrondissement—the nice district the band's management had chosen. Ornate, pale-stone buildings with balconies lined the wide Avenue George V and, at the end, the street opened out on the Seine river. The Eiffel Tower loomed to our right, across the dark water.

"Item number one on my list." Taylor gawped at the tower. "Shame it isn't lit up. It only flashes for a couple of minutes every hour."

"Maybe we'll be lucky. Let's get over there." I squeezed her fingers, and we put our heads down against the stiff spring breeze and half ran across the still-busy roads and over the Pont de l'Alma bridge. A long walk later, and we rounded the corner to the tower.

Taylor hopped with every step. "Look, look! William! Oh my God! I had no idea it was so massive."

Her excitement had me grinning. "It'll make a great shot if we stand underneath."

I'd left my camera kit at the hotel, not willing to get mugged on day one of my assignment, so we both snapped shots on our phones. The tower soared over our heads, the four feet giving acres of space underneath and a sweet view up into the ironwork.

Few people haunted the park around the tower, and the shops were all closed and dark, a sense of desertion hanging over the place.

Taylor put her phone away and hugged me. "Thank you for being here for this."

"Anytime," I murmured into her hair.

The lass pushed up onto her tiptoes, and suddenly my arms were full of her and her lips were meeting mine.

Finally.

Hours ago, on the plane, she'd tortured me with her game. Now, she tortured me with a hot, deep kiss, her hands gripping my biceps before sneaking under my jacket to untuck my shirt and caress my stomach.

"What are you up to?" I said against her mouth.

"Feeling you up. All night, I've had to watch these

muscles rippling under your shirt. Now I want to bite your skin."

One hand travelled south, and she took hold of my junk through my jeans.

"Fuck," I yelped.

"Ah, you're hard. Always ready. I want you so bad it actually hurts."

"We are not having sex here," I managed, though every atom of my being wanted otherwise.

"Who said anything about sex? I'm not getting my cooch out here, it's freezing. You, on the other hand..." She gave me a meaningful look then darted her gaze around us. Then she took my hand and led me away from the tower and towards a stand of trees, large heavy blossoms creating a canopy.

"How do you feel about getting your mind blown under a flowering magnolia?" she quipped, ducking under the damp branches.

"You have to be kidding me." I didn't sound convincing even to myself.

Taylor pushed me against the tree trunk then kissed me.

"Taylor. We could get caught."

"I know." Her fingers made light work of my belt and jeans button, freeing my dick. "Doesn't that make this hotter?"

It did. Oh fuck it did.

She left my lips and kissed down my neck, then my chest.

"You're really doing this." I groaned, really wanting her to do this.

"Don't try to stop me."

"Wasn't." I slipped off my jacket then dropped it to her feet.

She knelt on it, her eyes bright with danger.

As soon as she took me inside her hot mouth, my last resistance crumbled. The heat. The wet slide. All my nerve endings caught alight.

She tongued the end of my dick and peeked up at me. "You better get off quickly. Who knows who could walk by."

"You're crazy." I squeezed closed my eyes and knocked my head against the tree bark. Still, I gripped her head and held on for dear life.

Taylor grasped hold of my thigh with one hand and my balls with the other. I muttered every swear word I knew and concentrated on the intense sensation of delight.

Oh fuck, she knew exactly how to work me.

Taylor pulled lightly on my balls, fondling them while she sucked on my dick. Sliding me in and out of her mouth. The suction driving me wild.

In an embarrassingly short time, I was breathing hard. I stole an anxious glance at the dark park beyond the trees. People moved under the streetlights, but they were far enough away not to be a problem. Yet.

The lass gave me no let-up. She moaned, and I thickened more inside her mouth. My orgasm closed in, frantic and surging.

"Taylor." I gritted out the only warning I could give.

She didn't slow for a second, instead ramping up her efforts until I was dragging in air, my whole body alight.

Just a little longer. One more slide...

Ahead of us, through the trees, the tower blazed into light. Two powerful spotlights shone across the city from the top, and each tier lit in a shimmering display. The tower fucking sparkled, and I lost my mind.

"Fuck!" I burst out and then I came. Hard. Gripping Taylor's head and thrusting into her mouth.

She drank me down, seeing me out to the very last pulse.

Dizzy, I stilled, acutely aware that I'd shouted. Luckily, if anyone had been around, hopefully the tower's light would've been more of a draw than investigating my roar.

"That was hot," she said, rising. "It was like you powered the light show with your dick."

My brain had fuzzed out too much to talk, so I choked on a laugh and hugged her instead. Then I righted my jeans and jacket, trying to steady my breathing.

"You okay?" Taylor slipped her hand into mine, and we stooped under the low branches and made our way back to the path.

"Perfect," I replied. "Mind blown."

"It wasn't your mind I was working on," she quipped. "But I'll take it."

Then a thought struck me. "Not that I didn't appreciate the fuck out of that, but it was risky. What happens if someone recognises you when you're out with me? Won't that screw up your plans?"

Her engagement would be a media circus, surely.

Taylor raised a shoulder. "No one knows me, not yet. And certainly not here. I'll keep away from the cameras at the gigs."

"Gigs? Plural? You're hanging around?"

She tucked in closer. "For a couple."

We passed a group walking the other direction, and heat and a certain smugness stole over me. We'd got away with public indecency. How about that? Plus, I had this wild and crazy woman for a while longer.

If I didn't think past the end of the week, things looked good.

At the hotel, we found a quiet corner and kissed goodnight, then I took up my bed for a few hours of rest before the circus started all over again.

In the bright sunshine of the following morning, snapping shots of the band under and on the Eiffel Tower, the sprawling city as our backdrop, I couldn't stop my grin. Self-preservation had me forcing down thoughts of the night before, or I'd never get a good shot, but the good feeling was there to stay. Later this afternoon, when I saw Taylor again, I'd try to work out a way to return the favour.

Either way, for now, the lass was mine.

12

LITTLE BIRD

Taylor

Outside a tiny street café, with crowds busying by, I sipped from a cup of scalding black coffee and picked at a croissant. It was midmorning, and boredom kept me draped over my chair. How was that possible with a whole city waiting for me to explore?

First thing, after I'd taken a quick shower and dressed in the shared bathroom at the hotel, I'd gone looking for William. He'd already left for his morning's shoot and texted me an apologetic reply.

We should've been sharing a room. I wanted that, wanted to sleep in his arms. Tucked up against him and aware of when he left. But I'd never thought for two before and I'd got it wrong.

As a girl, I'd never been bothered by being alone. My parents, after they'd split when I was tiny, couldn't agree on anything, so the constant battles over me often left me in the middle and without proper care.

In the school holidays, I'd be torn between my English mother and my American Father. Dad would summon me to visit him in the States, but he'd never fetch me. Sometimes he'd send an assistant, or he'd pay the airline to have a designated adult travel with me. The moment I was old enough to travel alone, I did, turning down the guides. Dad's political climbing took him all over the country, so sometimes I'd arrive at his home in upstate New York just to be on my lonesome for weeks on end.

Even that ranked better than spending time with my mother. God knows how she and Dad ever fell in love; they were so utterly different. Mom lived in England but had a string of boyfriends and took regular yoga or spiritual retreats whenever her latest relationship ended. She'd invite me to stay, but I knew she found my presence disturbing. I looked like Dad's side of the family. The spitting image of his mom.

And his sister.

So I found ways to entertain myself and to fund my exploits. I became adept at lying about my whereabouts and a pro at keeping myself safe. At fourteen, I toured Chicago with a local boy for a couple of days, exchanging kisses for company until my father noticed that I was in the US.

He never missed a line on my credit card statement, knowing where I'd been and who with. Which was why, for years, I'd been siphoning off cash where I could. I had a small, secret account with my savings. I doubted it would last long, but still, it felt wrong spending it on me when I'd saved it for Charity to maybe one day live on.

Tomorrow, William and I would be moving on to Italy. Perhaps I could fork out on a hotel room. Somewhere I could get the privacy and intimacy I craved. Not be alone for a few hours.

Under my table, a little bird pecked at my crumbs. I tore a chunk of pastry and tossed it down.

I was that little bird, but company and care were my crumbs.

Ugh. How pathetic.

I checked my email to distract myself and found a message from Mathilda, William's sister-in-law. It was short, but she asked if her reply to the company covered all the points we'd discussed. I checked it, adding a couple of questions and, just after I sent my response, my phone rang.

"Hey, gorgeous. Where are ye?" William's deep brogue sounded down the line.

My heart fluttered. "Taking a break from sightseeing. How's it going?"

"Good. I'm at the stadium, about to shoot the set up and the sound check. I'll be here all afternoon, so if ye tire and want to come join me..." He trailed off, clearly unsure of where I'd rather be.

"I'll come," I said quickly. "Is now okay? I can bring lunch."

"You're all I need," he said sweetly. Then he chuckled. "But, aye, bring food if ye can. I have no idea when I'll be done, and no one remembers to feed the photographer."

We said our goodbyes, and I leapt from the chair. In a few minutes, I had a feast of patisserie goods and was running for a cab stand. At the stadium, I gave my name and showed the Reportage One digital pass William had sent me the previous day—it had his details but no one seemed to care once I claimed to be his assistant—then I was through security and winding my way through to the wide-open gig space.

"Lass," a voice hailed me from amongst black packing crates and equipment. William lifted his head, and a grin broke over his face.

I yipped and ran the last few steps until I was in his

waiting arms. He gave a growl and wrapped me in a hug, then his lips found mine, and he stole a kiss, getting reacquainted.

"Missed you." He took the café's paper bags from me and placed them on a crate next to his heavy camera. Then he picked me up and spun me around.

"Argh!" I shrieked.

"Tell me you missed me, too," he demanded.

"Never! I don't respond to blackmail!" I howled, and he kept spinning.

Faster he went, until my head reeled and I gripped him.

"Stop! Or I'm going to fall!"

Then he did, abruptly, and weaved on his feet, still clutching me to his broad chest. "Fuck. Dizzy."

William dropped to the floor, landing hard on his ass.

I scrabbled free, wobbling to my feet, and gaped at him. "What happened? Are you okay?"

"Give me a sec." He put a hand to his head. Then he blinked a couple of times before lumbering to his feet. "Shite. Did I hurt ye?"

"Not at all. Are you okay?"

William hid a wince. "Other than embarrassed? I'll live. My head just flipped."

"Has that happened before?"

"Once or twice. Except I don't usually drop lasses."

Did I hug him or breeze over it? I chose the former.

William hugged me back, but an awkwardness descended on us. I wanted to ask more but could see he didn't want to share right now.

A tapping came from the stage. "Testing!" yelled an enthusiastic stage hand.

I flinched at the mic feedback.

William blinked, his colour slowly returning to his

cheeks. "Let's eat. I'll be shooting the band again in the sound check, then we can go see about car hire after."

"Car hire? I thought you said you had to go on the tour coach?" I'd planned to try to blag a spot for myself.

"Nope. They offered me a place, but I don't have to take it. It's not on the list of shoot locations, and I want to spend the time alone with you. We'll hire a car instead and share the driving. Or I can drive through the night. Whatever works."

A warm anticipation rose in me. On our drive, I'd have plenty of time to get to know more about my increasingly intriguing Scot. "You've got it."

We busied ourselves with lunch, then the bands appeared, and William snapped back into work mode.

I watched him, his careful, professional way as he got the pictures he was here to provide. Whatever had gone on in his head had cleared, and he was back in control. At least it appeared so.

The afternoon flew by. William and I hung out in between the action, and soon we were out of the stadium and at the car hire place.

We returned as night fell, right before the start of the concert. William murmured that he needed to take crowd shots, starting the gig at the back of the place then working his way through. I assumed he'd ask me to wait somewhere for him. I could go sit in the car we had the keys for, where we'd hidden our luggage. But he didn't.

Instead, with his face pale, he gripped my fingers. He peered at the rush of people making their way through security, and for one horrifying moment, I thought he was going to fall again.

"Can I stay with you?" I blurted. "Help you change lenses or something?"

William's darting gaze settled on me, and he drew in a long breath.

"I won't get in your way," I added, my voice smaller now. I could tell myself I wanted to be there for him, but that was only partially true. The loneliness I'd experienced earlier still lurked at the edges of my consciousness.

"Aye, if ye don't mind me staring through this instead of at you." He threw an arm around my shoulders and hefted his camera with the other hand.

We entered the hall, and the lights fell. Viking Blue appeared on stage, and the crowd roared.

A guitar chord shook the floor, then a frantic drum beat ushered in the first song.

My pulse leapt, and I hopped on my toes. I didn't even know this band, but the catchy rock anthem had me wanting to dance.

Like before, William got into the action, working the floor. In the zone, he was a true professional, getting wide shots of the musicians on stage with the crowd framing them.

He kept a grip on me, and when we finally emerged from the crush, popping out at the side, we flashed our backstage passes—I'd had one made earlier by Freddie, the sweetheart publicist—and joined the milling support crew. This time, I let William do his thing, and he strode out onto the stage, keeping a low profile but getting the live pictures he'd told me the band craved. Then the song ended, the stage lights dipped, and a spotlight fell on the singer.

Last night, while William had been busy with the crew and his work, Rex of Viking Blue had introduced himself to me. In the 'How you doing?' slow-look-over kind of way.

I'd gotten the impression that he'd expected me to fall at

his feet in hero worship, but effectively, he was William's boss, so I'd chatted politely.

The way he'd stared at me had creeped me out. I knew when guys wanted me, when all they saw was blonde hair and boobs. Now, on the stage, the vocalist strummed the chords of a ballad. And his gaze slid left.

Rex stared right at me, crooning a sexy tune.

Yeah, not happening.

With William busy capturing the moment, I stepped back until I found my way into the corridor, looking for somewhere I could wait out the gig. A number of closed doors faced me, plus busy rooms with people working or talking.

I tried one of the doors. A dressing room. Empty on first glance, with only a single lamp brightening one corner. I slipped inside.

"Hello," a voice came from behind a rail of clothes.

"Eek!" I leapt a foot in the air and spun around.

The singer from Hedonist regarded me from over the rail, a smirk pulling at her lips and her half-black, half-white hair in a frizzy updo. "What are you doing in my room?"

I laughed, shaking out my hands, trying to calm my speeding heartbeat. "I'm so sorry. I was... It's been non-stop for twenty-four hours, and I needed a minute."

The woman, Effie, gestured to a sofa. "Take a seat. I'll be out of here in five. We're onstage soon."

"You sure?" I sat lightly, maybe a tiny bit starstruck.

Effie emerged from her hiding place—I guessed she'd been privately smoking a joint from the smell—and sat on a chair in front of the mirror. She hit the switch for the lights then touched up her makeup, layering on glitter to her wing-tipped eyeliner, and I stared, fascinated.

"Gotta say, big fan here. Just putting that out there in case I accidentally fangirl."

In the mirror's reflection, the woman smirked, keeping her gaze on me. "No problem, you don't look dangerous. You know, actually, you seem familiar."

"I do?" My heart sank. I had email alerts set up in case my name appeared on any news or gossip articles, but so far so good.

Her eyes narrowed, and she examined me closer. "What's your name?"

"Taylor. Taylor McRae." I lied smoothly, marrying myself off to my Scot in my panic.

Effie shrugged. "Nope. That rings no bells. My mistake, I guess."

It wasn't. She'd played at a White House party last year. I'd been there with Dad and, though we hadn't done anything other than shake hands, the woman clearly had an excellent memory.

The door swung open, and a lackey stuck his head inside. "Two minutes, Effie."

She stood and slammed the door in his face, yelling, "I know!"

Then she blew a lock of hair from her forehead and rolled her eyes. "They keep doing that. Like one of them will catch me naked. Assholes."

With a final check of her reflection, the singer gave me a wink and exited the room, leaving me on the couch.

I'd been complacent, not expecting anyone to know me outside of the States, but tonight had been a close call. I hadn't been subtle with William. I'd publicly kissed him— and worse—with no fear of being recognised.

What if Effie remembered?

What if, after the engagement announcement, she sold

the story of my last weeks as a single woman? It would get her publicity.

That had consequences.

Dad had warned me to keep my affairs concealed.

Bringing my knees up to hug my arms around them, I gulped. Should I leave the tour? I couldn't risk my father carrying out his threats. And if the engagement didn't go ahead, I had no doubt that he'd unleash the vindictive side that fuelled his battles with Mom.

But leaving William...

Noise came from the hall. I straightened up. If Viking Blue had finished, we could get out of here. No way was I walking away right at this second.

As a minimum, I'd make the most of the drive time William and I were about to share. Our days together were numbered. There was so much we had to do.

Leaping to my feet, I swung open the door. Outside, Rex was passing, his arm slung around his bandmate's neck and their publicist in tow.

"Oi oi!" He spotted me. "What did ye think of that? We slayed, aye?"

Then he lurched forwards and grabbed me into a squeeze.

Sweat rolled off him onto me. I froze. If this had been anyone else, anywhere else, I'd have kneed him in the balls, but William had told me how important this job was to him. How he hoped it would be the foundation for his career.

So, with gritted teeth, I took the forced hug then politely stepped away.

Rex's mouth slid into a wide grin, appearing unaware of his boundary smashing. "The afterparty starts now. Follow me."

"I'll wait for my boyfriend," I stated, nice and clearly.

"Find him later on the tour bus."

"We're not getting the bus," William's voice sounded above my head.

Relieved more than was reasonable, I peeked back at him.

He ran his gaze over me then held me to his chest. "Everything all right?" he asked.

"The fuck? Ye are." Rex gave a laugh, but his smile dropped, and confusion took over his expression. "I want the party shots. Then the all-nighter we're going to pull on the road. People puking and passed out."

"Well, I'm not sure we want that extreme an image—" the publicist started.

"Not everyone has to dance for ye twenty-four seven. Use your phone if you want photos of your shite." His band mate, a grumpy big man, pulled a face. "Ignore him," he said to us. "He's overexcited by tonight."

"Fuck off," Rex said to his friend. "What's the fucking point of having a fucking expensive photographer if he's not around to capture the good shit?"

Rex's bandmate tried to reason with him, and I bit my lip because William had been around them, almost solidly since we'd got here.

"I'm working to what we agreed," William said, calm but serious. "The gig tonight was the last event in Paris. The next is the gig in Milan. No promo shots needed until there, ye said. That's tomorrow night. So we're out of here."

"Fuck." Rex weaved on his feet. His frustration melted, and he focused on the publicist. "Is he right?"

The publicist gave a wide-eyed but pacifying explanation, and then Rex waved him to stop before turning back to William.

"I still want those pictures. Are ye sure you won't get the bus? It'll be a riot."

William gave me a quick look, a question in his eyes. I gave a tiny head shake, and he turned on his heel, taking me with him. "See ye all in Italy," he called to the band and crew.

The group that had assembled gave their replies, but we were heading for the door and finally on our way to being alone.

Outside, in the cold Parisian night air, William clamped me to his side, and we marched across the venue's carpark. "What happened before I got there?"

"He only hugged me. It was gross but no big deal," I replied.

William stopped. "He touched ye?" His gaze leapt back the way we'd come.

"He seemed high more than handsy. Tomorrow, I'll steer well clear," I joked, but then I caught the look in William's eye, and my jaw dropped. I stared at him and the anger that glittered in his gaze.

"No man has a right to touch a woman."

Awe struck my heart. I liked this possessive side. "What would you have done if you'd seen it?"

"Grabbed him off ye. Smacked his face."

Delight filled me. "But you'd lose your job!"

William gave a short laugh, humour replacing a small part of the anger. "Aye, I probably would."

I pounced, throwing my arms around him, because that right there was way too much. As well as being a huge, ginormous turn-on. "Don't. Not for me. But thank you. I'm really touched."

William stroked my spine then pulled me with him, moving once more towards our car. Once inside, he turned that lovely thoughtful expression of his on me and sat for a moment.

"Ye know, I don't think you've ever had a single person in your life who'd put you first. Am I right?"

I blinked. "That's... I mean, I don't..."

He grinned and started the engine. "For as long as you're mine, Taylor Vandenberg, ye better get used to it. Because if that man touches you again, or anyone else lays a finger on ye without your permission, they answer to me. Fuck the consequences."

My answering giggle, made of nerves and a continuing sense of wonder, had him shake his head in amusement then take off into the dark night.

Fuck the consequences indeed. I'd never let him lose his job, but that speech was about the sweetest thing anyone had ever said to me.

13

LONG DRIVES

Wasp

We left Paris in the dead of night, heading out of the bright city and into France's dark countryside. The journey to Milan took around ten hours of solid driving.

On the wrong side of the road.

With signs I could barely read with my schoolboy French.

But the night was clear and, for the first four hours, it was one straight route that took us all the way to Lyon in the south of the country. The *Autoroute du soleil*. The highway of the sun? Sounded good to me.

I settled into my seat, a hot coffee, grabbed before we left the metropolis, in the holder, and a darling lass at my side.

"Let me know when you get tired and we'll switch." Taylor played with the buttons for the radio, finding a Europop channel and wiggling to the music though keeping it low.

"I'm used to long drives so I'll be good for a while. Ye can sleep if ye want. Or dance. Either is good."

Honestly? All I wanted was to get to the next port of call, find a hotel we could check into early, and take Taylor to bed. For as long as I could before Ally turned up and crashed our love-in.

"Maybe," she replied. "Or I can pepper you with questions. You're in the hot seat and you can't get away."

"I don't want to get away," I answered with a quick smirk. "And if you get to ask me questions, I get to ask you an equal number in return."

She studied me. I sensed her attention even with my focus on the rear lights of the car ahead.

"Favourite colour?" she finally said,

"Seriously? You have free rein, and that's your question?" She didn't respond, so I shook my head and answered, "Blue. Like your eyes. Darker around the outside and with all the intensity of a summer sky."

Taylor hummed. "Nicely put. Do you have a question for me?"

"Aye, but I want to go deep, baby. None of this surface-level shite."

"Fine. Have at me. I'm all yours."

Heat rolled through me. "Now all I'm thinking about is sex."

"Because that's our thing. It's what we're good at."

"Nah." I shook my head and tossed her another glance. "Only because of circumstance. Can I ask you more personal questions?"

"Go for it." She didn't move, no wrapping her arms around herself or curling in like she was wary of an intrusion, yet tension strained her voice.

"I know your parents are divorced, but do ye have any siblings?"

"Oddly, no. Dad wanted more but never had any. For a

while, Mom lived with a man who had two kids, but they broke up after a few months. She's kind of flaky. It's where I get it from."

"You're not flaky."

She'd picked up her coffee and now choked on a sip. "You think?"

The road curved gently, and I followed the arc, a good speed, the empty road, and the clear night letting us make decent headway already. "You finished your degree, right? You're always on time and you don't let people down."

"How do you know that?"

My sister-in-law had once made a passing comment about Taylor's timekeeping, and I'd carried it around, a little nugget of insight into a mysterious woman. "Ella."

Now, Taylor's body language changed. She gripped her knees, leaning forwards as if to peer out at the black surroundings. "After all that went down between us, I'm glad to hear that she still says nice things about me. Anyway, my question. You want deep? How's this: Have you ever been in love?"

"I had girlfriends I was fond of, if that's what you mean."

"No. I mean properly in love. With all the hearts and flowers. You know, said out loud so the other person knows."

Well, when put like that, I guess I hadn't. "No."

But now it was my turn again. I had such burning curiosity about what had motivated Taylor to seek an arranged marriage with her best friend's brother. It had to be the same problem that haunted her now. The reason behind her planned engagement.

Fuck it, if I didn't ask now, I might not get another chance. My mouth opened despite knowing I was about to be shot down in flames. "What made ye agree to marry James? Did something happen?"

Taylor stiffened further. "You could say that. A relative of mine got sick."

"Sorry to hear that." I stretched out and found her fingers, entwining them in mine. "The same relative whose diary you're carrying around?"

A soft laugh reached my ears. "You don't miss a thing, do you? Yep. Same one."

The next logical question fell from my mouth. "Then you getting married is to help this woman?"

She fell silent for a long while. "Her name is Charity. She's my aunt."

The moment quivered, tension drawing out. I knew, without a shadow of a doubt, that if I pushed her now, she'd crumple and close up. The indecision in her voice spoke volumes. I might not know her well, but I knew enough. I knew the difference between someone like me who had issues but a strong grounding, and someone who'd been left floating. Taylor didn't have strong ties, apart from to Ella.

I wanted to tie her to me.

I strengthened the grip I had on her hand. "Thank ye for telling me about her."

As expected, Taylor said nothing, so I continued, suddenly urged to share my own demons. "Ye know earlier, in the stadium? When you met me at lunchtime?"

She sat up a little. "Sure."

"My head..." Ah shite. I was about to make myself look weak in front of a lass I wanted to impress. I broke our hand contact to scrub my fingers through my hair, wavering in indecision. I forced out the words. "My head's fucked."

"What do you mean?"

The white lines in the road spat towards us and under the car like bullets. "I get thick-headed sometimes. Overwhelmed. I can't concentrate. It can even make me dizzy."

Taylor righted herself, bringing her full attention on me. "Is that what happened earlier? Did I cause it?"

"What? No! It's work. Crowds. People in general."

"Oh."

"Never you. Not once."

Silence reigned for a moment. A tentative question followed. "Is there a name for it? Your condition?"

I drew my eyebrows in. "Introversion, I guess. I don't think it's anything more than me not being able to cope."

She shook her head. "Did you see a doctor?"

"What could they do? They can't change the type of person I am."

"But you just said it yourself," she argued. "It has a physical side. You aren't that introverted. You like company, right?"

"Just yours." I threw her a grin, half wishing I hadn't started this conversation now.

"What would you have told Ally if he'd not sought help for his issue?"

My twin had a real condition. Ally struggled to read, dyslexia jumbling the words in his vision. For years, as brothers, we'd covered it up as Da considered it a weakness. Then, as a teenager, long after Da had died, Ally finally got tested and received help.

Was I masking something that could be treated? Could a doctor stop the buzzing in my head and the sheer stifling need to cut myself off?

"I didn't know Ally had told you," I muttered. "He doesn't often talk about it."

Taylor drew a short breath. "I asked him once where your nickname had come from. He said it was to do with him being dyslexic but to ask you yourself next time I saw you."

"You've never asked me."

Up ahead, the red brake lights of multiple cars shone, the traffic slowing in solid lines. We came to a complete halt, and I peered up the road, trying to spot the problem.

"Do you think there's been an accident?" Taylor's worried gaze sought mine.

The line of cars remained stationary, and doors opened, people emerging and staring ahead.

"Maybe. Stay here and lock yourself in. I'll go see if I can help."

I leapt from the car, pausing for the *clunk* of Taylor engaging the locks, then strode up the road. The issue became apparent at the front of the queue—a minivan had skidded across the lanes, the multiple car headlights shining on the empty wheel arch from where it had lost a tyre. Amazingly, no one had hit it, but a multi-lingual debate was underway. The couple, with their sleepy children in their arms, were clearly distraught and unable to understand anyone.

I dove in. At home, everyone helped everyone else. The remoteness of the Highlands meant we all pitched in when strangers needed aid. Now was no different.

With a bit of gesturing, I roped three people into a concerted effort to push the car to the side of the road. The family followed us, eyes wide and shock still apparent. I got my back into shifting the hunk of metal, and we cheered when it rolled onto the hard shoulder.

Then I ran to help a woman heft the broken tyre out of the way while another person kept the traffic from advancing until we were ready.

I was midway through a quick sweep of the now empty lanes when Taylor appeared, crossing the beam from a headlight.

"You are so amazing!" she squeaked. "I just sat and watched you do all of that. You calmed the upset family and you got everyone in line."

"I thought I told you to stay in the car." I frowned at her.

She bit her lower lip, her eyes gleaming. "Yes, master. So sorry to disobey."

I burst out with a laugh. "Actually, we're about ready to open the road, so bring the car up and park behind the busted one."

"On it." She sashayed away, and I watched her pert arse for a moment before finishing my job.

The cars moved on, and I waited with the broken-down minivan for Taylor to pull up. She killed the engine and joined me again, adding her phone torch to mine as I examined the wheel arch.

"Is it fixable?" Taylor peered in.

"Not by me." I gestured to the husband and wife, making a sad face at the wheel and a phone sign with my hand. "Broken. Phone recovery."

The woman heaved a sigh, patted my shoulder, muttered to her husband, and found a phone. The man put his daughter back into her seat then offered me a hand.

I shook it. "Glad to help."

"Shall we wait with you?" Taylor mimed us staying, but the man waved us away.

Whatever he said in response, I had no idea, but he was happier than when I'd first seen him, and we left them to their roadside pickup.

In our car, Taylor gleefully threw herself at me for a hug. A kiss followed naturally, but soon we were both breaking away.

"We have to stop. People can see us. Kids are looking," Taylor said, her cheeks pink and her eyes glassy.

"I know. Ye have no idea how close I am to throwing you onto that back seat and having my way with you."

"You are such a good man. The best. You are a fucking saint, you know that?" She dropped back into her seat and chuckled. Then she yawned, big.

"Glad ye think so. Why don't you rest now? I'll get us back on track, and when ye wake, it's your turn."

Taylor reclined her seat, and I spun us into the now free-flowing traffic.

"I might just close my eyes. It'll mean we get to a hotel room quick if I sleep."

In under a minute, she breathed softly, and I pressed on with the journey, buzzing with the need to find privacy, a soft bed, and a place to use up all my built-up energy.

* * *

A few hours on, and we'd passed toll booths and skirted Lyon, all without Taylor waking. We were closing in on the Italian border and five AM when signs for the Fréjus tunnel appeared.

It went under the mountains with no stopping for miles.

Man, I needed to take a leak before we drove in there.

The night had darkened to a predawn royal blue when I pulled over. The edges of mountains loomed, jagged against the sky and, when I opened the door, clear, fresh air flooded in.

"William? Where are you going? Jeez. How long was I out?" Taylor's voice followed on my dart into the trees.

"Pee break. Good to know you're still alive," I shouted back.

Her happy laugh had me rushing to finish and get back to the car. From my door compartment, I took a half-drunk bottle of water and washed my hands, then chucked the rest on my face to freshen up.

"We're about to go under the mountain, so you might want to use the facilities now." I tipped my head at the scrubby edge of the road.

"Roger, Captain." Taylor disappeared for a minute. When she returned, she booted me from the driver's seat. "I'll take it from here. You must be exhausted."

"I'm not." Not even the smallest bit. "It's a gorgeous night, the drive has been easy, and I've had you to look at. What more could a man want?"

She shoved my shoulder. "Sweet talker."

Taylor got us back onto the road, and soon, we were in the queue for the tunnel. I had the idea that my energy was boundless, probably because of her and all the things I had in mind to try. Even so, my eyes began to close, and I twisted to get my tall frame comfortable on the seat. I stayed awake long enough to pay the toll fee—money that would be refunded as part of my contract—but then the strobing effect of the tunnel's lights sent me under.

* * *

The bleeping of my phone woke me, and I swept out an arm, trying to find it, my eyes still closed. "Shut up. Stop it," I mumbled.

"Heh. You're cute when you're half asleep," Taylor said.

Fuck. We were still on the road? I groaned and stretched out my arms. Broad daylight had me wincing, but the sight of my bonnie lass perched behind the steering wheel, her hair swept up into a high ponytail, had my heart thudding faster. "In my dream, we were in bed together. But people kept knocking on the door and trying to get me to go to work."

"You were sleep talking."

I found my phone on the floor but shot a glance at Taylor. "Uh, what did I say?"

Her lips tweaked at the corners. "You said my name. A few times."

Outside, a road sign read: Novara. I peered at the satnav. "We're nearly there?"

"Sure are. You needed your sleep, so I just kept on going. Hey," she gestured to my phone, "start looking for hotels. Find us a room, baby. In an hour or less, I want to be under a hot shower with you. Then thrown onto soft sheets."

"Searching now." A message from Ally waited on my screen—he was already in the city—but I tossed back a quick reply to say we'd see him later in the afternoon then got on with finding us digs.

"Is it okay if we see my brother for dinner before I go to work?" I'd mentioned meeting Ally to Taylor at the airport, once I'd remembered.

"Yes! He and I can hang out while you do your thing, then maybe we can go out to a bar after."

"Plan." If she stayed with my brother, she wouldn't have to suffer being around Rex, too, so the idea suited me. I texted the suggestion, and Ally sent an enthusiastic reply. Then I got on with booking us a room. It took a while to find somewhere with instant check-in and parking, but eventually I made a booking, and we were on our way.

14
───────

FEVERED

Taylor
      I drove to the hotel in a fevered state, nearly taking a roundabout in the wrong direction, though I'd driven fine for hours while I'd been the only one conscious in the car. William silently pointed out La Sagra stadium— the location of tonight's gig—as we passed, but we didn't speak.

Too keyed up.

Too in need.

The very air in the car charged with sex electrons.

Then, after ten or more hours on the road, the long hotel building appeared. Finally. Leaving the car poorly parked in an alley bay, we snatched our bags, checked in a fast as humanly possible, grabbed the key to our courtyard room, in an old monastery of all places, and were falling through the heavy wooden door.

And oh *GOD* did we need this.

The second the lock clicked into place, William's hands were in my clothes, just as I struggled to wrench open his jeans.

Our kisses hurt where we clashed, but our laughs followed.

The room had its own bathroom, thank the heavens, and I pawed at my Highlander before yanking my dress over my head and half falling in my rush to get naked. "Shower."

"No time." He dropped to the cold tiled floor, taking me with him.

I landed on his chest in just my underwear and burst out with a giggle. "This is your fantasy?"

He'd described almost this scene, but at his crofthouse.

William rolled us, careful even in his urgency. He reared over me, the Devil in his eyes. "Yep. Hands up, hold the doorframe. We're doing this hard and fast, then we're going to spend the rest of the day doing it slow and easy."

I clenched, empty, needing him to fill me. Doing his bidding, I found the wooden door surround then gasped as he unhooked my bra with one swift move then tossed it behind him.

For a second, he just stared at my exposed breasts. I loved this, the anticipation. The care he took and his obvious desire.

"So fucking gorgeous." His hot mouth landed on me. I squirmed, my eyes shuttering closed of their own accord. "Your body has driven me crazy for days."

"Sorry not sorry. Go down on me."

"I'm there." He left my nipples and hooked my underwear, tearing it down my legs. Then his face buried straight into my core.

William devoured me. He sucked and licked, then his tongue slid south and forced its way inside.

"God!" I yelled. A tiny voice in my head reminded me that I was sweaty and gross.

But he didn't seem to care.

My guy growled his happiness at his work.

He knew just how to tease, but this morning, he was all fury. I was muttering curses and begging him by the time he next raised his head.

"Want to come like this or can I fuck you and get the job done that way?"

"Please. Now. Dick."

"Thank fuck."

A rustling came, and I opened my eyes to see him stripping his jeans to his ankles then rolling a condom over his weighty dick.

He knelt between my wide-open thighs again and gave himself a nice pump. "Missed this."

I had no chance to answer. William took my knee, lined himself, then sank into me.

"Christ!" he yelled.

"Oh!" I howled at the same time.

"Ah, lass." He gripped and lifted both my legs, giving short, hard thrusts until he was home.

We both paused, as if dazed.

In the sweetest move, he leaned forwards until his mouth met mine. And God, was he glorious. Even without taking the time to shed his shirt, his body tone stood out, his muscles stark. Bulky biceps. Hard planes.

"You're perfect," he whispered with the kiss.

I kissed him in return, wanting to claw him closer, but I kept my hands where he'd instructed. He gave me a savage grin and jacked his hips. And again, faster.

Blinding pleasure flashed.

"More."

The right words. He surged.

William fucked me like a train. Perfect angles. His fingers at my clit.

Never had I felt anything as good as him.

He read every moan and watched my expression. His powerful rhythm never wavered, and soon I was breathless and hanging over the edge of a furious orgasm. I knew it would go like this. The want had built for days. The teasing had escalated so even a kiss held too much meaning.

With my back arched to meet him blow for blow, I gave a broken cry and fell. Tumbling down into spirals of pleasure. Hopelessly gone as I throbbed around him.

Lord, this man was good.

William gave a grunt of satisfaction but no let-up from his task. He ploughed into me, his features, when I could open my eyes, raw with need and his gaze on fire.

I knew he loved it, sex, the act of giving himself to a woman. He'd told me before. I played witness now to the battle plain on his face.

He needed to come.

He held it at bay.

I wanted his orgasms, every one.

Unleashing my hands, I took hold of his arms and dragged him in for another clashing kiss. But I forced him to slow, and we made out, him still moving inside me but with added tenderness now.

Ah this. All of this.

His tongue slicked over mine, and we were joined, inside each other, writhing together.

"Roll us again," I murmured against his lips.

William complied, putting him on the cool tile floor and me over him, still joined.

Watching every move, I rose then crashed down. Knees to the hard ceramic. Slow. Steady. And again.

He hung over that same precipice, and I dragged it out until we were both breathing deep lungfuls of air.

"You're killing me." William's fingers left my hip, where I was sure I'd have marks from his fierce hold, and once again found my clit. He strummed me, maintaining the same fervent eye contact. But he moved slowly, too. Nothing lazy about it, but determined and intricately focused.

It was like we were stalling the world, giving ourselves a tiny piece of extra space.

Then a throb hit me deep inside. A moan tore out of me, my second orgasm taking me by surprise.

William took over control, and I surrendered. He rocketed home, once, twice, then three times and gave a hoarse yell.

I crumpled onto him, seeing stars, my second round of tremors stronger still. Inside me, his dick pulsed. Finally, we'd got there.

With my legs splayed around him, he nudged my head up and took my mouth again, swallowing little sounds I didn't know I was still making.

But my trembling didn't stop, and he clamped me to his chest for good measure.

I knew we'd clash. I guessed that we'd hit the floor or another surface and go at it.

I had no idea that a seismic shift was occurring.

An emotion I couldn't understand or explain said *him, this man. Now.*

"You... I..." I tried, but my words failed me, that strange new *something* holding my tongue hostage.

"Aye. All that. And more." He kissed me one last time, then sat, bringing me onto his lap.

"Whoa." Overbrimming with sensation, I shook my head then ducked again, hiding my confusion. I wanted to laugh it off, but no further words made it out.

When I peeped up, green eyes watched me. Then

William grinned like he'd discovered something.

"What?" My voice wobbled, but my verve returned.

"Nothing." His grin widened. He stood, lifting me with ease. "That was fucking mind-blowing. Thank you, my woman. Now we get to have a hot shower before we do it again."

"Thank God for that." I mock-wiped my brow, but everything was upside down. The new feeling sat wrong in my chest. I didn't know how to make room for it.

In the simple but thankfully clean bathroom, William got the shower going then deposited me inside. He smirked the whole damn time he soaped up our bodies, then he backed me to the wall to give me more of his devastating kisses.

It was an addiction, this man. This feeling.

I already craved him, even in the middle of his kiss.

Maybe that was it. Sex with William was my drug of choice.

"How you doing in there?"

I blinked to find him gazing at me, the same joyful light still in his eyes. "What?"

"You zoned out and were just staring at me."

The shower had stopped, and he held a towel in his hands. I forced my brain to engage because this was ridiculous. "Sex coma, I think."

William heaved a happy sigh and brought the towel around my shoulders. "Not a bad place to be."

He bundled me up then lifted me into his arms once again. "How about we start on round two? We've got six hours, and there's a whole lot we can get done in that time."

"You're not tired? Or hungry?" *Please say no.*

"Nope. Only for you."

Instant horniness flooded me, and I was myself again,

back in the zone I knew how to handle. I wound my legs around William's waist and jammed my fingers into his hair, tugging him in for a kiss while he stumbled out of the bathroom and to the bed.

Who knew that with more time to spend with a guy—as this was already the longest I'd spent with a man I was sleeping with—I'd want to make it last? I never did this; I'd always cut and run.

We hadn't talked about what happened after tonight. I should pick up Charity's diary to plot my next move. I'd only managed to tick off one item, and William would have his brother for company on the drive to Berlin, his next port of call.

Then again, he was doing a pretty convincing job of showing me I still interested him.

"Stay with me." William kissed his way up my body, biting gently at my hip, licking my belly, using his teeth on my nipple in a way that had me seeing stars. "Don't leave tonight when I'm working."

"I—" Like I would.

"Stay with me, Taylor. I mean it. We've got two days to get to Berlin. Then ages before the first gig in the States. We'll focus on your list. We'll enjoy ourselves."

As if trying to convince me with the skills of his body, he used his hard, bare dick as a tool, working my clit while he played with my breasts, making me crazy.

"Why?" I managed, drawing an unsteady breath, already too wrapped up in him to care if the solitary thing that interested him was what now filled his hands.

"I don't want you to go."

Good enough.

A number of earth-shattering orgasms later, before I fell asleep on his chest, I whispered a triumphant, "Yes."

* * *

*M*uch later again, William threw on shorts and a shirt and strode out to play hunter-gatherer and fetch us dinner. The timings wouldn't work for him to eat with his brother, and we both needed food badly.

In the plain cream-painted room, I got busy, pushing aside the odd feelings from earlier and feeling perky over my extended role as travel companion. This evening, I'd get to explore Milan with Ally, who was a hoot, and then snuggle down with William and spend the night with him. Tomorrow, we'd drive in daylight hours upcountry. Three of us to share the time behind the wheel and choose places to explore along the route.

What a riot. My own European tour with my favourite guys.

In the bathroom, I took another quick shower and washed my hair properly, thankful for the opportunity after a couple of days of wearing it up and spritzing with dry shampoo.

I blow dried it straight, put on careful makeup, then wriggled into a flirty, little black dress. Where Paris had been chilly, Milan was a good ten degrees warmer, and I opened the windows, taking care to keep the mosquito blinds in place, humming to myself as I worked.

Then I checked my email and waited for my Highlander to come back.

Mathilda had sent a follow-up message, and I happily tapped out a reply, smiling to myself for feeling both useful and wanted.

That had never happened before. I wondered how long it could last.

15

JEALOUSY

W *asp*
    With an hour until I had to get to work, I hustled back to the monastery hotel. To where Taylor and I had done things that should have brought thunder and lightning down on the place. Under one arm, I carried boxes of food I'd picked up from a restaurant, iced coffees in the other.

The sun shone, my body ached in the best way, and my smile hadn't left my lips.

"Well, well!"

I turned at the voice. Alasdair stood in the doorway of a large building, a collection of tall and skinny people around him, and Jennie, his agent, at his side. He'd given me the address of his audition in case I got there early and wanted to watch him in action—yeah, no—but I'd completely forgotten.

"Holy fuck, man. I'm seeing double. There's two of you. Except that one's wearing a beard." One of the other models thumped my twin on his shoulder.

Ally bounded down the steps and bear hugged me

around the food. "Nah, just my brother." He took me in. "And a very happy brother, too. Where is she?"

I smirked. "Hotel's just down the road. We needed fuel. Are you finished up?"

Jennie joined us. I'd met her at the castle where she'd visited with her young daughter, ostensibly to bring a contract, but more likely because Ally had talked up the place and she wanted to see our home. They hadn't been disappointed and, since, he'd gotten more than his fair share of work.

"Ah, William. Every time I see you two together my heart thumps. Do you know how popular identical twins are? How much work you'd get together?"

I gave her a wry smile. "Nice to see you, too. But still no modelling for me."

The woman sighed dramatically. "Pity."

Ally turned to her. "You don't need me until tomorrow morning, right?"

"Correct. The last audition is at ten. Don't be too hungover if you can avoid it. And for God above's sake, don't get into any brawls. This one is the big one. If you get it, you'll get more work than you can shake a model-skinny stick at."

"Lover, not a fighter." My brother tipped a fake hat.

His agent rolled her eyes and tucked her purse stuffed with papers under her arm. "At least it's only for a face fitting. The rest of it will be my negotiations. See you then. Work on your twin for me overnight, if you can?" She waved and returned to the crew on the steps.

I elbowed Ally. "Come with me now? Taylor will be hopping up and down to see you."

"Done."

We fell into step, heading back to the hotel.

"So what the fuck happened to your hair?" I began. Ally usually wore his hair long on top in a floppy boy-band style. Now, it had been cut back to a severe military style like our older brother Gordain used to wear when he was in the RAF.

"Had to shear it back for the audition. My beautiful locks are gone!" He slapped the back of his hand to his forehead in a pretend bout of drama.

"And the face fitting Jennie mentioned? What the hell is that?" Modelling was great money and an enormous trip for him, but that didn't mean he shouldn't endure endless teasing about it.

Ally wrinkled his nose. "It's the last shortlist. Ye stand still in a pair of boxers while the director looks ye over and makes their final decision before hunkering down with the pack of agents."

"Huh." Examining him like he was a piece of meat. "How... Um..."

"Dehumanising? Aye. It's the industry, though. Ye get used to it if ye want the money." He shook his head. "How's it going for you following the band? You're a couple of days in, is it working?"

"Shite. I'm coping but I don't know for how long. The drive we did overnight helped, but my head's still stuffed."

I shifted my grip on the coffee holder, and Ally took it, helping out. Then he extracted one of the cups, checked the contents, and took a sip.

"Ye wee scrotum. How do ye know that isn't Taylor's?" I barged him gently.

He grinned. "I'd lay any money you bought her a fancier drink than your black coffee."

I had. Well, fuck.

"She's staying with us for the drive to Berlin," I added.

Now, my brother's concerned gaze deepened. "That'll be fun," he murmured, but his tone held an unspoken question.

We took a right onto the hotel's road, and I pointed out the monastery ahead. "Can ye do me a favour? Ye know I need to work tonight? Taylor had some unwanted attention from one of the band, so she's not coming to the gig. Can ye hang out with her until I'm done?"

"Sure thing. I'll take her skydiving or whatever's fun around here. What kind of attention?"

I rolled my eyes at him, only half knowing that he was joking. "The singer has an interest in her. Then last night, he grabbed her after he came off stage."

"Cheeky arsehole. Ye had a word with him, aye?"

I should have gone back. Or called Rex and warned him off. "Not yet. But I will."

"And have ye fallen head over heels for her yet?"

We'd reached the glass doors of the stone hotel building.

I stopped and ran my hand over my hair, blowing out a breath before returning my gaze to my brother. "No. I know the rules of this. She hasnae talked about her plans, but her mind is made up."

"And you're still okay with that?"

I gave a shrug. "Aye, I'm good." I was all about proving myself, but I couldn't help the gnawing in my gut that I had the potential to fail hard. In both areas.

Ally pushed the glass door, moving into the air-conditioned lobby. He didn't reply, but I knew where his mind had gone from the frown marring his brow. I directed us down the open-sided corridor that looked out on a courtyard, found our room, and knocked.

"Taylor? Are ye dressed? I found a stray on a street corner."

Ally elbowed me, his grin reinstated. The door flew open, and Taylor appeared in the frame. I expected her to go straight to Ally, but she hugged me, hard.

"I missed you," she said against my lips. "And you!" She turned to my twin. "Bring it in."

Ally claimed her from my arms and gave her a squeeze, advancing into the room and spinning her around. "You and me tonight, baby. We can go dancing and drinking while this one works, aye? Milan won't know what hit it."

Taylor beamed, gorgeous in her joy. In the time I'd been out, she'd transformed herself from my tousled bedmate to a knockout preened version of herself, her hair glossy and straight and her makeup perfect. A short, black dress displayed her long, tanned legs. The lass was a vision.

That my brother was still holding.

It hit me like a bolt of lightning, a savage, atom-splitting burst of jealousy.

I needed his hands off her.

Oblivious, Taylor chattered happily to my twin, sitting on the bed while he took a chair. She started a story about our drive through the mountains, taking her coffee from him, all while I stood in the doorway, heat winding through me and infusing my limbs with adrenaline. Ah Christ. This wasn't like me, I'd never been jealous over a lass. Certainly not with my brother. She was as safe as houses with him.

I trusted them both.

But a fact struck me. Something I'd always thought true.

If Taylor had met Ally first instead of me, they'd likely have slept together.

"William?" Taylor's voice roused me from my thoughts. "You have the fiercest expression on your face. It's super-hot, but are you okay?"

I focused on her again but still couldn't speak.

Slouched on his wooden chair, my brother burst out laughing. "I think he's having a moment."

Taylor swung her gaze between us. "What? What kind of moment?"

I deposited the food bag on the table inside the door and shoved my hands into my pockets, kicking the door closed behind me before leaning back on it. "It's nothing."

"Oh yeah, you're so good with it." Ally threw my words from earlier back at me. "You're seething, man."

"Fuck. I am."

"Will someone fill me in? Seething over what?" Taylor leapt up and came to me. Her arms wound around my waist, and her blue eyes held mine. "Talk to me."

"You'll think I'm messed up." I gazed straight into those eyes.

"I promise I won't." She twisted to look at Ally. "Could you give us a minute? I know you just got here."

"Nae problem. There was a coffee machine in the reception. I'll go grab myself a cup before I drink all of this one. You'll need it more than I will, bro?"

We stepped aside to let my twin from the room, and Taylor moved straight back into my arms.

"Talk to me," she repeated. "Is it your head?"

I groaned and banged my stupid head on the door. "I didn't like seeing Ally's hands on ye, that was all. And it should be me taking ye out, not some other guy, even if he's my brother. I'm sorry, I know this isn't part of our deal."

Recognition dawned in her gaze. "You got jealous?"

I grunted agreement. "Pathetic, aye?"

"Nope." She grinned and pushed up onto her tiptoes. Then her mouth landed on mine in a single, tender kiss. "It's actually really sexy. If I saw you with your arms around another woman, I'd be pulling hair and spitting teeth."

"Really?"

"One hundred percent." I got another kiss for my troubles. "The only question is whether you genuinely believe I'd chase your brother."

"Not for a second."

She inclined her head once. "Good answer. Can we make a new deal then?"

I watched her, my jealousy settling to a more urgent kind of sensation. I'd had her all day and I immediately wanted more. "Tell me what you have in mind."

"This is working out okay between us, right? You asked me to come to Berlin. How about in that time we push it to the max? As much as we can fit into the time we have together. Then," she drew a breath, "we fly to the States and have more fun there before we go our separate ways."

"Taking this as far as it can go," I murmured, lost in the intensity of her pretty blue gaze.

This escalated our arrangement to another level. I'd had the idea in the back of my mind but I hadn't dwelled on it, never expecting her to stick around. She'd said that she worried I wouldn't want her around for that long, but she held all the cards.

She always had.

"Aye, lass. I want that," I finished.

Taylor hummed a happy sound, then we lost a few more minutes kissing against the door.

A tentative knock broke our love-in. "Uh, guys? I don't mean to interrupt, but I think ye have to get to work soon. And I'm getting hot under the collar listening to you make sex noises out here. Quit now or be prepared for me to make this awkward."

"Oh my God." Taylor knocked her head into my shoulder, her cheeks reddening.

I huffed a laugh then moved us aside to open the door. "Jerk," I said to my brother.

Ally pulled a ridiculous sex face, easing past us to take his chair again.

"We weren't up to anything. But you're right. I need to eat and run."

In a few minutes, I'd wolfed down a burger and grabbed my camera bag.

With a last kiss to Taylor and a promise to find them in a bar after I'd finished, I was out the door. My angst had gone, but the energy remained. Milan, watch out. Because I was gunning for action.

* * *

At the stadium, crowds already milled, and I flashed my pass to get through security. Backstage, in a large white room, the production teams busied at their various tasks. I found Freddie, the publicity manager, and gave him a chin lift. "Any direction for this evening, or do I have free rein?"

He chewed his lip. "I'd suggest you ask Rex, but he's pissed off."

"What about?"

"I took photos of the tour bus party last night, and they weren't exactly brilliant. He's got this idea that they've got one shot to make their name as a top band and therefore need all the bells and whistles."

Yeah, similar to my aim for the job. I took my camera body from its compartment and clicked a lens into place, a small measure of guilt creeping in that I'd left them. Not at Rex being in a mood, because screw that guy, but at Freddie no doubt getting it in the neck. "Did he yell at ye?"

Freddie grimaced. "A bit. Just get some great stage shots tonight and a few at the party after, and we'll be good."

Tonight, I was down for the party. It was taking place at a famous bar, and a number of celebrities were invited. With any luck, I'd get away with an hour of work, capturing the arrivals, then I could escape. I wanted to be professional; I also knew this would be trouble for my fucked-up head.

"Wasp McRae." Rex's voice sounded behind me. He sneered, standing a little too close. "Good of ye to show up."

I'd wondered how he'd be today. Turned out shithead was his attitude of choice.

Instead of answering, I raised the camera to my eye. Instantly, the man's expression melted, and he smouldered at the camera, changing position a couple of times while I clicked.

Then I dropped it to my shoulder. "Have a good night, aye?"

Rex grunted and swung away. Then he paused. "Christie Banks will be there tonight. We are going to cause a scandal. Make sure you get that down on film."

My camera was digital, but whatever. I gave him a curt nod, and he strolled away.

"Christie Banks is a model," Freddie informed me. He wrung his hands. "I don't think Rex has met her before, so what kind of scandal can he be expecting?"

Who knew, but I'd have to make sure I got the shot. I put my game face on and got to work.

16

PROBABLY FUELLED BY ALCOHOL

Taylor

"Jeez, lass, give me some space. Nah, come on, what are ye doing?" Ally shoved me away then dragged me back to his side, playing the joker and teasing.

I cackled a laugh, staggering on the pavement and nearly losing a heel to a tram track. Maybe that last glass of wine had been one too many.

"Idiot." I tucked in against Ally, anchoring myself by gripping his shirt.

At two AM, the medieval streets of old town Milan thrummed with people, everyone dressed to impress, though the day's warmth had lifted. We'd been out for hours, living it up in bars. I could've picked up Charity's diary, but it felt wrong ticking off items without William present. Ally had friends in the city—models, not intimidating at all—and we'd met for cocktails but had since moved on. Now, my feet ached in my stilettos, and I just wanted to find my Highlander. His twin made me laugh, but he was no substitute for the real thing.

"Ooh!" Ally hooted. "Nightclub up ahead! Want to dance?"

"Sure, but when is William going to be done?" I checked my phone again, blinking at the screen. A new message landed, right in front of my eyes. I read it then groaned. "He's still at the afterparty. It's at some place called Boutique."

Ally stopped. "You mean the place right in front of us?"

"No way!" I stared. Ahead, people queued outside an impressive building, velvet ropes separating them from the passersby. A thudding beat hummed. William was inside. "Yes! We have to go in!"

Ally wavered on his feet, gazing between the enticing club and me. "Wasp said the singer of his band is a dickhead. He wants to keep him away from you."

"Rex? If he touches me again, I'm going to knee him in the balls."

"Wasp didn't say not to come here, but—"

"Then we're going in! Come on. You want to dance. I need your brother."

Ally's grin returned. "Yeah, ye do. And I know he'll be missing you. Let's do this thing!"

Without any kind of coordination, but probably fuelled by alcohol, we marched to the head of the queue. I eyed the doorman, rolling back my shoulders and pushing out my boobs. "I'm a photography assistant to Wasp McRae. He's onsite already with Viking Blue."

The stony-faced man switched his gaze to Ally.

Ally gave a one shouldered shrug. "I'm a model."

The man blinked then stooped, unclipped the rope, and gestured us to go inside.

Well!

I hustled into the plush red corridor and peeked at Ally.

He winked at me. "This face opens doors. You should've said the same. He'd have ordered us drinks, too."

Any reply I could've given was lost to the pulsing beat that shook the walls around us and vibrated up through my shoes. A further doorman waited by a pair of double doors at the end of the corridor. He nodded at our approach and pressed a button on the wall. The entrance swept open, ramping up the ear-shredding beat to monster proportions.

Oh man, I needed to dance.

Lights swirled over a darkened, wide room. Humidity rose from the crowd, instantly sticking my dress to my skin. I searched the corners first, expecting to find William with his back against a wall, observing.

Ally nudged me then gestured to the dance floor. I shook my head as I really needed to find his twin. Just to look at him, even if I couldn't steal him away from his job. A waggling finger stole my attention again, and Ally pointed across the room to where William moved through a group of people.

My heart leapt, and I clamped Ally's hand in mine then dragged him forwards. But as soon as we'd descended the single step onto the dancefloor, bodies obscured our path. I pressed up on my toes to track William, but already he'd vanished.

We moved deeper into the throng. Ally took out his phone, and I gathered from his gestures that he was messaging his brother. The music changed as the DJ upped the tempo. Happiness infused me, and I threw up my arms, getting into it.

I hit someone in the face.

Horrified, I spun around, ready to apologise.

Rex stood right behind me.

Ugh. This guy?

Glassy-eyed, he looked me over, a sour expression on his face. He leaned in and yelled something.

Alcohol fumes hit me, and I wrinkled my nose. Then I shifted my posture, ready with a knee if he tried to grab me. *Try it, buster.*

Rex tried to speak again, but this time I stepped back, pressing closer to Ally. He raised a quizzical eyebrow.

"Rex," I mouthed and jacked a thumb at the jerk who still stared at me like he was considering something. Surely he didn't think I was still an option? Oh no, Mr Rock Star obviously thought any woman was fair game.

Ally narrowed his eyes at the man, clearly not impressed with what he saw. Then, oh, thank the lord and the heavens and all the pretty angels, I caught a glimpse of William a few metres away in the crowd.

How it should've gone down was he'd take those few steps, I'd kiss him, we'd all go grab a drink, then dance our asses off. But no, my vision dissipated as a hand landed on my shoulder again, pulling me the other way.

"Get off!" I yelped at Rex.

The blue-haired singer held both hands up, but that odd, twisted set of his features was still there.

Anger, hot and ready, built in my gut, and I squared my shoulders.

But I didn't need to do a thing.

In slow motion, Ally's arm passed me, and he shoved Rex in the centre of his chest. Rex stumbled, catching himself on a table at the edge the floor.

Then William was at my side, whipping me around to create a barrier in front of me.

At the same second, Rex leapt forward, fist flying. His punch glanced off Ally's cheek.

William surged, his expression one of terrible anger. He

grasped Rex by his shirt, lifting him from where he'd half fallen from the lucky strike.

Then he hit Rex.

If you'd blinked, you would've missed it.

Rex was on his ass, and a furious William stood over him, glowering, his fist ready to lay a second hit.

A man darted over. Two more barged through the crowd. Road crew. Staff.

Oh God, this needed to be over. This was all going wrong. I lunged for William and took his arm. Ally grabbed his other, then we were moving. Through the club. Down the corridor. Into the fresh air and the no-longer-beautiful night.

"What happened?" William demanded as soon as we'd cleared the end of the street. He shook us off and marched ahead a few steps. Then he spun around, and his gaze took me in. Checking me over. Putting me into one piece as though I'd been scattered apart.

I had whiplash from how fast that had all taken place and a big case of the guilts.

"I'm so sorry. That was all my fault." I ached for the comfort of his arms around me. I didn't deserve any of it.

Because I was ninety-nine percent certain I'd just lost William his job. I'd said I'd stay away from the band. I hadn't. I'd wanted to do everything I could to support him. I'd failed.

"What are ye talking about? I saw both your faces. I know he did something."

I wrapped my arms around myself, the cold creeping in. "I'm sorry," I said again, smaller this time.

William gave his brother a frustrated look. "Alasdair, talk." Then he stepped up to me. "You," he said, quieter, depositing his camera bag at his feet. "Come here."

That closeness I so badly wanted descended. Despite myself, I clutched on to him.

"That dude with the blue hair tried to corner Tay. He wouldnae leave her alone. He was the singer you told me about, aye?" Ally replied.

"Yeah, him."

"Then he deserved the hit. I'm fucked off that he got one on me, though."

"My fault," I said again, muffled by where my face was smushed against William's chest.

"No. That wanker has form this evening."

I raised my bleary gaze.

William gave me a quick kiss to his forehead then winced at his brother. "Fuck, that's left a mark."

"You're kidding me!" Ally clutched his cheek. "It can't. I have my audition in the morning. Christ on a bike."

"Quick. We need to ice it." I waved at a passing taxi. "We have a machine in our hotel."

In a few minutes, we'd sped through the winding streets to the monastery and filled a cup with ice. In our room, I slipped into the bathroom with a t-shirt and shorts to change into while the brothers treated Ally's face.

When I emerged, makeup removed, alcohol burned off, and feeling shit in fifty different ways, two identical faces raised to watch me. William with his thick thatch of hair and beard, and Ally with his shorn head and black eye.

Oh boy. This had all been going so well.

"I was just telling Ally what Rex's plans for the evening had been." William patted the bed next to him.

Gingerly, I sat. Ally stood at the mirror, running a lump of ice over his bruise.

William continued, "He invited a woman along tonight

—a model—with the single idea of getting into the gossip pages by a well-timed photo of them kissing."

I blinked, a distasteful picture forming. "Was she in on the plan?"

"Nope. He had me follow him around until she showed up. It was so fucking clear what he was about to do."

I gaped. "He kissed her?"

William shook his head. "Again, nope. I caught her and told her what I thought was about to happen. Do ye know the fucked-up thing? The poor lass rolled her eyes like this was commonplace. She posed for a single photo with him but then left the club, thank God. Rex was fuming, but he hadn't heard the conversation, so he just stormed off and hit up the bar. All night after that he was stalking women. One or two of them obliged, but I wouldnae take the shot."

"Fucking creep," Ally muttered.

"Ugh. Then that's why he was looking at me strangely." Not that I was a prize. Though in a few weeks, he would've had a golden shot if it was publicity he was after. Him with the presidential candidate's daughter-in-law-in-waiting? That'd serve him up a nice row.

"He really didn't touch you?" William took my hand. His frustrated expression turned gentler at my head shake. "I was glad to see ye."

"You were?"

His fingers entwined with mine. "Aye. Always have been, always will be."

"Even if I lost you your job?" And my sanity.

William raised a shoulder. "I was gunning to hit him. I'm just sorry you had to see his ugly mug again."

"Talking about ugly mugs..." Ally stepped closer to the lamp. "Is it bad?"

His bruised eye shone.

I grimaced. "Maybe it'll be better in the morning."

Ally gave a groan. "It won't. Which means I can't audition. Ye have to be perfect or they write you off. Fuck! I needed this job." He shook his head then collected his phone from the table, frustration in his moves. "I'm going to go to bed. I'll see ye both tomorrow."

"Ally?" William stopped his brother. "There's another option if ye can't model."

Ally stared at his twin, then his shoulders went down a notch. "You'd do that?"

William shrugged, but his expression was anything but comfortable. "I could try. It'd be just like old times."

Ally whistled low. "Something to consider. We'll judge in the morning, aye? There might be no need." He blew me a kiss. "Night, Tay. Sleep well, you two."

Then he was gone.

"What did you mean? You'd step in?" My mind whirred. "You'd model for him? You can do that?"

William dropped back on the bed and covered his eyes. He gave another laugh that was half humour and half crazy. "Perhaps. We used to do it all the time. I sat exams for him. I even took his driving test as he can drive fine, but he'd never have passed the part where you read a licence plate."

"This isn't the same, though. Won't this be a lot of pressure on you?"

Darkness passed over his vision, but he masked it with a quick grin. "My brother took a hit on my behalf. I owe him one. And that one would be me strutting around in my underwear. Baby, you could be looking at Europe's next top model."

* * *

I clambered under the covers while William made a call to Viking Blue's publicist. He left a message then did the same with his photography agency. Then he slid behind me in the cool bed, instantly surrounding me with heat. We'd both wanted this—the night together, the time to explore and connect. It felt like I'd waited all my life.

"Don't even think about it." He nuzzled my neck.

"Think about what?" I replied.

"Anything other than me. This."

In the dark, his steady hands took my hips, finding the waistband of my shorts and dragging them down.

His dick prodded my ass. Automatically, I pushed into him, needing this. Him. William's fingers found my core, and he leisurely explored me. His hot mouth laid kisses on my skin.

"Fast or slow?" he murmured. "You're so fucking wet already."

"Fast," I said, and the bed dipped as he moved away. "Don't wait to get inside me."

Then the foil packet crinkled, his weight returned and, from behind, he fitted himself between my thighs. Both hands came around me, and he took my breasts in his palms, sliding his cock through my wetness. In one thrust, he was home.

I made an indecent sound built of gratitude and relief.

"All I thought about, all night, was you." William held me close for a second, stretching me and crushing me in glorious equal measures. His thumbs played with my nipples. "Have ye any idea what ye do to my head?"

I snaked a hand to find his neck then twisted to kiss him.

With our mouths fused, we moved.

Our easy start turned rough and ready.

Ah, God. This was what I'd dreamed about. In the big bed, we tussled, gripped, groaned, and bit. William fucked me so hard I yelled the place down before I put him on his back and had him follow me over the edge.

That, I adored. The easy way we came together. But after...

After, once we'd settled again, sweat cooled and pulses slowing, we stayed. William stroked my bare arm, whispering sweet things until his drowsy voice drifted off. I lay awake, wallowing in the sensation of it all.

I'd never done this.

I'd never slept overnight in bed with a man. Even when I'd slept with him at the castle, I'd always returned to my own room. In the crofthouse, we'd been on the floor. A new reality settled, one I could no longer avoid recognising.

Ah no. Anything but that.

"This is all your fault," I told William's heavy form. "You're making something happen, and I can't handle it."

But even as I spoke, I knew I liked this new thing far, far too much. Which meant it was doomed from the start.

17

DANGEROUS TALK

W *asp*
Something was up with Taylor. A phone call from my brother had us scrabbling to dress before he showed up with his agent to our hotel room, and though Taylor had returned my snatched kisses, she wasn't meeting my eye.

A fresh text from Ally told me they were nearly with us, so I only had a minute before things got crazy. He'd confirmed that his eye had only worsened, so I knew what I had to do.

Even if it had my stomach in knots.

"Tay?" I stopped the lass and held her in front of me.

"What's up?" she asked brightly, but she still wouldn't look at my face.

"Eyes on me, lass."

That worked. She stopped moving and raised her gaze. For a moment, I studied her, seeking for any sign of whatever was bothering her. But the emotion lurking under her surface kept itself well hidden, her perfect makeup concealing her from me.

"If I have to do this thing this morning, can ye make me a promise?"

Taylor inclined her head, inviting me to continue.

"Don't leave me." I was already halfway to being a wreck. A headache built over my eyes, and worry for my career had me in pieces, let alone concern for fucking up my brother's livelihood, too.

If she left in the time I was working, I'd lose my ever-loving mind.

In the weirdest way, that was another reason I volunteered to help Ally. I could do nothing for Taylor. She hadn't given me an inch of headway into her thoughts or problems. All the angst I had to fix her went to helping my twin instead.

"What are you talking about?" Her gaze gentled, and she raised her fingers to touch my face. "I wasn't going to leave."

I huffed in acknowledgement but moved a little closer. "Then why is there this distance between us this morning?"

With a smile forming, Taylor eclipsed the space between our bodies. "What distance? Don't know what you're talking about."

My own answering grin came unbidden, and I ducked to rest my forehead on hers, liking the closeness more than I could say. In fact, I needed it. Right now, her touch anchored me. "I know we haven't had any time to go out together. This wasn't the trip ye had in mind."

"I'm not worried about that." She traced lines in my beard. "Is today going to be a problem for you?"

Fuck. This, I didn't want. Her worrying about me and my messed-up head. "Nah. It's no big deal."

Taylor kissed me, once and carefully. "Please don't do that."

"What?"

"Lie to me."

"I didn't mean to." Though I was diminishing a cluster-fuck of shite spinning around my brain. I slid my arms around her and lifted her from the floor. "Maybe we can try something else today. Total honesty."

Taylor wrapped her legs around my waist and settled into my hold, gazing into my eyes. "I have no idea how to do that."

"Try it, aye?" I swallowed, sensing a precipice I was primed to fall over. But hey, what else could the universe bring me that it hadn't already. "I'll tell ye how I'm feeling right now if you do the same."

"Dangerous talk, but okay," she agreed, her words slow.

"I'm worried that hitting Rex last night will have me booted from the tour. I'm worried that Ally won't get this job because I'll flip out and mess it up. I'm half expecting my head to explode with the pressure coming in from all sides..." I drew a hard breath. "And then there's you."

"Me?" she whispered, her face open but her gaze wide. Almost terrified.

"And this. This *us*." I hadn't intended to open up a conversation about feelings, but here we were, square in the middle of them. And I wasn't about to declare my undying love, but there were words I had been thinking that I'd kept to myself.

Emotions had risen for sure.

Hungry, greedy, possessive ones.

"Do you mean the jealousy thing?" she said.

"Amongst others."

"What—how many others?"

"More than a few."

Taylor nodded, sliding her gaze right like she was working out how to respond. The moment stretched out, and I clamped down on my impatience, giving her the space to speak.

She wasn't freaking out anymore. This was a good sign.

A knock rattled the door.

For Christ's sake. This conversation had been timed spectacularly badly. Or maybe the interruption was good. I wasn't sure I could take being shot down in flames right now.

"To be continued." Trying to reinstate the guards I'd put around myself, I pecked her on the nose then placed her down.

"Wait." She took my hand, and I paused in my step. "I have a few, too."

My heart gave an almighty thud. "Ye do?"

"Honesty, right?"

"Right."

"Then yeah. A few. Or more."

I stared at her, then another more impatient knock came.

"You'd better answer that and see what your morning looks like." Taylor flashed a smile, but it didn't reach her eyes.

She now looked how I felt: wary and on the edge. I had the idea this was bigger for her than it was for me, and I had the ground shifting beneath my feet.

But I couldn't leave my brother and his agent waiting. "Time to talk later, aye?"

"It's a date," Taylor said, quiet and pale.

Right. I opened the door. Ally waltzed in, Jennie hard at his heels. Then another man followed with a case in his hands.

"Hey," I greeted them. I winced because my brother's eye shone, a dark purple contusion marring his skin.

Ally grunted in reply, misery on his face. "So sorry. This is on. Jennie thinks it'll work."

"Set up on the dresser there." Jennie directed the stranger. "We've got thirty minutes, so quick and precise, if you please."

"Wasp." She turned to me, and I tore my gaze from my brother. "Alasdair said you'd stand in for him this morning. Do you have any scars on your head or neck?"

"What? Um"—I ran a quick mental check—"not that I remember. I do on my arm—"

"Won't matter. Face is king today." She gestured to the other man. "Antonio here will cut your hair and beard. I've been told our timeslot has been reduced, which is lucky, but we will still need to shave your upper half. Waxing would be so much better, but there's no time to reduce the redness. Now, I'm anxious to see what's under the beard. Take a seat, please."

"Shave my upper half?" I turned, tracking the woman as she circled me. "Wait, cut my hair?"

Across the room, Taylor's hands flew to her mouth. "Oh no!" She pointed at Ally. "Can't you use makeup to cover the bruise?"

"No makeup allowed. So sorry." Ally sat heavily on the bed and fell backwards, his arm over his eyes.

"It's very simple." Jennie tapped her foot, a model of brisk energy. "Wasp, all you have to do is be your brother for the meeting. You don't smile. You don't need to take the catwalk. All you do is listen to my commands. They've already chosen your brother on the strength of his form. Today is for the head honchos to come in and give the nod. You'll go into the building, strip to your underwear, walk into the room, stare straight ahead, I'll say some things, then we'll walk out again."

The other man, Antonio, placed a hand on my shoulder, guiding me into a chair that had magically appeared behind me. He picked up a pair of trimmers and slid the button, producing a *buzz*.

I had a moment of *what the fuck?* before coming to my senses and giving him a reluctant but resigned nod. Then my beard disappeared, and my hair followed.

And a whole new Wasp McRae emerged.

* * *

Thanks to my brother's pestering, I kept up the same physical routine as him, working out in the castle gym every day and watching what I ate. There was little between us when it came to appearance. With Antonio finished, I took a pack of razors to the bathroom and shaved my chest and arms.

"And armpits," Jennie called from the bedroom.

Great.

A light knock came, and Taylor cracked the door open. "Can I help?" she asked.

I gave her a swift nod, and she joined me, taking the razor and catching bits I'd missed.

"I'm grieving the loss of your hair, but there's something I need to tell you," she said.

"Go on."

"You are so hot right now. Your cheek bones are popping."

I grunted. "Ally's look."

She pawed my bare chest, her grin spreading. "Yours now. I didn't like it on your brother. On you? Whoa."

I watched her. "That's because you like me."

"True fact. But now you have to go."

I did. Under my hard surface I was quaking.

Her gaze found mine in the mirror. "If you want, I can come with you?"

It was that, that tiny offer of support, in the midst of being together for days that had something click inside me. When we'd kissed at the crofthouse, Taylor had told me she wasn't capable of love. Then the conversation this morning had thrown me for a loop. She *did* feel. She cared.

My objectives turned on their head.

I lifted my chin, accepting her offer, and we left the room together. Antonio and Jennie gave me a once-over, approving the plan, and then we set off for the modelling studio. Ally took himself off for a sour-faced stroll, and Taylor stayed with me. She didn't know what she was doing —this shoring me up—something my family instinctively gave.

I'd never have asked.

She did it anyway.

At the building, our cab came to a halt, and we climbed out.

"I'll be here." Taylor indicated to the steps outside. She gave me a quick kiss and then took her phone from her pocket.

"Showtime." Jennie slapped her hands together.

We entered the cool reception, and I put on a game face like I never had before.

18

BABY STEPS

Taylor

The door swung closed behind William and the modelling agent, and I made a call, a little frantic and a whole lot confused.

"Tay! What's up?" my best friend answered.

"What happened when you first met Gordain?" I descended the steps, pacing the hot street.

"Which part? When he flew in to rescue me or when we met again a few months later?"

"When you knew you had fallen for him."

I'd known Ella since we were little girls. There wasn't much I could do to shock her. She'd watched me lie effortlessly to schoolteachers in order to get out of trouble; she'd heard how my father talked to me and knew why I was the way I was. But still, a pause came, and her voice uttered, "Tay? Are you asking me how it feels to fall in love?"

Relieved, I leaned on a wall. "Yeah. That bit."

"I'm... Just... Wasp? You're in love with Wasp?"

I gave a short laugh, sounding crazy to my own ears. "I didn't say that. It's the falling part. Describe it to me."

"I don't know! What are you even...? I mean, this is a revelation! I hoped, of course I did, but Tay!" she babbled nonsensically.

"Ella!"

"Okay, okay. Hang on, let me catch my breath." She breathed dramatically. "Right. Um, well, I had nothing to compare my feelings to but I wanted him. In every way. All the live long day. It was like an obsession, both physical and emotional. I'd never felt anything so strong. It changed everything. Do you feel like that?"

"Pretty much." I sighed. "What is that even about?"

"I didn't know for a while." Then she added quickly, "Don't be like me. Don't doubt if you feel it. I kept G waiting for a year until I was ready, but you're not seventeen. You can't pretend to yourself it's a crush. You and Wasp have known each other for years—"

"I know! Why is this only happening now?"

"Is it, though? Look at how you are with him: you never used his nickname, and you started avoiding him on your last visits. That isn't something you'd do for someone you don't care about. You set him aside as special. Maybe you just didn't notice before."

I stopped my mouth, considering her points. I'd been instantly attracted to William, that was for sure, and I'd kept coming back for more.

He'd never left my head.

"Argh!" I bit out. "I didn't know! This was the reason for not having a boyfriend! I can't have feelings because I can't follow them."

"I know why you think this, but what options have you tried?"

"I've asked Dad outright to give me Charity's care. He said no. I begged him. He told me that she could rot in Hell for all he cared, and if I didn't shape up, that's exactly what she'd do."

Ella sucked in a breath. "Have you told Wasp?"

"Which part? The blackmail Dad's had me under for years? Or that fact that William makes my heart race every time he looks my way and the thought of our time together coming to an end is killing me."

"Oh, honey."

I closed my eyes and rested my head on the wall behind me.

We both remained quiet for a while.

Then my friend said, "If you want, I can give you some advice?"

"Please. I'm willing to beg." My pulse thrummed with my frustration. "Keep talking at me. Say anything. I'm trying to work this out and I don't know how to do it."

My friend sucked in a breath. "You really want this, don't you?"

I had no idea what I wanted. I was balanced on a ledge and I needed to find a way to walk it or fall to my death. A tad dramatic, maybe, but things couldn't continue as they were. If I had *that* conversation with William, the one that said we weren't just fucking and those feelings had names, I couldn't walk away. He'd told me he could handle a fling, but I knew that wasn't true.

"If I don't, I have to walk away from him now."

"The fact that you called me rather than packing a bag tells me you already made that decision." Ella hummed. "You've always been a loner. We're best friends, but this is probably one of the only times you've come to me with a problem before you'd decided how to fix it. Charity is important to you. But Wasp is, too. I think previously, you'd never let yourself get close to anyone so you wouldn't have to choose."

My newfound emotional state had tears pricking my eyes. "I can't choose. She means the world to me."

"And your dad knows that. He's a fucking asshole. Just saying."

"He's the worst."

There was one fundamental point to wanting the best for my aunt, and that was my lack of choice. Charity's illness meant that she'd signed over power of attorney to my dad. He'd give it to me, now I was over twenty-one and could take responsibility, but only if I did what he said.

If I didn't, he'd punish her. It had always been so simple.

Ella spoke again. "If she knew about this situation, she might have other ideas. If Wasp knew about the situation, he might, too. Stop being the island your dad tried to turn you into."

Wow. I blinked, the moment of realisation stark. In the warm Italian sunshine, I shivered. My stubbornness was my father's. Through and through. "What if I can't be any different? What if I'm too much like Dad?"

"Oh, shut up. You are not. As your best friend, I get to tell you when you're being an idiot, and that time is now. You're just confused and scared."

I snorted a surprised laugh at Ella's indignance. Then the surprise simmered into apprehension. "I am scared. It was easy before. I knew my path, and so long as I followed it, I got what I wanted."

"Change is terrifying, but if you don't ever try, you miss out on so much potential."

"Thank you," I said, because she'd helped more than she knew. "You've always been far wiser than me."

She clucked her tongue. "I'm not sure that's true, but if it helps you fall in love with my brother-in-law, then I'm all for it."

I cradled the phone, loving the idea.

Ella continued, "And talking of change, Mathilda was here earlier. She told me you'd been helping her with a contract. She said you knew your stuff and you'd really saved her."

My cheeks warmed. "She did? I always thought she hated me, so this is a big turnaround."

"Hated you? Don't be daft. Besides, she's pregnant again and loves everyone and everything right now. That's why I need to ask for your help for her."

"She's pregnant? Aw!" I grinned. "What can I do?"

"Did she mention her office manager quit? There's a backlog of work building up. When you come back, do you think you can help out?"

"Sure. I'd love to. Except, I'm not sure when I'll visit again. Can I look at it remotely? We're driving to Germany today, so if she sends it through this morning, I can download it and work on the road."

"I'll call her and make the suggestion." Then my friend paused, and her breath hitched. "She told us she was pregnant a few days ago. It got me and G talking..." She trailed off.

I stood tall. "You? Are you going to tell me you want a baby? Oh my God!"

Ella snickered a laugh. "Yes! We started trying already. As soon as Mattie told us, I had the biggest kick in the ovaries. When we got home, I leapt on G then told him what I'd been thinking." She gave a groan. "Can you imagine his grey eyes on a baby? They'd be so beautiful."

The image came unbidden of William's green eyes. I'd never thought about having kids, other than as a practicality of an arranged marriage. But to have one for love? I sighed long and hard. "I bet Gordain was all over that idea."

"He was! He said he'd been thinking about it for months but didn't want to mention it until I did."

"This is huge! Did you start trying right away? You could be pregnant now!" I grinned big, and a laugh escaped me.

"I know! I mean, it probably takes a while, but we'll have fun trying."

After a little more baby chat, and a promise to call her again in a couple of days, I ended the call to Ella. It was easy to envy her—she had an incredible home, an adoring husband, and a career she'd built all for herself.

For the first time, taking baby steps, I wondered if there was a way I could have the same for myself.

* * *

A few minutes later, William and the agent emerged from the building. I dragged in an excited breath and skipped over but then I stopped short of offering him a hug. With his body held rigid and his eyes fierce, William exuded a spikiness I'd never seen on him before.

A cold trickle slid down my spine.

"Did it go okay?" I asked, forcing the words to sound bright.

"Fine!" The agent beamed, seemingly unaffected by whatever bothered William. "We'll know the final results tomorrow. I'll call Ally then. I'm flying home now. Wasp? It was great you stepping in like this. You have my card if you ever change your mind about your career."

She patted William on the arm, and he offered her a semblance of a smile. Then the woman waved to me and strolled away, leaving us alone.

"Should I get us a cab?" I pointed to the street, like he didn't know where cabs were usually found. Nerves had me babbling. "Or we can walk?"

William nodded briefly, but his gaze darted away.

He didn't reach for me.

He didn't look at me.

The chill took over my stomach, but I busied myself in setting our direction. Side by side, we made our way back to the hotel. For fifteen minutes, he didn't say a single thing, and it was the most exquisite form of torture after all the soul searching I'd done on the phone with Ella.

My mind wrangled thoughts of the night before. Of the way he'd looked at me. Defended me. Of the conversation we'd started to have this morning. I wanted to ask him so much. I wanted to know why he used a nickname. I wanted to ask how come he'd had girlfriends he'd been fond of but hadn't fallen in love. All the questions I could've asked before crammed into a long list, stuffing my head full—

Then I got it.

Realisation slapped me in the face, and I jerked in my step. He'd told me his head scrambled when overloaded by people. And what had he done this morning? The most exposing activity possible.

Oh, I was the most self-centred woman in the world.

We neared the hotel, and I slid my hand into his. William jumped, but his fingers took mine, gripping hard.

"You did good," I told him calmly and firmly. His eyes widened, but he still didn't speak. "Now we're going to pack up our things, find your brother, and get on the road. You can sit in the back if you want. You can sleep, and we'll stay quiet. Sound good?"

He swallowed then gave a tiny chin lift.

Right then.

Energy renewed, and with utter, sheer relief driving me, I marched us to our room and bagged our stray clothes and products from the bathroom. As I worked, I called Ally and told him to return.

"Jennie said it went well. Is Wasp there? Put him on, will ye?"

I eyed William where he sat, his eyes closed and his head against the wall. The muscles of his neck strained, his sharp biceps defined and rigid.

"Uh, maybe later when he's not so maxed out. We'll take the first driving shifts, so can you bring coffee and pastries?"

There was a pause on the line. "Can he hear me?"

I switched to loudspeaker. "He can now."

"Good. Wasp? We're going to drive until we find somewhere peaceful. Maybe a little village, or we could even buy tents and sleep on a lakeshore somewhere. Whatever ye need, aye?"

"Aye," William answered.

"Be back soon. Love ye, bro."

We hung up and, with a quick final search, William and I were good to go. He lumbered to his feet and shouldered our bags, keeping with me as I checked us out. Before we left the hotel, I used the WIFI to download a spreadsheet and several files sent by an enthusiastic and grateful Mathilda, then we loaded up the car.

Ally arrived a few minutes later, and his concerned gaze instantly swept over his brother.

"You'll be okay. Tay and I have got you," he murmured quietly.

William's attention jumped between us. Now I understood this a little more, he seemed frozen, but like he'd purposefully locked himself down. When he got better, I wanted to talk this out with him. I was only guessing at how to help and I didn't want to guess. I wanted to know.

But now was not the time to ask.

Ally gestured for William to get into the big car then arrived at my side, glancing to the keys in my hand with a questioning eyebrow raised.

"I'll take the first shift," I said. "You can both catch up on your beauty sleep."

In an hour, we were on the A2, passing Lake Como and heading into the mountains that made up Italy's northern border. I hit the gas and put the metropolis behind us.

If William needed space to fix his head, I'd deliver.

19

WHITE NOISE

W *asp*
        In the rear of the car, from behind a veil of white noise, I watched Taylor. With quiet efficiency, she drove us to the Italian/Swiss border, buying the toll pass that we needed for Switzerland's motorways before taking us into our third country in about as many days. She brought food, though I couldn't eat, and throughout the drive, she'd sent wee glances my way but made little conversation.

Almost as if she didn't want me to miss out before I got myself under control.

I needed exercise. A run. Through trees. Alongside a river. That was what I'd do at home to focus myself and clear some of the wool.

The other option was sex. But I didn't think Ally would appreciate the show.

Another hour on, and Ally suggested trading up on the driving. Taylor agreed, pulling over, and, to my huge relief, she joined me in the back, clipping herself into the middle seat.

"Sorry to treat you like a chauffeur, Ally, but I have some

work to do and a man to snuggle," she said, balling her ponytail into a bun in a way that showed she meant business.

Ally shrugged. "Lucky the voices in my head make interesting conversation. I'll get us into Germany, and we'll stop when we get hungry, aye? Then we can work out where to spend the night."

"Perfect. Let's do it," Taylor agreed, ignoring his idiocy.

As my brother drove, she took out her phone, plugged it into a charger on the seat, then busied herself with what looked like office work. All the while, gently pressing into my side.

She didn't chat.

She made no demands of me.

I could fucking weep for how good it felt to just be able to rest.

For the next couple of hours, I let her warmth sink in and alternated closing my eyes and watching either her or the scenery. Lakes. Towns with unusual architecture. Mountains everywhere and road tunnels through them. We left Switzerland and crossed into Austria, keeping on going until we swept straight through into Germany.

After a total of six hours travelling, at Ulm, a small city in Baden-Württemberg, Ally got off the motorway and drove us into the winding medieval side streets. Half-timbered houses lined our route, and Taylor stopped her work, eyes wide at the pretty scene. I caught sight of a cathedral and restaurants. Many, many restaurants.

It must be nearing dinner time. My stomach growled.

I hadn't eaten all day.

Then, with a lurch, Ally halted the car, reversing into a just-appeared parking space on the busy high street. He killed the engine and twisted in his seat. "We just passed a burger place, and I'm about to die if I don't eat. Orders, please. I'll get food to take away, then we'll find somewhere quiet to eat."

"Meat," I uttered, surprised to find my voice working after so many hours.

For good measure, I pointed at Taylor, extending my Neanderthal persona. "Woman."

She burst out in laughter. Relief shone in her eyes, and I felt like the worst kind of man.

"Burgers sound great," she said to my twin. "Cold drinks. Fries. Stick the works on them."

"Got it. Sit tight, kids." My brother left us for his mission, and I stared at the lass.

She waited for a beat then gestured to her phone. "I've been working on something for Mathilda. Sorry if I've been boring."

"You're perfect," I muttered. Her, boring? Impossible.

"Yeah? Good to know." Taylor eyed me, then, like she was coaxing a wild animal, held out her hand.

I took it, closing my eyes once more. Traffic whizzed by, my heart beat too fast, and my head hurt, but I had an anchor. My fingertips on her pulse. A slow and steady *thrum, thrum* that centred my wayward thoughts.

Ally returned, bringing the rich scent of food with him, then we were moving once more.

"I asked in the restaurant where we could go. They said we're near the river Danube, and not far away is a swimming lake. It's warm enough to be outdoors, and I thought the space would be good..." He trailed off, seeking input.

"Let's do it," Taylor agreed.

On the short drive, I sat forward, needing to get out of the car. When we stopped, I was scrambling from my seat, sliding the door open before Ally had even taken the keys from the engine. Then I paused and turned back to Taylor, trying to focus over the whooshing in my ears. "Gonna run."

She nodded her understanding. "We'll find you."

I took off across the open ground. Fuck my stupid head. Fuck this shut down. "Argh," I bit out to no one, flying through the thick trees along the only clear path. At the end, the track opened up on a lake.

Cool water.

At home, I'd jump straight into the loch.

Aye, this would have to do.

A deck stretched out into the deep. I jogged to the end and kicked off my shoes, shed my jeans and shirt. The gentle late-afternoon sunshine brushed my skin.

I stood in just the fucking boxer shorts I'd posed in at the audition.

Then I leapt.

20

CRISP, CLEAR WATER

*T*aylor

A splash sounded from beyond the trees at the end of the track where flashes of sunlight shone on water.

"At least we know where he went." Ally stuffed a final bite of a burger into his mouth, rooting in one of the paper bags he carried and finding a handful of fries.

I adjusted our towels under my arm—our makeshift picnic blankets, one of which William had given to me in New York—and picked my way down the path. Part of me wanted to race after William and hold on to him until he was better. But I knew that wasn't what he needed.

He'd be hungry. And probably cold from his dip in the lake. Those things I could help with.

"Can I ask a question? How long does this, um, issue last?"

Ally drew out another burger but stared at it for a second then tossed it back into the bag. "Eh. I've lost my appetite." His brow crinkled. "It takes him a couple of days. Sometimes more. Usually he knows when he's getting stressed and can do something about it like freeing up time to go running."

I blew out a breath. "It all happened so fast between the nightclub and the audition. I guess he didn't have time to recognise it."

"I should've. I know him better than anyone." He threw me a glance. "Currently, at least. I know when it started and I've seen him do this a few times a year since we were kids."

"Wait, something caused this?" We cleared the trees, emerging onto a grassy bank. Ahead, William swam, carving up the water halfway across the lake with smooth and powerful swings of his arms. Bright spray arced behind him.

Ally palmed his neck. "Aye. Ye remember ages ago when you asked me about his nickname? It's all linked. And it's all my fault. When he comes back in, I'll tell ye. He won't mind."

We continued until we reached the bank then the wooden dock. At the end, I sat cross-legged on the planks and tidied the discarded clothes into a pile. The sun warmed us and, if it hadn't been for William's state of mind, it could've been the prettiest, most relaxed part of our trip yet.

William cut through the crisp, clear water. I watched him for a few minutes then gave in to my appetite and ate.

After a little while, he swam over. When he reached the dock, he took hold of the edge, resting for a second. Water droplets ran down his shorn head, catching on the tiniest hint of new beard stubble.

Ally took a burger and unwrapped it. He held it out to his twin. "Bite."

William took a mouthful, chewing and swallowing like he was starved. He reached out and seized the burger, demolishing it, one hand keeping him steady in the water.

I grabbed my drink and offered it. He winked at me, taking a long draw, continuing until the straw rattled in the empty cup.

"Bro? I don't mean to judge, but did you know you're naked?" Ally peered into the water.

"Nice in here. Come in?" William replied.

"Not with your naked arse."

"I will." I stood, kicking off my sandals. We had towels, there was no one else around. He needed me. "You," I pointed to Ally. "Look the other way."

Ally swung his gaze between us then cocked his head to one side, as if making an assessment. He pressed up from his lounging position. "Actually, I need to make a couple of calls. My phone's almost dead, so I'll go back to the car and plug it in. I can search for a hotel nearby and book a couple of rooms for the night. Sound good?"

William lifted his chin in silent agreement. I gave him a smile, and Ally leapt to his feet, taking one of the food bags with him.

"See ye both later." He clattered away down the dock.

I waited for him to hit dry land then grasped the hem of my sun dress. William rested his cheek on his folded arms, watching me.

I raised my eyebrow at him, then I pulled the frock over my head, discarding it to the deck. William's attention bounced behind me, no doubt checking on his brother's progress, before snapping to me once more.

He ogled my chest.

With a practiced move, I unclipped my bra and let it fall to the ground. Then I took the straps of my bikini underwear and slid them down my legs before stepping out.

I had no problem with nudity, and with William glowering at me the whole time, I grew heated from the intensity alone.

Yet I didn't move.

William's face lost the small amount of humour it'd held. "Get in before Alasdair turns around," he ordered.

A shiver took me. I hesitated. "Hmm. I'm not so sure. It looks cold."

His barked command was the old William. The one I could never say no to. But I'd push the boundaries a little if it helped bring him back.

I widened my stance, a frisson of excitement hitting me right at the juncture of my legs. Right where his gaze clung. The light breeze glanced off my skin, cooling me where I was already wet. "If you want me to do something, all you need to do is ask."

"In the water. Now, lass," William uttered.

With a sharp inhale, I held my breath and jumped.

Water rushed over me, filling my ears and blinding me. Oh *God,* it was cold. I struck out, trying to right myself.

Two hands grasped my shoulders, hauling me to the surface. I broke it and dragged in a breath, treading water.

William clamped me to him, but I put both hands on his chest and pushed. He instantly released me, and I swam a metre backwards. Then another. Eyeballing him. Making it a game.

"If you want me, you're going to have to catch me," I said, and with a flip, I powered away.

There was no chance I could outswim him. None. But I tried.

Tried to help him burn up his energy.

Tried to get him into a place where he knew what to do.

The way he'd stared at me told me this was an option

and, when he'd held me, I felt the evidence. He'd been hard for me. Solid. Turned on to the max.

A hand took my foot. I shrieked, the sound amplified by the bowl the lake sat in.

I kicked, twisting right and ploughing on across the flat surface. My stomach tightened with the thrill, and my skin electrified. The shock of the chill evaporated, and I shrieked when his fingers gripped my ankle.

"Never!" I yelped, spinning around.

I splashed out, sending a wave of water over his head.

William swept in, crowding me. He released my foot but captured me in his arms. The wildness in his eyes had my heart pounding harder. The tiny smirk on his lips had me melting.

"Always," he replied. Then his lips crashed onto mine in a soul-seizing kiss.

I met him measure for measure. Wrestling him, digging into his muscles with my grip. Our lips moved in sweet unison, even as our bodies battled for closeness. Under the water, I strangled his waist with my legs.

We'd somehow neared the dock again, and William reached out, taking hold of the rungs of a ladder. Giving us purchase.

His dick pressed against me, right where we both needed him to go.

Then, he slid inside, just an inch, but it stopped us both in our tracks.

He was bare. No condom.

William opened his mouth. "We've never—"

Right as I said, "I haven't—"

We both stopped. Then he tried again. "I've never done this before. Gone without."

"Same here. I want to." He knew I was on the pill. I'd

taken one in front of him this morning and I'd seen it pique his interest then.

"Are ye sure?" He stretched me further, the water moving us closer, like nature needed us together and strong. And why not? It was a powerful thing, the way my Highlander and I came together. I'd never get over the exquisite feeling of his body taking mine. The rapturous way every cell lit up, pleasure bent and exhilarated.

And I had never needed anything more than this moment with him.

I inclined my head then loosened my hold on his neck and found my own grip on the ladder.

Now we could really go for it.

William made a guttural sound, and his mouth fitted over mine once more. Now, his tongue slicked in as he fucked deeper into me. His free hand found my ass, and he groped me, enjoying my body.

Around us, waves rippled, created by our lovemaking. The forest watched on, tall green sentinels guarding our moment. Oranges and yellows stretching over the sky as dusk crept in.

My heart hurt with the beauty of it all. Of him.

I worked my body in tandem with his moves. Meeting his thrusts, upping the tempo. It felt so good. Different, as the water made it challenging to hit hard, and it forced us to slow.

"Need more," William said, pausing, resting his head against mine. "Hold on to me."

He took my weight

"What are you doing?" I gasped.

Then he climbed the ladder into the cool air, taking us both onto the dry wood of the dock.

He crouched and tossed a towel down before laying me out on it.

How the hell he could lift me was a miracle.

I glanced around his side, scanning the banks for people. For his brother. "We could be seen."

"I don't care if you don't. They'll see my back if they look. I need ye and I'll have ye." William spread my legs wide. Then, with a single hard thrust, he was home once more. His wet body taking mine. Only this time he had no restrictions holding him back.

"Nng," I answered, insensible and wanton.

He took two handfuls of my breasts, moulded and massaged me, a grin spreading over his face. Then one hand flew to my clit, and I got a whomp of extra sensation.

In no time, I was moaning.

William full-on smirked now, the happy expression after his emptiness doing unknown things to my mental state. My orgasm hit me entirely unaware, a slamming, throbbing head rush that had my eyes closing by themselves and me gripping the towel, forcing myself not to scream his name to the whole area.

"Oh fuck. Christ, Taylor. I want to… Can I come?" Wild-eyed, he jacked his hips, building up steam.

"Do it. Please," I begged. "Come inside me. I want you to."

The gloves were off. William gave a series of staggering, hard thrusts, then growled out my name. Inside me, his dick pulsed, and he stilled, his muscles quaking with the effort.

Then he collapsed, clutching me to him as his orgasm blew his mind.

I drew a sharp breath at the newness of it.

We were instantly sloppy with the effects. A strange sensation I couldn't have predicted. Then there was something else. A chemical reaction maybe, that had me wanting to keep him inside me.

To never let me go.

"Fuck," I uttered. Then I kissed him on his lake-water-wet shoulder. "That was just magical."

"Aye." With his eyes closed, he nudged my face to find my mouth for a kiss.

We hugged, keeping together. Kissing endlessly. The approaching dusk brought glorious colours to the sky. The faint streaks now burning overhead and the surrounding trees darkening.

"The only problem we've got," I said, conversationally, "is no condom means a mess. I need to clean up and get my clothes back on before your brother comes looking for us."

William raised his head. Then he glanced at the water. "Easy solution for that."

"No." I glanced between him and the cold lake. Before, I'd been burning up to get him to focus on me. The cold hadn't mattered. Now, I was nice and cosy in his arms. "Not again. It'll be— Wait!"

My squeal came too late. William rolled, taking himself —and me—off the dock and straight into the lake. We hit with an almighty splash, and I floundered to the surface.

"You dick!" I splashed him hard, laughing even as I wiped water from my face.

"What?" He took a mouthful of water and squirted it at me. "Problem solved, aye?"

Then we just smiled at each other like dopes.

The mask had gone from William's expression, and he no longer seemed lost. He was back. My William. At least mostly. I didn't imagine one swim and a screw would solve all his problems. Gently, I sent another wave his way. "Glad to see you smiling."

He sent one back. "I was always smiling at ye. I always will. It just won't always be visible. And for that, I can only apologise."

If hearts made a noise when they broke, mine would've boomed around the valley, crackling south over the mountains, causing chaos on its path. Devastating the land like it devastated me. I think I needed it, the swift pain of his vulnerability. The hurt he'd been unable to hide presented as a burden. I needed it to change me. To force a restart and to make me new. Better.

As a girl, I thought I'd never fall in love. Simply because no one had ever fallen in love with me.

What a tragedy that had been.

William still watched me, so I took on that ache to puzzle over later and leaned in to kiss him. "Don't say sorry. Just let me in," I said.

"I already have."

"Then don't let me out."

His breath hitched, and emotion passed over his features. "I'm sorry for this. For what I am. Up until now, the worst I thought this could do was lose me my job, which would be a fucker as I'm nae good at anything else. But now, I'm more worried about you."

I shivered, the cooler evening air chilling my shoulders and my wet hair. "I'm not going anywhere."

William kissed my cheek. "Come on. Let's get ye out," he said gently.

We climbed out of the lake, and I watched the shoreline for movement. Far more aware now of being naked and in plain sight. Quickly, we dried off with the towels, then we dressed, quiet, but exchanging glances. Grinning when we found the other doing the same. I sat on the sun-warmed boards and towelled my hair.

A whistle came from the forest. A loud, tuneless melody.

"We've been a while. That'll be Ally." William hopped up and hauled his jeans over his bare ass. Then he checked me over.

"I'm decent." I winked at him.

He winked back and put two fingers in his mouth and whistled as Alasdair emerged from the trees, looking anywhere but at us.

Ally swung his gaze around then waved and jogged to join us. Our moment was over, for now, but something huge had changed for me, and I felt it through every cell. I'd become thin, a fine glass version of myself, needing to resolve into a more substantial woman.

For too long, I'd been a shell. Now, I had to work out how to grow.

21

SOME HURTS NEVER WENT AWAY

W asp
"Twice today I've seen your lily-white arse, and that's two too many. What happened to your boxers?" Ally approached, a hand over his eyes and another extended, like he was afraid of what he might see. "Wait, maybe I don't want to know. You decide."

I snorted a laugh. "Moron. I kicked them off. They're floating out there somewhere."

Ally dropped the act then joined us, sitting at our lazy perch. "Symbolic."

"Aye, exactly. As I swam, in my head they became the constraints I'd been under. Now they're fish food."

My brother's smile dialled back, and his swift gaze took me in. "You seem happier already. You'd normally be at the grunting stage and disappearing off to be alone."

I glanced to where Taylor finger-combed the tangles from her hair, and then to my twin. "Nah. Not from you both. The rest of the world can keep its distance for a day or two more, but you two can stay right here."

"Good to hear," my lass said.

Her blue eyes held mine for a moment, and my heart skipped a beat.

There was far, far too much still buzzing around my head to make clear sense of everything that'd gone on, but I knew one thing for sure. She cared for me. To some extent needed me.

She'd asked me to keep her. *Aye, lass. Watch me.*

I sensed Ally's gaze on me and instantly felt bad for his worry. "Did ye hear from your agent?"

He stared out over the water. "Not yet. But she thinks it's in the bag, thanks to you."

"So have ye been sitting in the car and moping?"

"Ha. A wee bit."

"Moping over what?" Taylor asked.

"He feels guilty over my meltdown. Like it was his fault that I took it upon myself to go to his audition."

Ally's silence confirmed it.

Taylor tilted her head. "Can I ask a question?"

We both nodded, probably looking ridiculous now I'd undergone my shave and haircut. We hadn't looked this similar since we were lads.

"Ally, you said earlier that you felt guilt over the Wasp nickname. I don't even know how it came about."

Ally sucked in a breath. "Ah, that. Bro? Care to explain?"

"I copped a beating for him," I said starkly. I had no problem with Taylor knowing this, though it wasn't my favourite topic of conversation. Depending on who was asking, I told different versions of the story. Taylor could have the facts. "Da got drunk and grabbed me, thinking I was my brother. He whipped me, screaming shite about how dense I was. How I'd failed at a test and needed good sense beaten into me. I remember wondering what the hell he was going on about, then he called me 'Alasdair', and I got it. Eventually, Callum stopped him, broke the fucker's nose, but I had a back covered in black and blue lashes to show for it."

Taylor's mouth gaped open, her expression one of shock. Ally had closed his eyes.

I continued, "Gordain put ointment on the cuts and commented how I was striped like a wee wasp. It made me laugh, and from there on in, I used the name."

Darkness gathered around us, night replacing the evening. Even so, tears were plain on Taylor's cheeks. Ah, Christ, I hadn't wanted to upset the woman.

"How old were you?"

"Eight."

She gave an unhappy little gasp.

"That's why he," I indicated my head at my brother, "carries around this permanent guilt. Despite us all knowing it was Da's fault. Callum and Gordain talked to us both about it, over and over. Making sure we understood how neither of us had done anything wrong."

"Ye didn't stop him, though," Ally said to the stars. "Ye could have just told him he had the wrong one of us. It would've stopped it."

Ah fuck, he was breaking my heart.

Some hurts never went away. This was ours.

For over fifteen years, this argument remained.

"Then two of you would've been beaten by that motherfucker." Taylor rose from her position and sat between me and my twin. She put an arm around his shoulders then leaned against me.

Such a simple gesture, but it broke the invisible barrier between me and him. I'd say it was okay. He'd still look sad. Taylor's move changed up our dynamic.

I wrapped them both in a hug, taking their weight.

"She's right," I told Ally. "And she's smarter than me, so you should listen."

Ally huffed, letting it all happen. Letting Taylor hold him. The tender moment stretched out, and around us, the calm lake air seemed to gentle further.

This time, no jealousy struck me.

Everything felt right with the world.

"Love you guys," Ally murmured.

A loaded silence met his words. I loved them both, too. But this wasn't the time to say it. Not to one of them, anyway.

Under my arm, Taylor tensed.

My brother sat up and gave an amused chuckle. His eyes sparkled. "I just made this super awkward, didn't I?"

Taylor didn't move, and I hugged her a little harder, just in case she wondered.

Ally leapt to his feet and planted his hands on his hips. "Well, it's getting late, and we have another long drive tomorrow. I booked us into a hotel. One room with a king-sized bed for all of us, aye?"

"Shut the fuck up." I aimed a kick at his leg, but he danced away.

"What? I'm trying to lighten the atmosphere."

Taylor's delayed laugh startled us both. She held out a hand to Ally, and he helped her to her feet. Then she slapped his chest. "You might look like your brother, but don't push your luck."

Chuckling, I joined them, and we collected our items and left the dock.

Emotionally, I had bruises, sustained in the water and shaped like Taylor's heart. I needed more food, sleep, and a couple of days of relaxation.

Then we'd see about that whole love conversation.

* * *

*A*t the car, I retrieved my phone from where I'd stashed it in the bottom of my bag. I hadn't had the brain space to handle the callbacks from Freddie or Reportage One so hadn't checked it since the morning.

The screen lit. Missed calls and voicemail messages loaded.

Ally drove us back towards the town. Taylor placed her hand over mine. She'd taken a seat with me in the back, just like before.

"Want me to make any calls for you?"

Freddie liked Taylor. He'd happily added her to the tour lists for things like backstage passes. He'd probably be fine talking to her on my behalf.

Not that I would go there. I had to reclaim my pride somehow.

If I was lucky, this event would be it for a while. It sometimes went that way with maxing out. I'd be steady for months until the next episode.

Squeezing Taylors's fingers, I gave her a soft smile. "I've got it. Thank ye."

First, the voicemails. Amongst much humming and hawing, Freddie told me that he was going to talk to Rex, who'd apparently left the club in a temper. His second message was even vaguer. He said Rex had punched me first, which made no sense, and they'd see me in Berlin for the evening performance.

Reportage One's message was curter. "Mr McRae, you'll no doubt be aware that the incident you have reported breaches our terms and conditions of service. We'll be discussing the matter further and will be in touch to advise of the action we'll take."

How ominous.

I relayed the messaged to my brother and Taylor.

"If they don't need you until the gig," she mused, her gaze on the road ahead as my brother made a left into a square, "we have time to kill. All tomorrow and until the following evening, right?"

I confirmed it.

"Then tomorrow, we should do something spectacular. We're in the middle of a huge country. We have the time, and it'll be better than hanging out in Berlin worrying about the band. Agreed?"

"Aye," Ally and I replied in unison again, though I had a small blip of apprehension. I still craved isolation but I'd fight my way through it if she wanted to have a good time.

My brother parked the car outside a small hotel. In the reception, he checked us in and gave me our key, then told us goodnight.

We made our way upstairs.

"What did ye have in mind for tomorrow?" I stole an arm around Taylor's waist, pulling her close.

She grinned. "Let me worry about that. It'll be outdoors and in peaceful surroundings. The rest will be my surprise."

My concern dissolved, and happiness replaced it. I needed a shower, room service, and a hot date in bed with my lass. One who knew me, despite the short time we'd been together.

Then I needed sleep. Hours and hours of deep sleep.

* * *

The next morning, while I showered, babbling noise filtered through the bathroom door. My brother's and Taylor's voices. When I emerged, a towel around my waist, the two of them were sitting in bed, the blanket over their legs, Ally at the bottom just like me and him would chill in our rooms at the castle when we were kids. They had the TV on and were cackling over a reality show.

Taylor swept her gaze over me. We'd woken up naked and entwined and fallen into a slow, semi-awake, highly pleasurable screw.

Christ, did I need the lass. All the time.

"Ally's made a decision." She shook off her open lust and gestured to my twin. "He says he's going home."

I raised my eyebrows at him. "That so?"

He stretched his arms over his head. "Aye. I already booked a ticket from Stuttgart. It's only an hour away and in the right direction for ye. If ye can drop me there this morning, I'll let you love birds continue on alone."

"I already told him I didn't mind him being with us." Taylor shook Ally's foot.

"Eh. You two need time together. I have stuff to get on with. Callum and Gordain are busy with a project, and they could do with another pair of hands."

I loved my brother, but this news meant I had two days alone with Taylor before I needed to work again. I grabbed fresh underwear and joined them in their den. We ordered breakfast to our room, and it wasn't hard to picture this becoming a regular thing.

It was all I could do to stop my mind moving Taylor into the crofthouse with me and having Ally stay over sometimes.

Taylor drove the stretch to Stuttgart, and we dropped my brother at the airport. Outside the car, he hugged me then pulled me back a few steps. Concern filled his gaze.

"Will ye be okay on the flight?" I asked.

Ally had long hated air travel.

He waved me off. "Fine. Listen. I need to give you a heads-up on a question Taylor asked me this morning."

"Aye?" I shielded my eyes against the morning sun, my brain already a little frazzled from being in the busy car park.

"She asked if ye could handle an angsty sort of conversation or would it harm ye."

I furrowed my brow. "What does that mean?"

My brother shrugged, shouldering his sports bag. "No clue. I didn't pry."

"Sounds like she's going to dump me."

He winced. "Are you two even dating? I didn't want to break the mood, but she's still meant to be getting married, right?"

"As far as I know." But I didn't know it anymore. Not for a fact. I knew she cared about me and I trusted her not to hurt me. So where did that leave us? "We'll talk," I added, understating what needed to happen next.

"You do that."

My brother gave me a friendly punch to the shoulder then disappeared into the crowd, while I put together another *please don't leave me* speech and worked out the best way to deliver it.

* * *

For the next several hours, Taylor and I took turns at driving, heading for her mystery location. We both seemed lost in our thoughts. She read emails from Mathilda and then made a call to my sister-in-law. They appeared to be plotting out a new business venture and, when she got off the call, she explained it to me.

"Mathilda has all the staff she needs to run the catering part of her business but not the time. Plus, with her baby on the way, she doesn't want more hassle when she isn't going to be handling it."

"What did you suggest?"

She tossed her phone back into her bag. "It's such a waste to pay money to the companies she has shortlisted. I think she needs to change the job of her part-time office manager and have them manage that section of the business, too. It's not that much extra work. Originally, I thought she should package it all up and outsource it, but I've come full circle now I understand it better. It would save her a heap of money."

Taylor could do that management job, I was certain. A terrifying kind of picture built up in my mind. One where she worked with Mathilda. Lived with me.

One where she was mine.

She got on with her work, and I focused on the traffic ahead and shut down that train of thought. That was a road to nowhere and only fucked with my head worse than I could ever do myself.

Just after lunchtime, we rolled into a small village. Behind, mountains soared over the quaint hikers' town. Taylor directed me to park up, and I squinted out of the window.

"Cute, huh?" She indicated with her head at the scene. Milling people in hiking kit, families, and day trippers.

I gave her a half-smile. Sure, it was pretty, but I still had the urge to get out of town and away from all the noise. This wasn't a city, but it certainly wasn't the refuge I sought.

Taylor unclipped her seat belt and blew out a breath. "This is just a quick stop off so we can pick up supplies." She gripped her fingers together, impatience crossing her expression.

"Uh-huh. Supplies for...?"

"Our hike."

I stared, and she hurried on.

"We're going to climb one of those mountains. Or walk up a beautiful part of it, anyway. The hiking store will give us the map and water bottles and everything else we'll need. Even shoes." She pointed to her pretty sandals. "We'll be completely alone, and by early evening we should be at our cabin."

"Cabin?" I gaped now. This was so perfect, and a weight lifted from my mind. The impact almost staggered me.

"Yes! It's a little mountain shack and totally isolated. The place will even have a food delivery with all the ingredients we'll need for dinner tonight and for tomorrow's breakfast."

"You organised this. A hike. In the mountains." She hated hiking. She'd told me so back in Scotland.

"Well, you said when you get stressed your home is the best place for you." A red flush crept over her chest and up her neck. "Oh God. You hate the idea. I know this isn't the same, but I thought—"

No. No way was she thinking like that. "Come here." I reached out and grabbed her from her seat, dragging her over to straddle me in mine.

She gave a startled laugh but settled on my lap, her knees either side of my hips.

Then I took her lips with mine in a hard kiss that left us both breathless. To hell with being in public. She'd done this for me? My mind was blown.

"I thought you were going to dump me," I told her.

She gaped. "Why?"

"Because I'm a wreck. Because you have other plans, and

this thing between us has got so intense. I've been expecting you to back away."

She rested her forehead against mine. Around us, people got on with their daily lives, shopping in the little stores, herding kids, being normal, and Taylor only had eyes for me.

"How could I leave you? I'm falling in love with you." Her gaze fierce, she stared deep into my eyes. Then she drew a shuddering breath and crumpled, dropping her face into my collar. "I had this whole idea of telling you tonight. We'd be sitting outside our shack, drinking a glass of wine and watching the sun set. It would be perfect, and I've just blown it because it wouldn't stay in anymore."

She... I...

My brain stalled, and I tried again to let it sink in.

"I love you," she repeated. "I don't want to exist in this world for a minute longer without you knowing."

Ah fuck. Dizzy, I closed my eyes.

Taylor pulled back and placed her hands on my chest. "Oh no, I broke you," she whispered.

She almost had. Shattered, I couldn't even look at her because of the answer to the next question I had. But that either made her declaration a thing of beauty I'd treasure forever or the straw that finally broke my back.

"Are you still going to marry someone else?" I managed and, with my hands to her hips, I grabbed hold of her like she was all that was keeping me on the earth. "All I need to know is that one thing, then I'll share a thought of my own."

"I really want to hear that thought," she whispered.

"Taylor!" I growled out, opening my eyes to her perfect, gorgeous blue ones.

"No," she answered, unblinking and appearing entirely

terrified. "No. I don't see how I can. I love you, and I won't marry anyone else."

My skies burst open, and I flew untethered. My brain an empty space, a trail leading from her heart to mine.

"Then I'll tell you what's on my mind. I'm in love with ye, too. Heart, soul, body, and mind. And Christ knows it has been a long time in the making."

Taylor stared at me and gave a happy laugh. Then a single fat tear rolled down her cheek, and I knew, I just knew, that this love had cost her.

I kissed it away.

Whatever it was, I'd solve that problem. Whatever it took, I'd fix this for Taylor. For my lass. For my life.

22

EVERYTHING

*T*aylor

When I'd been around seven or eight years old, on school vacation and unable to sleep, wandering around Dad's vast New York home, I'd overheard a conversation my father had been having with a friend. The guy was another politician, and Dad had been bragging about his long-term plans.

He'd called me a pawn.

He'd arrogantly stated, to that man, the building blocks he needed for his career. A significant policy change attributed to him. A spotless record in office. Taylor married to someone of influence.

"What about her own career?" Dad's friend had asked.

"Too much like her mother: Dumber than a box of frogs."

I'd tiptoed away, stunned. It hadn't been a surprise in itself, as he'd said as much to my face previously, but it hit home. I'd rebelled, of course, barely speaking to him and growing up cold. Dad's tactics simply shifted to blackmail. How lucky for him that Charity had become ill.

It left a mark, though.

My shaky self-worth. My lack of settling down. It had all stemmed from this half existence.

What the hell had I been doing?

Sleepwalking, that was a fact. But now, I'd woken up. This didn't mean any of my problems with Charity had gone away, but I'd been manipulated into thinking there was only one answer. I couldn't accept that. Not now I had my own personal goals.

I wanted a job.

I wanted my own home.

I needed the man at my side.

Breathtaking fear gripped me, and I had to pinch myself to listen to the woman in the hiking store talk us through our route. William listened carefully, pointing out lines on the map and nodding along to her description, but I was away with the fairies. My brain scrambled by the sheer effort it had taken to let go of years of bad ideas.

I *loved* him. Somehow, I wanted to keep him in my future. But it had been a life-changing, earth-shattering decision.

It shook everything up.

With our backpacks sorted, the very last thing I did in the store was buy a pair of cargo pants. I never wore jeans, I didn't even own a pair, and I couldn't recall the last time I'd worn anything but a skirt or a dress, so a whole new me was being birthed, and I wanted to yell out the consequences.

We got back on the road, and every so often, William glanced at me and squeezed my hand, like he needed to know I was still there and this was real.

After parking up on the foothills, we took a few of our own items with the supplies we'd been given, locked the rest in the car, and set off on foot.

"Do you really hate hiking?" William strode along the gravel track, exuberant in his joy.

"No. Hard exercise was frowned upon at school because it left you muscular or, the horror, with calluses. I've always done yoga. This is actually really lovely."

"I had it in my head that you could never live in the Highlands. What with hating mountains and the outdoors." He slid me a look, passing a water bottle between his hands.

"You've thought about me living in the Highlands?" Warmth pooled in my belly.

"Aye. I have. I told you so when ye visited my home."

He'd told me that he'd pictured me as his bride. I choked on a startled laugh. "I thought that was a joke."

"Naw. It was always you, sweetheart." He grinned big and picked up his pace.

We climbed through green, glorious nature, cool mountain air and sunshine surrounding us. For a few hours, I put aside my fears and just enjoyed myself.

In the pretty, low sun of the early evening, hot and sweaty, we came across our lodge—a wooden structure high on the mountainside, with solar panels for power and a metal chimney for the wood-burning stove. Inside, in a tiny fridge, we found chicken and vegetables for a stir-fry, with fruit and oatmeal for breakfast. I nabbed a bottle of wine while William cooked, then, at last, we got my wish. We ate our meal with the chilled wine, sitting on a tiny deck, gazing across at the valley below us and the mountain range all around.

"I have so much to explain to you," I said into the fresh air.

William drew his chair closer to mine and moved our empty dishes to the boards. Then he topped up our glasses and just watched me, waiting for me to go on.

I told him everything. From the role Charity played in my life—my sole visitor for months on end—to the time she'd called me to say she'd had a diagnosis.

"What ails her?" William asked quietly.

"Motor neurone disease. A really nasty illness with no cure. She's only thirty-two. Dad's sister by an affair his dad had. My father never really knew her, but she made every attempt to make a relationship with him. Here's the thing: My grandmother drank herself to death after my grandfather's affairs came out. After he lost his mom, Dad blamed Charity. Irrationally, but Dad's always been led by his passions. She found me at my school, and oh my God, she was the most amazing aunt. She was so much fun. She took me and Ella out. She bought us alcohol. She had this amazing car and she let us have turns behind the wheel."

I took a deep pull on my wine. "But now I know she did it all because she'd already started getting symptoms. It never occurred to me to wonder why she never ate in front of us. And we'd always go for drives. Never walks. Her disease weakens muscles and affects breathing. Even damages the brain. She was already hiding it then."

William blew out a hard breath. "I've heard of it. What treatment is there?"

"That's the kicker. There's no cure. Patients only get worse." Hot tears welled in my eyes, and I sliced them away with the side of my hand. "She's in a care facility in the Hamptons. But it's more like a hotel, and she has dignity there. The care they give is second to none, and it's keeping her alive, I'm sure of it. Life expectancy can be as little as a couple of years, and she's had it for nearly ten. I try to see her as often as I can, but she's getting increasingly frail. She was sick with a bug on my last visit."

Pictures flooded my mind. Stark, contrasting images of

my beautiful, glamorous aunt who took an interest in me when no one else did, and the thin, crumpled figure in a wheelchair.

"Can I meet her?"

I glanced up to see William's kind expression gentle. "When we go to the States, we'll try to find time to go to see her." If he met her, he'd understand, and maybe I wouldn't seem so weak to him.

Something crossed his vision and, though he produced a smile, pain or frustration lurked.

"What is it?" I asked.

He shook his head. "I'm stuck on your dad and what he's been doing to ye. He knew you cared for the woman and he used that against ye, aye?"

Taking another healthy swig of wine, I switched my gaze to the middle distance, to light clouds and mountaintops, trying to work it through. "Dad's world is a strange place. It helps that I didn't grow up with him or I might think it normal. Politics turns everything—every person—into a playing piece. And political marriages are common."

"But you're his flesh and blood."

"So is Charity. He doesn't care about either of us beyond what we can do for him."

The emotion on my Highlander's face switched to anger. I held out a hand, entwining our fingers.

"How?" he ground out. "How could anyone not love ye?"

Despite the heavy conversation, warmth and a buzz of happiness suffused me. "Easily! You're the third person ever to have said that to me. Charity, Ella, now you. I don't even really know what it means." My voice dried up at the end of the sentence, but I forced out the honesty he deserved. "I don't know if I'll be a good person to love. I don't know how. Look at how I treated Ella."

William tugged my hand, and I stood, leaving my glass on the small table. He pulled again, and I dropped onto his lap. A wiggle of my hips, and we were face to face, almost nose to nose.

"Tell me how ye feel about me."

"I love you."

"What does that mean?"

I thought it through. "That I want to be with you."

"Always? Or just for now?"

"God! Always." That required no thought at all.

A smug grin took his lips. "Good. Because I want ye. I don't want to be apart from ye."

"Ever?" I stared, agog, my spiralling emotions dizzying.

"Nope."

"How can you be sure about that?"

"Oof." He sucked in a breath. "Already, ye doubt me. But I get why. Then here's the thing."

A pause followed, and I kept up my stare, on the edge of my nerves, waiting for him to say something that could ground me in the shifting sands that were my life.

"On the drive up, I worked something out. I've loved ye for years."

"No!"

"Aye. Think about it: I never fell for anyone else. Despite the fact we hardly saw each other, each time we did, it got stronger for me. Do ye know I told my brothers to keep me from running to Braithar and finding ye?"

I laughed, perking up and placing both hands on his chest. "No!"

"I did. I didn't want to make a fool of myself in front of ye."

Now that rocked me. "A fool? You are without a doubt the most solid and steady person I know. I think that's one of the reasons I kept gravitating back to you. The first time we met, you took charge of me. You know what it does to me when you boss me around."

"Oh aye?" Under me, his dick hardened.

Heat flared.

"Ignore that." He waved a hand before bringing it back to holding me. A little firmer now. "We're trying to have a serious conversation about commitment, so just pretend ye can't feel me."

"Can we jump to the end of the discussion and agree we're a thing?" Even after everything he'd said, I needed to hear that.

Then I needed to take him to bed.

Green eyes held mine. "A couple. Aye. In love and with a future. Facing problems together. Being fucking happy."

"You'll leave me." The words left my mouth before I even knew I'd had the thought. I slapped my hand over my face.

"Never," William disagreed. "I know you love me. I will never, ever let ye go."

With that, he took my wrist and removed my hand, then laid his lips on mine.

I'd known, all through our climb up into the mountains, that we were heading for a spectacular summit. I also knew he'd catch me from falling from this brave height.

I could fly from this. I'd already started.

Our tender kiss rapidly descended into indecency, and he tore his mouth from mine, standing, holding me in his arms. "Bed?"

I gave a single urgent nod then kissed him again, harder. Faster.

He stumbled into the shack and up the open wooden steps that led to a small platform in the roof space. A comfortable bed awaited us, and we fell into the blankets, not letting each other go. Gripping and tumbling with our efforts to free ourselves of our clothes, enjoying the kerfuffle. Then, for a while, we just kissed, embracing naked, charging ourselves on the feel of each other and getting slowly more and more turned on.

Then, bare, he nestled between my legs, a grin on his face.

I held my breath, waiting on that incredible feeling. The one where he slid home and stretched me. Filled me. Made me his.

Instead, William kissed my cheek. "I'm in love with ye, Taylor Vandenberg. Every last bit of ye. I have been for the longest time. I built a home with you in mind." He took my hand and laid it over his heart. It thundered. "But you were always in here, too."

This man... "I love you," I uttered, no speech ready because I'd already told him far more than I'd shared with any other person. But that was okay. He didn't need it.

There was more than enough time in the world for me to let William McRae know just how wonderful he was.

A beautiful self-satisfied grin stole over his face, and he rolled his hips, pushing inside. "How many kids do ye want?"

A laugh burst out of me, interrupting my moan of pleasure. "Shut up." I giggled, pushing myself onto him, manhandling his thick biceps.

"Four? Five?"

"William!"

He moved faster. "Six? Christ, woman. We'll be run off our feet."

"Stop talking and just... Oh!"

His hand joined in the action and made fast circles over my clit. William watched my face intently, choosing his angle to maximum effect. His devilish expression mixed with signs of his own raw hunger, his powerful rhythm giving away his need.

"Over six and I'll have to build an extension on the croft-house," he ground out.

Nearing the edge, I reached out blindly and pressed my hand to his mouth to stop his words. "Can you go back to being alpha? Boss me around."

He opened his lips and took my fingers between his teeth. He sucked on them, and I gasped. Then he rose and, in a flash, I was flipped over, ass in the air.

"Ye want alpha? Done. Hand to your clit. Now."

Facedown on the quilt, I snapped to obey, poised and waiting for him to fill and stretch me again. "Come on!" I begged, empty but so turned on, my fingers moving fast.

"I'm enjoying the show. Ye look so fucking gorgeous."

I glanced back to see him stroke himself, his other hand to his balls. That sight...

"Please!"

Just as I needed to slow or come alone, William grabbed my hips and thrust inside me in a single, punishing move.

"God!" I yelled. My orgasm hit with a roar.

Eyes screwed shut, I clawed onto the quilt for dear life, my nerves shattered and my muscles pulsing around his rock-hard dick. On and on, my orgasm struck, elongated with my Scot's clever moves. When I dropped down, boneless and spent, William gave a satisfied chuckle, withdrew a few inches, then pounded into me. In a minute, he was growling out his pleasure, his fingers digging in like I was his world.

This, I needed. Being this close to him overrode my fears. He centred me.

As he collapsed down onto me, hugging me, I wrapped my arms around his, trying to provide the same for him.

"I've got no idea how to do any of this, but I'll learn," I whispered. "I've never had a boyfriend. I've never lived in one place long enough to know how to do that."

He kissed my cheek, his eyes hazy and his expression blissed out. "How are ye with rain?"

I blinked, trying to work out the subject change.

"It rains in the Highlands a lot. Ye get used to it but you've only visited Ella for a few days at a time. Just giving ye prior warning."

I snorted a laugh. "How long will I be there on my next visit?"

"Permanently."

Now, I reared up, pushing him off me. "What?"

"You heard." No humour in his face now. Nothing but the solid strength I'd come to love in him.

"Are you asking me to, to move...?" My mouth stopped, and my sentence failed. He didn't know it, but his offer filled a gap, no, a rip inside me. No one had ever done that. Neither of my parents had ever made a home for me. Never asked. I had a room in Dad's house, but it was generically decorated, and I'd slept in hotels more than I had there. When I visited Mom, I slept in whatever spare room she had going. She moved too often for me to carve out a space.

"Don't freak out." He eyed me with humour, sprawling his long form beside me on the bed.

"I'm not freaking out!" I squeaked.

"I undersold it when we talked about it before. I really did picture you living with me. Every decision I made about the place, I asked myself what would Taylor like? Before this job, I finalised the interior design—the layout of the walls, what room went where. And in all that, do you know whose influence I sought?"

"Mine?" I whispered, excited.

"Yours. Even though, at that point, I had next to no hope of you ever setting foot in the place. Still, it didn't stop my heart leading me." He took a lock of my hair, kissed it, and set it on the pillow. "Aye, move in with me. When you're ready. Help me finish the place. Make it ours."

I just stared.

"Ye look like I've offered ye a prison sentence." He rose on his elbow, his brow furrowed in the most adorable expression.

"Doesn't this terrify you?" I finally found my voice.

"Utterly. But in the best possible way."

"Best possible way," I muttered. Then I tightened my grip on him like a monkey.

He whispered in my ear, "I always figured when I fell in love, it would be the works. On-the-spot happiness. My whole future wrapped up in one sweet lass."

"I'm not sweet."

"Aye, ye are."

The mire I was wading through resolved to a clearer path. It was my own mind resisting the image he painted. My own beliefs that I'd already decided were no good. "Fuck. Yes. Yes, I want all of it. The fricking works. Marriage, babies, a house on a rainy mountainside with a warm fire and my friends nearby. I want a job. I want to come home to find you waiting. I want to learn how to cook—"

"Wait, you can't cook?"

"Nope."

"Deal's off."

I kissed him, hard. "But most of all, you. I've wanted you since I first met you."

"Now you have me. Completely." There was nothing in his expression but the honest truth.

It hurt to see. No, it hurt to *feel*. But I believed him.

"I need to see my dad. I need to tell him I'm upturning all his plans and still try to persuade him not to carry out his threats. This isn't going to be easy."

William rolled off the bed and took a moment to tidy us up from our new post-coital messiness. He gave me his t-shirt and pulled on his boxers then switched on a lamp, dusk having stolen the light, and sat cross-legged on the bed. "In recent years, I've spent a lot of time with James, getting to know him as my own friend rather than just my brother's."

I winced at the name, the memories still raw of debasing myself in the offer of marriage to that man.

William continued, his expression kind. "He told me how he nearly lost his home and his family's inheritance after he fell in love. He had to choose between being sure he would inherit and not, and being with Beth or not."

"That can't have been easy."

"He chose Beth, and whatever the outcome had been, they would've had each other. I'm not saying that a house and money compares with your aunt's life, but you've chosen me, and I don't take that lightly. Whatever there is to come, we'll face it together, and it will be good."

"My worst fear is Charity suffering then dying alone and in pain." I gripped the soft blanket and gave voice to my nightmare. "I can't know what Dad will do."

William pushed his fists into the bed at his sides. "The man was trying to blackmail you. His own daughter. I doubt he ever had good intentions."

"You don't think he'd have lived up to his promise? But I meant to hold him to it. Sign the papers. Give over a fund."

"Do you trust him?"

"He's a politician, so no, not for a second." Reality struck me. Had Dad been lying? Would he have gotten me into a political marriage then forced me to stay there? Always held Charity's care over my head? "God, maybe you're right."

"It's our problem now. You don't have to worry about this alone."

Scared over what my father might do, I knelt and crawled the couple of feet to sit with the man I loved. He welcomed me with open arms and an open heart.

"I won't hurt you," I swore to him. "Even if this all goes to hell, and I only make bigger problems for myself, I'll protect you from it. I want a life with you, but—"

"But nothing. That's it. You want a life with me, and I want a life with you. So that's what we'll have."

That was the last words either of us said for a while. Our newfound love put a bubble around us, leaving us safe in our mountaintop perch. But it couldn't stay that way. William didn't know what my father was capable of. Neither did I, but I suspected trouble would be coming our way. I just had to work out how to make the best for the two people I loved most.

23

FRAIL

*W*asp A lazy morning saw Taylor and me sleeping late, cosy in our loft room in the shack and tucked around each other. I made us a hearty breakfast which we ate overlooking the mountains, and happiness had my chest so tight I could barely breathe. Twenty-four hours ago, I couldn't have imagined this feeling—the sheer fucking joy of knowing she loved me.

My life had turned a corner.

My existence now centred around this silky-haired lass.

Perched on a white-painted wooden bench, tiny mountain flowers in clumps around her, she paused in her efforts of twisting her hair into a braid. "Will you do something with me?"

I glanced at her from where I packed the last of our things into the backpacks. "Anything. Always."

That earned me a grin. Taylor finished the braiding job and leapt to her feet. "Follow me."

I did, and we took the barely visible path around the

shack and over to a rocky ledge. A rope marked the way to stop anyone from wandering over the edge.

Taylor stopped just in front of it and peered down. "Not quite a cliff, but it'll do."

I furrowed my brow. "What are ye talking about?"

"One of Charity's diary entries was about standing on a cliff and yelling into a storm." She waved a hand at the clear-blue sky. "The weather might be great, but I'm about to walk into a storm, so do me a favour and yell with me."

I blinked at her then drew a breath.

"Aghh!" we both roared. Then I added a wolf howl, just in case anyone was listening and got worried.

Taylor faced me, small tendrils of hair framing her bonnie face. "I don't want to leave."

"We can come back one day. Or you might like the croft-house just as much."

I'd laid my heart on the line last night. Aye, I wanted her to live with me. I wanted everything with her, starting yesterday. She'd said the same, but now we had the broad light of day to contend with.

She had an existing life to unpack. Maybe jumping from that to life with me would be too much to handle. She gave me a wary look from under her lashes. Gone was the ballsy exterior she usually wore. "I had this idea that I could go home with you. After I've seen my dad and when your work is done. Not to sound too pathetic, but I don't want to be apart from you."

"Aye, come back." My heart raced. "We'll call it a visit, then if ye want to stay, ye stay."

Slowly, she nodded. "I don't have much to bring. I could have my clothes and things shipped over, assuming Dad will kick me out. But I don't own furniture or much of anything else."

"I don't own much either. Only what's in my room in Castle McRae. The crofthouse doesn't even have interior walls or plumbing yet. But it'll be the priority as soon as we get back. We can stay at the castle until it's ready, Callum and Mathilda won't mind."

Everything we'd buy would be ours. A bed, sofas, cupboards, plates.

Taylor inclined her head again, her hesitancy a counterpoint to my enthusiasm. I wanted this. She did, too. But baby steps. We had all the time in the world.

Fingers and lives now entwined, we made the hike back down the mountainside. After we'd handed in our rucksacks and thanked the outdoors store owner for the incredible stay, we returned to the car, ready to drive to Berlin. I felt a thousand times better.

Then I picked up my phone which had been abandoned to my luggage. "Missed calls from Reportage One," I told Taylor.

She frowned, and I made the call.

"Mr McRae," Claire, the office manager snipped. "I'm sorry, but we're not going to change the plan now. Your replacement has been sent in for tonight."

"My replacement?"

"You can resume the tour in New York but only once you've formally apologised to Mr Hamilton."

Hamilton was Rex's surname. "I'm not working tonight's gig?"

"Did you listen to any of your voicemails?" Her tone turned sarcastic.

Well, fuck. I was in the shite. "My apologies. I've been out of network reach. I'll guess I'll head straight to the States."

"Do that. And try not to hurt any customers on this leg of the tour." She hung up, and I swore at the phone.

Taylor pocketed her own phone and gave me a hug. "They cancelled your job?"

"Just for tonight." I kissed her forehead and gazed into her eyes. "Where does Charity live? Can we visit her before my next job? I'm working the day after tomorrow in Manhattan."

A smile spread over her face. "You really want to do that?"

"Aye. She's important to you so she's important to me."

"You know, you are something else, William McRae. I doubt there's another man alive who's as perfect as you are. You must be worrying about your job but all you're thinking about is how to make me happy."

"So that's a yes?"

"Yes!"

We pooled our efforts and found flights leaving Germany in the afternoon. Then we drove to the airport and got on a plane.

Taylor was right—I was worried about my job. My whole career, in fact. My chances of making it through probation were reducing with every step I took. Smacking Rex might've felt good, but I needed a career, and this opportunity had been hard fought.

"Note to self," I said out loud as we settled into our seats and found an old movie to watch together. "Don't hit the band. Repeat: Don't hit the band."

Taylor giggled then lifted my hand and kissed my knuckles. "I'll stay far away so you just do your thing."

"When will ye call your dad?" The plane sped down the runway, the G-force pulling us against our seats.

Taylor's happy exterior evaporated. "Soon. I had a dozen

missed calls and messages from him, so if I don't speak to him, he'll be looking for me. After we've seen Charity, though."

"And together, if ye want," I finished for her. "Then maybe if I still feel the need to punch someone, it can be him."

We took off into the skies, heading for the US and a whole load of trouble. I had no idea what to expect from Taylor's change of plans, but one thing for sure was I'd be at her side every step of the way. I'd make it right for her, if it was the last thing I did.

* * *

*J*n a secluded, exclusive part of the Hamptons in New York, at a long, low building, Taylor rang the bell, her face pale and her fingers crushing mine. After our flight, we'd slept the night in a budget hotel then driven out to meet her aunt. All morning, Taylor had been quiet, her features pinched and an air of distress around her.

A small man dressed in a smart uniform opened the door. He took us in, then recognition dawned.

"Miss Vandenberg! I am delighted to see you again so soon. Please come this way."

"Hey, Stefan." Taylor greeted the man who gave me a handshake, and we followed him into a pleasant, modern hall then to a desk.

"I came here before I flew to Scotland," she said in a low voice. "It was meant to be a reminder so I didn't try to change my plans. Look how well that worked out."

I gave her a squeeze. "I happen to think you made the best decision."

"Oh yeah?" She grinned, but it was tainted with that same worry.

"Charity wasn't feeling great when I saw her last. How's she doing?" Taylor asked the receptionist.

"She's still suffering, I'm sorry to say, but a visit from you will perk her up no end, I'm sure."

The man signed us in then ushered us beyond another set of secure glass doors and into a sunny, wide lounge. A green lawn spread beyond open doors, and patients sat with carers or visitors. Not one of the patients looked over forty. One woman played video games with headphones on, and a suited assistant read business emails to her charge.

"This is a care facility but also a rehab place for people who've had strokes or who have long-term conditions." Taylor's gaze skipped over the people as we passed, and she smiled at one or two. "It's specifically for younger people. Charity used to say, before she lost her speech, that she would die of boredom in an old people's home or a hospital."

"I didn't know she couldnae speak."

We exited the lounge and, in a colourful corridor of multiple doors, and with pop art on the walls, we came to a stop. Stefan poked his head around the door, and a nurse appeared.

She eyed me but spoke to Taylor. "Miss Allan has been under the weather. You can see her, but be aware that she's become more vulnerable in the past week."

Taylor's shoulders rose an inch. But she blew out a breath and opened the door.

In the room, on a hospital bed with a bright blanket over her knees, Taylor's aunt waited. Frail, she raised a shaking hand in a greeting. With her faded hair and high cheekbones on a gaunt face, she resembled Taylor so much it was like I already knew her.

But Christ, I didn't expect her to be so poorly.

"Hello, I'm William McRae. I'm so happy to meet you," I said gently and crossed to her bedside. I held back from taking her hand, not sure if I'd hurt her.

"My William. The one I told you about," Taylor added, sidling up. Her gaze flitted over her aunt, her happy expression melting at what she saw.

"Ye talked about me before?"

Taylor bit her lip, and her aunt gave a weak nod, her eyes gleaming, and a sense of humour shining through her wasted exterior.

I chuckled, stifling emotion from witnessing this woman —Taylor's most loved one—clearly so ill. So unlike the vibrant, joyful creature Taylor had described. All around us on the dresser and on shelves were pictures of them together. It was a shrine to their connection.

I clapped to dispel the heavy atmosphere. "Now I'm going to have to hear all about this. Come on, give me details."

For the next thirty minutes, we sat at the woman's side and talked, Taylor sharing stories of their previous adventures before starting on our more recent ones. Charity's nurse joined us and explained that the woman usually used an electronic speech programme but had been too tired after her recent illness to try. Her hints were noted, and we made our goodbyes, leaving with a promise to visit again soon.

At the reception desk, Stefan approached Taylor, his mouth a thin line. "May I have a quick word with you in private?"

She flicked her worried gaze to me. "Be right back."

They vanished into a room behind the desk, and I could only wonder at what news she was hearing. One thing about the morning's visit had been patently clear—Charity wasn't just in long-term care, she was gravely ill. I couldn't imagine her leaving that room without suffering.

After she emerged, Taylor's expression had changed from upset to anger. She strode outside, barely pausing for the doors to slide open.

I followed. "What happened?"

"Dad has stopped paying the bill for this place." She gripped her elbows. "After I agreed to the engagement, he was meant to pay for a year in advance. He didn't. I think you might be right in that he never intended to."

"What does that mean for Charity?"

"The money runs out in under a week. They'll transfer her to a state facility. They're a business, you know? They don't have a choice."

I palmed the back of my neck, sticky with the humidity. "How much is it to stay here? Can we work something for a couple of months?"

Taylor named a figure. It was more than I'd earn for the whole of my Reportage One contract.

"That's per week. The prices are insane. It didn't mean anything to my grandfather who started her treatment here a few years ago before he died, but what normal person can afford that? I just handed over almost the entirety of my savings, and it has bought her a month. A month! It's because she needs around-the-clock nursing care now. She didn't before but she's had pneumonia and—" Her voice broke, and she stopped. "I asked Stefan how long she'll need the extra specialist care for, and he put on this sad face, and I just knew he was about to say permanently. I didn't even get to tell her about her diary. Ask her about the things she'd done or tell her how I'd followed them. Do you know one of the longest entries is all about me? She wrote how much she adored our visit. I can't just walk away from her. I can't."

I wrapped her in a hug. "We won't. When I get paid, we'll add that money to the pot, too." But at the rate this place spent money, we needed a longer-term solution.

Taylor remained rigid in my arms. "You'd do that without even blinking. You're so wonderful. Do you want to hear the kicker?" I nudged her to continue. "Stefan isn't even sure he can accept my money. Dad holds the decision-making powers over Charity. He can move her anyway."

"Would he do that? Is there anything we can do to take over that control?"

Taylor didn't answer; instead, her gaze distanced, and I didn't like the look on her face.

We drove to the city, returning the car to the rental place. With an hour to kill before I had to go to work, we needed food and to hug it out. After the six weeks I'd spent in NYC, I would've been glad to steer clear of the place for a long while, but here I was again, in the centre of noise and fuss and just wanting to hold my woman until the angst went away.

"We'll find a hotel for the night," I decided, shouldering my camera bag and our holdalls. "When I get back, we'll work on this."

"I need to see my father." She stared down the busy street, not meeting my eyes.

"Aye, we'll go together. Call him. Set it up for the morning." If she went now, I'd go with her, which meant a no-show for the gig. I'd lose my contract for sure, then I couldn't help anyone.

For a moment, I expected Taylor to refuse, but instead she simply lifted her chin in agreement.

A wee while later in an overpriced box room of a hotel in Lower Manhattan, I kissed her goodbye. "I have to go."

"I know."

"I don't want to leave you."

She offered up a ghost of a smile. "I know that, too."

Pressing my forehead on hers, I stared into her blue eyes and tried to make an impression. "Don't leave me, aye? I know today was rough, but we will find a way to make it work for her."

Taylor pushed me to the door of our room then kissed me thoroughly. She stopped my heart, this lass, with her soft kisses and the tragedy she'd been trying to avoid facing.

"Go. Make your apology to that asshole Rex. Get your career back on track and stop worrying about me."

That was impossible, but I left all the same. And every step I took away from Taylor, I felt the pull back to her. I just had to hope like hell that she'd still be waiting for me when I was done.

24

EVERYONE WINS

Taylor

Mad, bitter, and utterly confused, I had calls to make. First, I telephoned Charity's home, confirming what I'd told William. If I was going to make this right, I needed all the facts, and I'd hardly been listening before. Then I dialled up the source of several of my missed calls: Pippa, Dad's loyal assistant.

"Irene! I've been trying to get hold of you for—"

"Why did Dad stop paying Charity's bills?" I interrupted, not needing her questions.

"He, er... Well... I'm not sure I can answer that. Your father has been trying to speak to you for two days—"

"Tell him to pay up or the deal is off."

The line went silent for a moment, then a new voice came on. "Irene."

My blood boiled. "Dad."

"Where are you?"

"What does that matter? I've been to see Charity and—"

"I know. And you took a friend. A Scottish man."

I snapped my mouth close. "How do you know that?"

"My Manhattan office. Thirty minutes." He ignored my question.

"No. Pay the care bill." I had a whole speech prepared. A damning argument that called his bluff and showed him how awful he'd been. I had to be able to convince him. If I couldn't, Charity would be out of her lovely home and into a place that couldn't afford to keep her alive.

She'd die in a place where no one cared about her.

"William 'Wasp' McRae," Dad said blithely, cutting my thoughts in half.

I dropped onto the bed, clutching the phone.

"Son of Laird Hamish McRae, deceased, brother to Callum McRae, the current laird. Twin brother Alasdair. Recent graduate with a degree in arts specialising in photography. Working for an international agency under the recommendation of Josie Addlestein."

He paused for effect, and I pictured the smile on the motherfucker's face.

Oh God.

He'd not only given up on Charity, but he was going after William.

"My office, Irene. You have twenty-eight minutes, now," he added. Then my father hung up the call.

* * *

I have to see my father today. Sorry. I love you - T

I fired the text to William as my cab weaved its way through the slow, late afternoon traffic. Sweat pricked my brow, and nausea cramped my stomach. I hadn't predicted this. Not for a second.

No response had come back by the time we pulled up outside Park Lane Heights, Dad's private office in the city, but that was to be expected if he was working. That thought brought me back to Dad's words. His threat. As it had been a threat.

Did he mean to take William's career from him? Could he do that? I knew how important it was for William to succeed. I swallowed and crossed the busy pavement, entering the dark interior.

Pippa stepped forwards from the shadows. With a grim expression, she took my elbow and led me to the elevator. I didn't shake her off. On Dad's floor, still gloomy despite the tall windows, she directed me into the office. Inside the door, she plucked my phone from my hands.

"Hey!" I squeaked.

"I'll return that later." She had closed the door before I'd even moved.

Dad turned from his position at the window. On the right-hand side of his office, another man stood. Theo Miller. My would-be fiancé.

"Hello, Irene," Theo said politely.

"Thanks for stopping by," Dad said with a sarcastic smile, like he hadn't just threatened me. "Theo's father and I had a little chat this morning, and we thought it might be better to move things on faster than originally planned."

"What things?" I gazed at him, at the man who I shared DNA with but didn't know. He might as well have been a stranger.

"Your engagement party. It's happening tonight. We are attending a fundraiser at the Yankee Stadium in"—he checked his watch—"two hours and announcing our joint campaign after. Pippa has organised your outfit and everything else you need. You'll change in the room next door, then you and Theo can travel together."

I squeezed my eyes closed for a moment, trying to centre myself.

I couldn't do this.

But he'd threatened William.

Hadn't he? My eyes flew open. "You broke our deal. I'm not going through with this."

My father smiled with reptilian coldness. "Yes, you will."

"You can't make me." I glanced at Theo, embarrassed for him to hear this conversation. He had his phone in his hand and was scrolling, apparently uninterested in my declaration.

Dad put his hands behind his back and strolled to his desk. Then he peered at the screen before smiling at me. "If you don't do what I've asked, I will not only pull the plug permanently on that sick bitch, but I will also ruin Mr McRae's career. I have Ms Addlestein's business information here. As State Governor, I can cause her all kinds of problems until she withdraws her support for your Scot."

Theo sucked in a breath, not looking up from his device. "I love her work. That would be a real pity."

Dad continued. "Since your name was connected to his after the Met, I've followed his career with interest. Here, I have his contract for his first assignment. It seems he has a temper. I'm sure a report or two would kill off his probation. If not, I will make it happen in another way. Am I making myself clear?"

"You are awful," I choked, horrified by the lengths Dad had gone to. I vaguely recalled William sending a message to report us both as safe. That my father had tracked him since then alarmed me beyond reason. "Why would you go after William? You don't even know him."

Dad pinched the bridge of his nose. "I didn't invite questions. I just need my goddamned daughter to do as she's told."

"Fuck you," I bit out, my blood rising. "What the hell is wrong with you? Is your brain so twisted that you think this is okay? It isn't. It's one thing treating your own sister like—"

"That person is no relative of mine," Dad hissed. He glanced at Theo who'd ambled his unbothered way to the window.

I could beg, but it was pointless. The man was a monster. "So you're going to let her die and you're going to ruin a good man's career because you want to play politics?"

Dad stared me down, his gaze switching to calculating. "Go to the engagement party. Smile and fucking wave. Get rid of your boyfriend and do what we agreed, then I'll pay that bill."

"I don't trust a word you say." My words held venom, and I dug my fingernails into my palms.

He shrugged. "I don't give a flying fuck what you think. So long as you do as you're told."

Now, Theo interrupted. He raised both hands. "Sir, if I may? Irene, come next door and have a chat with me. I have a suggestion you might like."

He winked at my dad and, though I didn't trust him for a second, I followed him from the room. The distinct feeling that Dad had trapped me rose, and I couldn't see a scenario where I got away from here without hurting someone I loved.

If I stuck two fingers up to Dad, Charity wouldn't be able to stay in her home, and William's career could be harmed.

If I did what Dad demanded, I'd have to give up the new dream I'd had. The one where I married the man I loved.

In the next office, bare except for a wheeled clothes rail

with expensive dresses, presumably for me, Theo gestured to the couch.

"I'll stand." I folded my arms, pushing down my distress, because fuck letting him see.

He sighed and brushed over his neat hair. "I know this is rough, and your dad doesn't have the gentlest way about him, but I want you to know I understand."

I just stared at him.

"I have one, too. A girlfriend, I mean. Her name is Karen. She was there when we met last. We already had the talk, and she's fine with this."

"The talk?" Ah God, why did I even ask?

"About our ongoing roles. She's happy to stay out of the limelight and wait for me at home."

"While you marry another woman?"

He shrugged easily. "She loves me. If your boyfriend loves you, then he'll agree, no problem. One word of advice: Get an NDA signed first." He followed his sage guidance with a wink then collected a suit bag from the end of the clothes rail.

"Think about it." He unzipped the bag and peered at the suit. "You get your boyfriend and your relative all taken care of. You're happy, your dad's happy. Everyone wins."

This was the most ridiculous conversation. Maybe a couple of weeks ago, it wouldn't have seemed so odd, but now I felt like a whole different person. One who couldn't stomach living a lie.

The door opened, and my father stepped in.

Dad raised an eyebrow at Theo.

Theo grinned. "No big deal. We just need her boyfriend to sign an NDA, and it's all taken care of."

Dad grunted. "Whatever you think best, son. I have another meeting first so I'll see you there."

He glanced at me, but I'd had an idea, and I wasn't giving anything away. I stared him down this time until Dad sneered, turned on his heel, and left.

Then a woman arrived to do my hair and makeup, and I gave her the nod to begin.

Oh yes, this was the only way forward for me.

25

I COULD ACT

*W*asp

In the green room of Madison Square Gardens, a huge venue compared with the others on the tour so far, Viking Blue was holed up with Hedonist, having a pre-gig pow-wow. I hung by the door, prepared to say my piece to Rex but more than anything wanting the night to be done with so I could get back to Taylor.

"Rex will be up on a platform in the third and fourth song." Freddie ambled over, tapping his screen, reading through notes. "Make sure you catch it when he jumps back to the stage. He's got this thing about having an epic shot taken here. The start of their big US takeover. They've never played in the States before."

"Mm-hm." A kind of anxiety gripped me, no doubt after the shite day we'd had. I slid my phone from my pocket. A message from Taylor waited, received over an hour ago, while I'd been capturing the setup and the waiting crowds.

I read it and baulked. She'd gone to see her father? Adrenaline hit my limbs. I should be with her, except I had no idea where she was.

"Sorry," I muttered to Freddie. "I need to make a call."

My sense of unease growing, I dialled Taylor's number. It rang. A stranger's voice answered.

"Why have ye got this phone?" I barked down the line.

"If you are trying to reach Miss Vandenberg, I can take a message."

A group of stage technicians manhandled gear through the door, and I stepped aside. "No, I don't want to give ye a message. Is she there?"

"She busy preparing for her engagement party," the woman replied.

"Her...what?"

"Her engagement party. Tonight. Like I said, I can pass on a message, but I doubt she'll be available to return your call until tomorrow."

"Where?"

"I beg your pardon? I'm not at liberty to divulge—"

I killed the call and stared at my phone.

"Wasp?" Freddie hissed. "Rex is coming."

On the balls of my feet, I swung around and grabbed my bag, stuffing my camera inside. "I need to go."

"Go? Where?" Freddie clapped his hands to his cheeks. "You can't!"

"Wasp. How are ye doing?" Rex entered the room, his cocksure grin in place and his hair newly dyed a bright blue. "Look, man, apparently I hit your brother by accident—"

"Not interested," I uttered, needing to get out of there.

He grabbed my bag strap, jerking me to a halt. "Wait a minute. Where do you think you're going?"

"I need to leave!" I yelled and wrenched the strap from his hand.

"If you do, you're off the tour," he snarled. "I'll see you

replaced and I'll bad mouth you to every fucker I know. We're playing fucking Madison Square Gardens!"

"Taylor's missing," I snapped back. "I have to find her."

He blinked. "She's probably with her fiancé."

"What the fuck are you talking about?" I got into his face, irrational with my worry for the lass. How the hell did he, of all people, know about her old plans?

"Effie recognised her. She's engaged to Theo Miller. His dad is meant to be the next president. You're up against stiff competition."

Ah fuck, so everyone knew. No way would Rex keep this to himself.

"Wasp? There's someone here to see you," Freddie called from by the doorway.

I wheeled around to see a sharp-suited man at Freddie's side.

Despite the fact I'd never met him before, I instantly recognised my visitor.

And despised him.

It was Taylor's dad.

* * *

$\mathcal{I}$n a side room, away from the prying eyes of my colleagues, I stared with hatred at the man before me. With a steady gaze, he took me in.

"Where's Taylor?"

The corner of his mouth quirked up. "Using that name, is she? Interesting."

I stepped closer to him, very aware that with my shaved head and scowl, I looked like a thug. At half a head shorter than me and a good thirty years older, the man didn't blink.

"I asked you where she was."

"I have little time and more important matters than this to deal with, kid. Tonight, my daughter, Irene, is attending her engagement party with her fiancé. This is a long-standing arrangement which is of vital importance to both families."

"She isn't going through with it."

"She is. I left her choosing a dress with Theo at her side." He sized me up. "So you see, it's a done deal. You're just a complication, and what I need from you is your silence. What will it cost?"

Something was badly, deeply wrong. Taylor couldn't have agreed to this. I worked my jaw, debating over how I could prise out where this party was. If I could get to her, I could help her.

"I'm not for sale," I muttered. Politics wasn't my strong point. I had no idea how to cheat my way to information. But I wasn't stupid. I could act.

"Everyone's for sale. Let me make this perfectly clear." He slid an envelope from his inside pocket and unfolded a piece of paper. "This is a non-disclosure agreement Irene wishes for you to sign. If the two of you are to continue seeing one another after her engagement and subsequent marriage, you will abide by the agreement. If not, we will sue you into the ground."

I stared at the white sheet.

"Alternatively," her father continued, "you get the fuck out of her life, and I give you a payoff to stay away."

"What if I don't want any of those things?" I kept my gaze on his, testing his mettle.

Steel crossed his eyes. "You don't want to ask that question."

I wanted to keep pushing. To tell him how I loved his daughter and would protect her from fuckers like him until the day I died. But I wouldn't see her again if I did, I was certain of that.

"What's your offer?" I repressed my shiver and dropped my gaze from his, beaten into fake submission.

The man stilled.

I doubted that he believed me.

Then, with malice in his tone, he said, "I'll hire you for the evening. You'll receive twenty thousand dollars for one night."

"You want me to photograph her engagement party?" Christ, this man took the biscuit.

I met his gaze again, and he smiled. The cruelty there in his eyes told me all I needed to know. He believed himself. He thought he'd won. He planned to show Taylor that he'd bought me as much as he controlled her.

"Snap the happy couple. Then go and never darken her door again."

Yeah, I was about to take the pictures of my career.

* * *

*I*n the weirdest of parallel universes, I travelled in Taylor's dad's car, albeit up front with the driver, to her engagement party venue at the Yankee Stadium.

In my jeans, black t-shirt, and with my shaven head, I couldn't have looked less like a guest if I tried.

Inside the vast hall, noise mobbed me. Loud chatter, people networking, a film crew making the rounds.

Then, across the room, Taylor appeared.

In a sparkling blood-red dress, with her hair and

makeup inch perfect and stunning, she took in the room, the model of a politician's daughter. Or wife.

A man arrived at her side, and my breath caught. If he touched her, I couldn't keep up the charade. All I needed was to get her alone and to an exit and we were away. But if that arsehole in his shiny suit laid one finger...

Taylor smiled at a couple who approached her and her *fiancé*, then, before my very eyes, she took the man by his arm. And she laughed, bright and happy.

Horror glued me to the spot.

"Take a picture, kid. That's what I'm paying you for." Her father patted my shoulder then parted the crowd with his overblown ego as he crossed the space to join his friends.

I'd felt better since my meltdown of two days ago.

Now, it all came flooding back.

The stress. The tension in my head.

If I'd been anywhere else, I'd have made for the door. Found a street to run down or a gym to hit things in.

But I couldn't leave her.

Desperate to look at anything but the apparently happy couple, I scrolled through the photos on my camera's roll, flicking the wheel back and forth. Waiting for Taylor to move on or do something.

A particular shot caught my eye. Taylor lay on the bed in our mountain shack, grinning at me, her ankles crossed and her head tilted. In her hands, she held Charity's diary. Her own handwriting stood out clear above her aunt's. I zoomed in.

This was the benefits of quality kit: I could read every word on the page.

Make love to someone I'm in love with, read the original words.

And then some, Taylor had added. Underneath, and underlined, she'd added a new list item: *Then lock him down.*

Any uncertainty I had fell away. She loved me. I knew her.

Taylor and her would-be fiancé approached the stage, and I strode out onto the floor. Centre left, there for her to see. And if she didn't notice me, I'd march right on up and join her.

26

FREEFALL

Taylor

A crowd of expectant faces turned my way as I took my place on stage. Cameras snapped, reporters hovered, and Theo made a move to join me, but I put up a finger to pause him. He blinked but remained on the floor, his confident smile unwavering under the venue's bright lights.

Over the last thirty minutes I'd shaken hands with multitudes of Dad's colleagues. They all knew what was coming and were out en masse, jockeying for position ahead of the election announcements that tied our two families, placing Dad as Theo's father's running mate.

What a night to declare a second tie—their two kids' engagement. I could see the appeal for sure. What a coup.

At the back of the hall, I caught sight of Karen, Theo's girlfriend, in a pale-pink dress. She had her brother at her side, but heartbreak played out across her face. Earlier, when Theo had introduced us, he'd winked at her like this was all some sort of game. I remembered the look in her eyes when I saw her in his hotel room, and it was there times a million now. I guessed she must really love him to agree to what he'd asked her to do.

Stay home and be the little wife while he married me.

Funny, the things people did when in love.

And also funny how, under the glossy exterior I'd put on tonight, I looked so different to the old me, the shell. Everything had changed.

I cleared my throat and raised a hand. The murmuring stopped.

"Hi, everyone. For those of you who don't know me, I'm Irene Taylor Vandenberg, and I'm so proud to be here tonight. It's a special evening, and I'm sure you're all excited about the announcements to come, but first, I have an announcement of my own."

Dad moved purposefully in the middle of the crowd, drawing my attention. He stared right into my eyes, and I gave him a wide smile. Theo's dad stood at his side. This was perfect.

"Dad. There you are. Can you see him, everybody? My father has been a constant source of inspiration throughout my life. He taught me to go after what was important, and he showed me the value of wrong and right."

Dad's eyes narrowed, but he kept up his fake smile.

A frisson of excitement bubbled inside me, and I stifled the urge to laugh. "Of course, you all know the sort of man my father is. But maybe there are one or two facts that might be a surprise."

I paused for effect. Mastering the game he taught me.

For a second, I saw fear flicker over his features, and my excitement turned hard-edged. "I have a relative named Charity." I wrapped my mouth around her name. "Aptly named as, in recent years, she's been reliant on Dad to provide care for her. She has motor neurone disease, and if any of you are aware of the condition, you'll know how hard it can hit a person. Charity is only ten years older than me, but thanks to Dad, she's receiving the best care money can buy in a facility in the Hamptons. He's never sought publicity for his act, but doesn't this deserve recognition?"

A round of applause rippled through the crowd. Someone palmed Dad's shoulder, and his cold, crocodile smile returned automatically.

But his gaze held only danger for me.

It didn't matter. I was freefalling without a parachute. I knew in doing this, there was no way Dad could withdraw Charity's funding now. The press would want the story, and Dad would spin it because the eyes of the voting public would be on him.

She was safe.

I couldn't say the same about me.

"Irene." With his gaze dark, Theo took another step towards the stage.

"My second announcement." I snapped my attention back to the crowd, not focusing on anyone for fear of losing my nerve. "You might have heard rumours of my engagement. Well, they've been a little premature, but they're true. I've been lucky enough to fall in love, and tonight is all about celebration, so forgive me if I want you to share in my happiness."

People gasped; happy sounds abounded.

Then I saw him. The one person who shouldn't be here.

Dad crossed the floor to where William stood. He placed a hand on his shoulder, and the message couldn't have been clearer.

Even so, not for a second did the name on my lips waver.

"Theo, would you come up here for a second?" I said.

William's green-eyed gaze held mine, but I pushed on.

"With our dads being such good friends, Theo Miller and I have spent time in each other's company. We're lucky to have a lot in common."

"That's right. Which is why—" Theo started.

"The rumour mills have it wrong." I spoke louder and bolder, my crescendo of freedom crashing over. "We're very happily engaged. But to other people. Karen? Why don't you come on up?"

The crowd gasped again and babbled and, from the back of the room, Karen took a visible inhale. Then she gave a broad smile. I wouldn't have done this, outed her, if I didn't know how wrong Theo was about her happiness. Her sole crime was coming from a poor background. A non-political family. I pitied her for falling for a douchebag like Theo but, in a way, I pitied him, too.

He was stuck where I had been. Before life and love had opened my eyes.

Still, I didn't dare look at William.

Karen wove through the crowd and joined us on stage.

"The happy couple!" I raised an imaginary glass.

Karen smiled shyly at Theo, but he, to his credit, took her hand and forced a smile in return.

"Now if you'll excuse me, I'm sure you can't wait for the rest of the evening to begin."

With that, I left them to it and hopped down from the stage. Blood rushed in my ears from my reckless act, and I crossed to where William still stood with my father.

Pointedly, I offered my back to Dad and my smile to William.

"Call that a proposal?" he said, his voice taut with stress but his gaze full of love.

I didn't dare answer. We needed to leave, and fast, before

Dad made a threat he couldn't take back. Slipping my hand into William's, I led him out of the hall.

Halfway across the room, I spied Pippa. I approached her and held my hand out. "Phone," I said with as savage a smile as I could summon.

Stony-faced, she took it from her bag and handed it over. I snatched it and marched on, not sparing her a second glance.

My spine tingled with the daggers Dad threw, but there was nothing he could do. Not in this public place. Not with the cameras on us and his colleagues around, let alone his own big announcement due.

We had time to get away. But after that? "I might have just brought a shitload of trouble down on our heads," I murmured to the man I loved as he threw open the exit door.

"Wouldnae have ye any other way," he chuckled in response, then we were outside in the fresh air, free and flying.

Across the carpark, Dad's driver waited by his car, smoking.

"Terence!" I gulped and ran to him. "For old times' sake, can you give us a ride? Fair warning, Dad's beyond pissed at me."

Terence tossed his cigarette to the ground and tipped his head at the car. "When was he ever not? Hop in. Where shall I take you?"

I gave the hotel address. "Do you need to go back to work?" I asked William, suddenly waking up to the fact that he was meant to be at the gig.

"Let's go to the airport," he replied. "As fast as we can. Getting a country away from your father will help my thumping heart no end."

After we merged into the traffic, I made the introductions. William wrapped an arm around my shoulders, holding me close.

"I've already met this man. Your dad was kind enough to come get me and bring me to ye."

I couldn't even imagine how that happened. "We have so much to catch up on."

Between them, Terence and William shared a look. Then we were at our hotel, William darting inside to grab our bags.

I hugged our driver. "I'm not sure I'll see you again," I told him. "At best, Dad will disown me after what I did, so I won't be visiting for a while." I didn't add the 'at worst', because it didn't bear thinking about.

"If I can, I'll send on your clothes. And if I'm ever in your neck of the woods, I'll give you a call." He meant that he'd let me know if Dad came looking for me. That would help. "But there's something you should know." The kindly man I'd known all my life leaned in and whispered a secret and, by the time William had reappeared, my whole viewpoint had changed.

Terence drove us to JFK, and we booked onto the next flight to the UK. William called his family so they were expecting us, and I just watched him.

"What did Dad do to get you to the stadium tonight?" I asked as soon as we had a second to talk.

"He showed up at the gig, threatened me, then offered me twenty grand." William polished his knuckles on his jeans. "Not a bad offer, considering."

I snorted a laugh. "Cheap if you ask me."

His gaze turned serious. "I had to find you. Don't think that I took the money."

"I didn't. Not for a second. To be honest, I haven't had a

coherent thought in the past few hours. I'm acting on instinct."

An announcement had us joining the queue for the plane. I considered it from his point of view. "Did you think, when you saw me, that I was going through with Dad's plan?"

William shook his head. "Naw. I knew. I could see it in how your hand shook. And in how you gazed at me." He gave me the once-over. "You're stunning, if I didn't already say. You stood there like an angel and said your piece. You claimed me and told the world that we were in love, even if ye didn't name me." He shook his head. "And I didn't even take a single photo."

I pulled out my phone and took a selfie of the two of us.

"Is that an engagement photo then?" he asked, a new kind of tone to his question.

I stared up at him, at the gorgeous man. Without the beard and thick hair he used to wear, he was on display. Uncovered. Vulnerable in loving me. "I'll do better," I said quietly.

"Can't wait," he replied.

Then we were on the plane and in the air, heading for home.

* * *

A long night of travelling followed. We'd caught the first UK flight possible so landed in London and had a red-eyed wait in the terminal before the next flight to Inverness took off.

William held me up. He carried our bags and made the arrangements. I mustered the strength to call to Charity's care home, leaving a message for them to alert me if Dad got in contact, otherwise I was a zombie, stumbling around in my scarlet evening gown, drawing stares.

Finally, when we landed in the Highlands, he pointed out a familiar face in the arrivals. Ella and Gordain waited behind the barrier.

I gave a cry of excitement that quickly turned to real tears. Overwhelmed, exhausted, and still fearful, despite what Terence had told me, I fell into my best friend's waiting arms. Just as William got wrapped in a bear hug by his big brother.

"Let's get in the car, and ye can tell us all about it," Gordain said, and we followed him outside into the fresh Scottish morning and to their Land Rover.

But the second I was in the seat, I closed my eyes and was out like a light. My fitful sleep on the plane had been laced with nightmares. Now, finally, a sense of safety rebounded.

I woke enough to be aware of William collecting me from my seat like a child, but, when I next came to, I was alone in a bed that smelled of him. By the light, it was late afternoon, and I rose, stretching out my limbs.

Ah. It was his room in the castle. I'd been here before, years ago, when we'd first met.

One stone wall held shelves of books alongside a stack of photography magazines, another had movies, all old titles. Clothes littered a chair. It wasn't neat, which surprised me. And pleased me. So he had a flaw after all.

Slowly, the door swung open. William entered, balancing a tray.

"God, is that coffee?" I gaped at him.

"Tea. If ye want to sleep tonight, we'll stick to the light stuff, aye?"

He placed the tray on a side table and leapt onto the

bed. I squealed and opened my arms, pulling him onto me. A long kiss followed. He tasted of fresh mint, and smelled gorgeous, like he'd just taken a long shower.

"What time is it?" I asked.

"Six-thirty. We slept all day. I only woke half an hour ago. Your fault. You're too nice to sleep with." He snuggled closer, and my smile spread.

"I'm so rank. I need a bath, clean clothes, and a reality check."

"Maybe in a minute. I happen to like having you here in my bed. Might've been a fantasy of mine." William gave me a squeeze. "How are ye feeling?"

"Emotionally battered, but I'll survive." The warmth of him woke me up fully. My hormones jolted to life, and I slid my hands under his t-shirt.

"I bet you used to lie here with your hands in your boxers, picturing me doing this."

"Far too often," he admitted. "Dirtier versions, too."

I traced soft lines lower.

William rumbled approval, and I got another kiss for my trouble.

Then, in a flash, he jumped up and backed away to the door, eyebrows raised to his hairline. He swore low. "God, woman. Have ye any idea how hard it is for me to keep my hands off ye?"

I eyed the bulge in his jeans. "Why are you trying?"

"We don't have the time. My family are waiting. Dinner's almost ready."

I rose on my knees and gave him a lewd look.

"Nope." He smacked his hand over his eyes. "Go get in the shower. I'll wait here."

Pity. "Sure you don't want to join me?"

William dropped the hand and took a heavy inhale. "I

do. Always. God knows that since the day I met you, I've never stopped wanting ye. But the next time we're together in bed, I want time to do every fantasy that we can dream up. I want my own solid walls keeping us safe. I want ye wet and willing and for there to be no one waiting on us. Nothing but you and me."

Well, put like that, he made a convincing argument.

I swung my legs off the bed and padded over to him. "Thank you."

"What for?"

"For loving me. For being you."

I earned a soft smile and a swipe on the backside that had me hustling to get ready. One reviving shower later, and I was back in the room. Still, I dressed slowly, letting him sweat over my disappearing flesh. Enjoying his ardent attention and open admiration.

But then, outside his bedroom door, nerves hit me. "Do people know what happened?"

"Aye. Mostly."

"Will they hate me for putting you in the firing line?"

"Naw. They'll love ye because I do."

Hand in hand, we walked the stone-walled bedroom corridor. Before we rounded the corner, William stalled.

"Ah, there's something you should know. James and Beth are here."

"Oh." Well, didn't that make this ten times more awkward. Not only had I drawn William into a world of potential pain from my father, but now my previous mistake had come back to bite me in the ass.

At least I could do something about that now. Pushing up onto my toes, I kissed William's cheek and gave him a reassuring smile. "Let's go say hi."

We descended the big staircase that led down the inside

wall of Castle McRae's great hall. Noise came from the dining room at the head of the hall, and the scent of roast chicken wafted to my nose.

My stomach growled. Loudly.

I picked up the pace, William chuckling at my back. I'd eaten a meal, of sorts, on the plane, but my appetite had been stifled by the events of the evening. Twenty-four hours on, and it roared back to life.

A feast spread out across the heavy wooden dining table. Mathilda's twins carefully carried bowls in from the kitchen. Mathilda herself appeared after them, a stack of plates in her hands that William instantly took from her.

"Can I help?" I spoke to the lady of the castle, but my eyes strayed to the dishes. Succulent roasted chickens. Trays of root vegetables and bowls of broccoli. Jugs of gravy.

God, roast potatoes. I couldn't remember the last time I'd had them.

"Nope. It's all ready. Grab a plate and tuck in before everyone gets back."

William took up a long knife and fork and carved slices of chicken.

A second woman strode into the room, carrying a small girl at her shoulder. Despite being tiny, the woman's presence grabbed my attention.

Beth.

I drew in a breath, searching for something to say. Anything. Last time I'd seen her, I'd been in such a different place. I'd cheerfully explained how my arranged marriage to her now-husband could work. I'd confidently described how he and I wouldn't have to sleep together but she'd need to be in the sidelines in certain situations.

What an asshole I must have seemed.

"Taylor!" She adjusted her grip on her sleepy daughter. "You're up. You must be famished."

"Hey, Beth," I croaked. "Can we talk?"

"Not right now." Her daughter grabbed a handful of her hair, revealing a shaved side, and she disentangled the little one's fingers. "I need to get Isobel to bed. If you want, we can talk later, but believe me, once the hoards descend, this food will be gone. And from all the strife you've been through, I imagine you need feeding up."

"Truth." William started on the second chicken.

I gazed at the little girl, a perfect blend of her mother and father. "She's gorgeous."

Beth hefted her, a proud grin spreading. "Isn't she? I'll be back. We can talk then."

Beth vanished, and I took up one of the plates of chicken William had made up and offered it to Mathilda. Then I took a chair, grabbed another plate, and we all loaded up on vegetables and potatoes.

Halfway through the happy task of devouring our glorious meals, Beth returned, and the rest of the party showed up. William's two older brothers, James with a small boy at his side, and then Ella. The boy fled, joining Mathilda's twins who played a noisy ball game in the great hall.

Ella swept over and hugged me from behind. "You're alive!"

I waved my fork, my mouth full of food.

"I have so many questions, but I guess I'll let you eat first." She took a plate from Gordain and kissed him on the cheek.

"Where's Alasdair?" William handed a jug of gravy down the table.

"Still there." Callum carved off what looked like half a

chicken onto his plate and tipped the tray of vegetables around it.

"Still where?" William asked.

"See what I mean?" Beth said to me, gesturing at the vanishing food.

I grinned at her then glanced up to see William's two older brothers exchange a meaningful look.

"What's going on?" William put his cutlery down.

Callum, the enormous laird of the castle, ran a hand over his pale hair. "We might have done something for ye."

"Done what?"

"When we heard about you and your lass, we thought ye might like to have a home to come back to," the laird continued.

William swung his baffled gaze to me then back to the two men. "What the hell are you talking about?"

"We put up the walls in the crofthouse," Gordain explained, a happy expression pulling his cheeks.

Ella bounced on her seat. "And one of the bathrooms is in. And the plumbing for the kitchen!"

William stared. "Ye did that?"

"In two days. Ally came back all fired up, but we'd all had the same idea. It's taken ye so long to get that place watertight it seemed a waste to wait another month to start the next phase."

They'd worked on his home. Oh God. I found William's hand under the table, right at the same second he sought mine.

"We helped," Mathilda's son told us. Lennox. I remembered his name. "It was a family effort."

"Can't wait to see it," William replied, choked.

"You need a place of your own," Mathilda said. She dabbed at her mouth with a cloth. It was only then that I noticed how pale the woman was. "Particularly if you'll both be living there. It's one thing you camping out without heating or plumbing, Wasp, but you can't expect your fiancé—"

Ella gaped, waving a hand. "Back the truck up. You two are engaged? When did that happen? Why did nobody think to mention this to me?"

I winced. "Last night, I told a roomful of politicians that I was marrying someone other than who they were expecting me to say."

"I'm still holding out for a proper proposal." William flashed me a wolfish grin that went straight to my heart.

I squeezed his fingers tight. "I'll bear that in mind."

We shared a moment, just watching each other. Here, in the huge, solid castle, surrounded by his family, we had breathing space. But there was so much else to consider.

Ella heaved a sigh. "I really need those details of what's gone on in the last few days."

"Aye." Callum stabbed the remaining bites of food on his plate then pushed it aside. "We've been talking this afternoon, but with the two of ye asleep, there are gaps in our plans."

I felt it then, the sort of love that came with a real family.

And for the first time, I didn't feel like an outsider.

In as succinct a way possible, I laid my tawdry family history on the line. As I spoke, William added his own take, and soon everyone was up to speed.

"There are two main problems," I concluded. "Dad has nothing on me. I don't have anything. No job he can destroy. No money he can take or reputation he can ruin. He might still find a way to carry out his threats against Charity, even with the press attention. But William, he can hurt."

"Fuck him. I don't care." William scrubbed his hands

over his face. "I'd already screwed up my own career. I punched my subject then walked out of the job. Any hope I had of staying with that agency is long gone."

"I'm sorry," I uttered, the loss of his dream a hard pill to swallow.

He shrugged a shoulder. "I wouldnae change a thing. This past couple of weeks has been the most fun I've ever had."

"What do you think your dad will do next?" Ella asked me.

"That's the thing. I'm not sure he'll carry out his threats at all." The news Terence had given me flashed into my mind. "His driver told me something which I haven't even processed."

Everyone leaned in.

"Dad's been attending a private healthcare clinic in the past month."

"What for?" William stroked his thumb over my hand.

"His heart. Terence said Dad has been diagnosed with advanced coronary heart disease. I looked up the treatment, and do you know what he needs to do most? What the doctors have ordered for fear of him dropping down dead?"

Every face around the table waited on my words.

I felt like laughing.

"Reduce stress."

* * *

With dinner cleared away, I took the opportunity to waylay Beth. She turned her bright eyes on me, bobbing her head when I asked her for a minute. We took refuge in the room the McRae's called the den, and I warmed up to saying my piece.

Beth took a seat on a green sofa, and I paced.

"I know it was years ago, but I've never forgiven myself for the way I treated you and your husband."

Beth waved a hand. "I know what you're going to say, but when I look back at that, I see a young woman of, what were you, eighteen? So young, and trying to get something she desperately wanted. I guess now it was your aunt's healthcare."

I lowered my gaze. "It was."

She grabbed me on my next pass and brought me to sit next to her. "In a weird way, you did me a favour that day. You forced me to acknowledge what I felt for James. Our lives together started there. Neither of us blame you for anything."

A weight lifted from my shoulders. "Really?"

"Yep." Beth reached out and wrapped me in a hug. "Stop beating yourself up. You're part of the family now, and we don't hold grudges."

A knock came at the door. Mathilda peered in. "Taylor? Wasp is chomping at the bit to go see the crofthouse. Are you ready?"

I eyed her and made a decision. Out of all the trouble I'd brought, maybe I could do some good, too. "Actually, if you have a moment, I'll tell him to go on ahead and I'll catch him up. I have a proposal for you," I said.

Mathilda gave me an interested look, and I readied myself to outline my plan.

I'd never liked Taylor Vandenberg, but that's because I didn't know her. I'd begun to love myself and now I intended to be the best I could. In all things. Including getting myself a job.

27

POWER

*W*asp Callum and I drove out to the crofthouse in contemplative silence.

"The risk this father of Taylor's poses, do ye think he'd hurt her?" He palmed the wheel, avoiding the potholes picked out by the headlights in the gathering dusk.

"Honestly? I have no idea what he'll do next. But he'll have to go through me to get to her."

Callum snorted. "He'll have to go through all of us, ye ken?"

I hummed, staring out at the landscape, the glens and the mountainside I loved almost as much as I loved my lass.

"Then the next question I have is about work. You had your hopes pinned on this career. Ye trained for it and are bloody good. Ye won't let one agency's opinion shut ye down?"

"No. But it makes life more difficult if they won't give me a reference. Or worse, give me a bad one." My career issues sat on the outskirts of my thoughts. Tomorrow, I'd get on the phone and see what I could salvage. The single message I'd left Reportage One before getting on the last flight had gone, so far, unanswered.

"Ye always have a job here. There's more than enough work between the estate and Mathilda's business. If you and your lass are settling down here, both of ye can find a place."

"I'm pretty sure that's what Taylor and Mattie are discussing right now." I loved my brother, and I appreciated the offer more than he could know, but I couldn't stifle the dismay that rose at the thought of losing the career I'd trained so hard at.

But if it had been a choice between Taylor and the job, she'd always win.

We drove up the final slope, and ahead, my home sat on the hillside.

Excitement stole through me, replacing the angst. "Tell me again what ye did."

Callum grinned. "Let's get inside, and you can see for yourself."

We parked up, and I was out of the car and into the front door, hanging on the door frame as I gaped at the inside of my home.

Fuck me.

For one thing, it had an inside that wasn't broken tiles and dirt. In my head, I'd pictured this many times, and I'd drafted the layout on paper. The framework of the rooms. The big lounge with an under-heated stone floor and views to die for. But now it had become a reality. Beyond the door, a room structure had been built. Still just the frame but it let the space take shape.

A floor had been laid. Thick stone tiles. Grouted, swept clean and polished.

Then to my right, the kitchen had been entirely boxed

in, and I staggered a few steps and poked my head in the doorway.

Spotlights shone. I had power!

Units had been built. Ones I'd chosen. Sleek and rustic grey wood with metal handles.

"Fuck! I have a sink!" I stared then rubbed my eyes. I'd slept hard, but an underlying exhaustion still held me in its grip. I could be dreaming.

A clattering heralded Ally half falling down the stairs at the head of the hallway. "You're here! What do ye think? Are you cross that we did it without ye? There's plenty more work to be done, but we wanted the bones in place as a surprise."

I wrapped him in a hard hug, knocking the wind out of him.

"Ah, bro. You're happy, aye?" He grinned into my shoulder.

"Happy?" I started and stopped my sentence. "Very. Over the moon."

Ally's gaze softened. "I got the modelling job. Ye did all that for me. I wanted to do something for you."

Ah, thank Christ for that. It had been worth it, then.

At my back, another set of wheels trundled down the road.

"I think your lass is here." Ally peered behind me. "We'll get out of your hair so you can give her the grand tour. Then, over the next two weeks, we'll finish it. You still need to choose paint and buy furniture and a shed load of fixings. And the downstairs bathroom is the only one working so far. There's lots to keep us all busy."

"Thank ye." I choked again, and my brothers laughed.

Callum slung his arm around my twin's shoulder. "It was

Ally's doing. He suggested it when you had the call for the job, as you'd be away. Gordain and I were just the labour."

"Yesterday, we even panic-bought ye a bed and put it together." Ally shook my shoulder once then passed me, heading out of the door. "Better check the bolts before you're too rowdy with it, aye?"

They left, and I slowly followed, stopping at the door. Taylor hopped down from Ella's car and hugged her friend. My brothers wrapped her in fond hugs, too, then my family drove away. Leaving me staring at the woman I loved.

She approached, the house light spilling over her. "Are you going to invite me in?"

I had another idea. Striding out onto the flagstones, I swept her into my arms. Taylor gave a delighted giggle.

"Like this, is it?"

"Welcome home." I crossed the threshold, holding her, and made straight for the stairs.

"Nice place you've got here." Taylor laughed again. "I love what you've done with the space."

She couldn't hear my heart, but it beat for her.

She didn't know my long-held dream of doing this exact thing.

"Tell me you love me," I demanded, finding a partially built airy hallway and diving for an open bedroom door. Sure enough, inside was a bed—the only piece of furniture in the room—but it had pillows and blankets, and if we broke it, I'd repair it before my brother found out.

"I love you, William McRae. Wait, do you have a middle name? I should know that."

"Cameron." I placed her on the bed, busying myself with pulling off her shoes then my own.

"William Cameron McRae. Owner of a huge heart. And a big stone house."

"Lover of Taylor Vandenberg," I muttered, adding to her list. "Long-time fan and now fervent devotee."

Taylor took the hem of her t-shirt and, in a scene reminiscent of our refuge in the photography studio, lifted it. This time, I didn't even consider stopping her. Instead, I let my eyes take their fill of her gorgeous tits.

"I hate that surname," she uttered.

I swooped in and pulled down her bra cup, licking her then sucking her nipple. "Take mine then."

Taylor moaned, pushing her breast against me. "I thought I was the one doing the proposing."

I stopped and moved to gaze into her eyes. "I'm serious. Marry me. Live here with me. Have my babies. Be mine. It's everything I've dreamed of for years."

She covered her eyes with her hands, and I snuck a hand around to undo her bra clasp, freeing her from the constraint. She giggled from under her arm.

As always, the powerful swell of heat she gave me flooded my system, and I was a man obsessed. Fever spiking, I returned to my task, moulding and shaping her and driving myself nuts. Taylor shivered and breathed hard, giving up her hiding.

"Maybe," she ground out a few minutes later. "Take off your shirt."

I did, and her eyes widened. "Quick, now your jeans. Don't keep me waiting."

I wanted to turn her maybe into a yes, but I knew we'd fallen head over heels and fast. She'd need time to feel secure with me.

Well, with no job and a house to renovate, I had plenty of time to prove myself.

I removed the rest of my clothes in record time and stood before her, stark naked, my dick hard and ready for her attention.

Taylor bit her lower lip, her eyes gleaming now. "Remember we wrote a list of fantasies on the flight to France? We ticked the first one off—fucking on the hotel room floor. But we didn't get to the others."

I gave myself a nice stroke. "Which one did ye have in mind?"

She tapped her lip then rose up onto her knees, bare breasts swaying. Picking up her skirt, she moved forwards on her knees until she was at the edge of the bed. With a flick, she pulled out the tie holding her hair up. It fell in a blonde sheet around her.

Ah God.

Taylor beckoned me in.

As soon as I was within reach, she had my dick in her hand and then, oh, thank Christ, in her hot mouth.

What a sight. I dug my fingers into her silky hair and wrapped it around my fist as she blew me.

"You're so good. So fucking beautiful." I groaned, resisting the urge to roll my head back so I wouldn't miss a thing.

Taylor worked me in and out of her mouth, sucking me and using the end of her tongue to do things I could hardly stand. With my teeth gritted, I stood it for as long as I could bear without blowing my top then I snapped my hips back and swooped down on her.

"Turn around. Arse in the air," I bit out, picking her up to speed up the action.

Taylor did as she was told. Her long skirt had to go. I wrenched it off her and then grabbed one side of her black lacy underwear. One short tug, and it broke, falling off her.

"Sorry," I mumbled.

"Don't care. Fuck me, please," she begged.

"This first." Kneeling on the bed, I took her thighs in my hands and gave her a long lick. Ah, that taste. Her. Sweet as Heaven.

Taylor yelped a happy sound, and I got into my game, licking and teasing her clit then fucking her with my tongue.

But I needed more. Everything.

"Please. Now." She whimpered, and then the thought struck me that we'd done this before, been in this exact position. The only other time she'd visited my house.

Our house now.

And I'd left her hanging.

Pointedly, I stopped, flipped her over to her back, and set her head on the pillows.

"Better," I told her and knelt between her legs.

It might've seemed tame compared with the wild positions we could try, but I needed to be face to face. To watch the woman I loved fall apart under me. To show her with my eyes and my body what she meant to me.

Lining up, I stooped and kissed her, saying against her lips, "Love you."

Then I thrust into her tight, welcoming heat.

"William!" Taylor uttered. Her lips sought mine again, her tongue sliding in a gorgeous dirty kiss. We tasted of each other.

We kept it like that. Mouths fused, lips locked, while we ground our hips, making love.

I set a steady rhythm, denying the urge to speed up, to go hard. All I needed was this connection. This open-hearted adoration.

Sweat broke out on my brow. Taylor moaned, sinking her nails into my shoulders.

"What do ye need?" I asked, low and sweet.

"This. Forever."

Around my dick, her internal muscles clamped down, her first orgasm of the night beginning. It ignited my hunger, but still I kept it slow, resisting the need to move. Killing myself with denial.

She arched into me. "And for you to make me come. Now. Please."

"Tell me you love me," I asked again, because I could. And it would have the effect she wanted.

Taylor gazed straight into my eyes, her lids heavy with lust.

A tremor ran through my taut muscles.

Her chest heaved as she dragged in a breath and said, "I'm wildly and utterly in love with you. You, William. I love you. I love you!"

I surged, gripping her hips and hoisting her to meet my thrusts. Again and again, I slammed into her. In no time, she was howling her pleasure.

In short order, I followed her over the edge, pulsing inside her and filling her up.

My eyes remained open and on her to the last before I surrendered, collapsing down. Blinded by the most powerful orgasm I'd ever known. Her welcoming arms held me close. Heart to heart.

It was all so clear now. Her being here in my imagination hadn't been me tormenting myself. Taylor's role as my wife had been a premonition.

Dopey with good feelings, I nudged her, rolling us so I could stand. Then I carried her downstairs. All the time we'd been here, we hadn't turned on a light. Only the kitchen lights illuminated the downstairs. On the way to the new shower room, I paused at the kitchen door, and we gazed inside.

"I can't believe how much this has changed." Taylor craned her neck.

I indicated at a gap against the far wall. "A big stove will go there. The worktop will go snug up against it. I figured the chimney breast could be painted a bold colour as everything else is muted."

"Classy. I can picture it. Where does that little door go?" She pointed to the far wall.

"Laundry room and mud room. Also where the downstairs shower is. Let's check it out." I hopped over the cold tiles—I guessed the boiler hadn't gone online for the underfloor heating yet—and Taylor leaned to open the door and flick a light switch.

In the bathroom, I hit the shower button, and it sprang to life with instant hot water. Steam rose.

"Such a luxury." I put Taylor down in the spray, noting my brothers had even thought to bring a stack of towels and installed a rack on the grey-tiled walls. "I've slept here on and off for months, imagining the night I could take a shower and sleep in a real bed."

Then I stepped into the jets and kissed my woman.

"I'm scared of falling in love with this place." She placed both hands on my chest and gazed into my eyes. "Everything I see, I instantly adore. It's so solid and homey. I can picture muddy kids running in the kitchen door and being herded into here for a wash before dinner. I'm imagining deep plush couches in the lounge and a TV on the wall. But we'd never watch it because the view outside the doors is far prettier."

My smile spread. "Aye? Keep going."

"That's what I'm trying not to do!"

"Why?"

"Because!" she squeaked. "I should be freaking out but I'm choosing paint colours."

"Naw. Get used to it. You've always been part of this place. You just didnae know it."

We glared at one another, and I loved it.

"I talked to Mathilda about taking over some of her tasks." Determination shone in her eyes. "Her pregnancy is hard on her, and she needs someone to take over. Beth is staying here for a couple of weeks, and she's going to help, too. I'm going to have a job! I'll earn a salary for the first time ever!"

"We'll need it. I'm broke."

Taylor reached up and ran her fingers over my creased brow. "I'll work something out with my dad. My mind is running over a million and one ideas for ways to make this right. I can't decide if I've been the worst thing to happen to you or the best."

She dropped her hands to hug me, and I rested my chin on her head, letting the water cascade over both of us, our naked bodies aligned, warm steam washing away the suddenly heavy conversation.

"The best. Always. Without you, I was a man building a family home for one."

"How poignant."

"Isn't it?"

We finished up and bundled ourselves in towels. Like kids in a sweet shop, we poked our noses into every corner of the crofthouse, inspecting what my brothers had done. Then we made noodles in the kitchen using supplies Ally had left.

On our bed, we sat cross-legged and talked for hours until I pounced and had her on her back again. Or perhaps she pounced on me. Either way, we both got what we wanted.

If this was my life from now on, I was the luckiest man to breathe.

If ill will followed our love, we'd stay strong and fight it out.

28

FACING THE MUSIC

Taylor

A soft breeze played with my hair, and I picked my way down the heather-strewn path from the crofthouse, my best friend at my side. Ella had texted this morning then brought William and me lunch. He'd then taken her car to go to see his brothers, leaving us to walk, like I'd asked.

I wanted to explore my new backyard, but we really needed a car if we were going to make a go of living here.

My friend looped her arm through mine and pointed to a village on the other side of the loch. "There's a lovely little church in the town. My brother had his wedding there, and it was so pretty. Just saying, you know, in case you and Wasp are making plans..."

I sucked in a breath, faking concern. "Careful, you might hurt yourself with all those fishing hooks."

She gave a bright laugh. "I can't believe you're here, and staying. I'm just going to put this out there and say I've never been this happy. To have you on my doorstep, it makes everything perfect. I'm going to need you around, and you're here! I can't even..." Her voice caught, and I swung my gaze around.

"You're crying? Oh my God!" We stopped, and I examined her face. It crumpled, her bottom lip trembling. Then something twigged. "Oh, honey. Are you...?"

A smile broke through her tears. "Pregnant? Yep. We took a test this morning. Positive."

"Ahh!" I screamed, startling a small flock of birds from a nearby tree. "I can't believe it! You only just starting trying!"

Ella laughed now. "We know! Gordain's been marching around all puffed up. He's going to tell his brothers now. But do you see why I need you? So you can't go anywhere."

She threw her arms around me, her dark curls against my straight blonde mane. We hugged it out on the side of the gorgeous glen that was somehow my home. My first real home.

"I'm not going anywhere. I don't think William will let me out of his sight." Then I quickly admitted, "And I'm worrying about him, and he's not even left the estate. I'm beyond freaked out about all of this."

"But it feels right?"

"One hundred percent."

She nodded, pleased. "Then tell me, what happens next? Have you heard anything from your dad?"

"Not yet." Earlier, lying in bed with William, I'd scanned the news, and Theo's engagement announcement had been on a few sites, but the election plans were missing. Clearly, it hadn't been made. "I think I scuppered his chances of running for vice president."

"Nope. He did that all by himself by being a douche canoe."

I snorted agreement. "William said to let Dad come to

us. But he still hasn't heard back from his agency, so what if Dad's messing that up for him?"

"Does he have that power?"

I stooped and picked up a small stone on the track. Rolled it around in my fingers. "I don't know. Probably? I think he treated my mom pretty bad."

"Call her. Ask. She'll know him better than you."

I grimaced, but Ella was right. I'd had it in the back of my mind that I should speak to my mother, though with no real expectation that she'd be able to help. I slid my phone from my dress pocket and made the call. It rang for a while, then Mom answered, sounding a little drowsy.

"Hi, Mom, it's Taylor." I trod carefully down the slope, reaching back to take Ella's arm.

"Oh!" Noises of flustering came from the other end of the line.

"Don't panic. You haven't forgotten anything. I just need to ask a question."

The noises stopped. "Certainly. I'm listening."

God, it was always so awkward with this woman. The path underfoot levelled out, but Ella kept hold of me.

"I've got a problem with Dad."

Mom sucked in a breath, but I pushed on.

"He wanted me to marry one of his politician friend's sons, but I've refused. He threatened my boyfriend."

"Taylor..." Mom's hesitant tone held a warning.

"I just want your advice." I palmed that piece of Highlands stone in my hand. "How likely is he to go through with it? Is he as vindictive as he claims?"

"I don't want anything to do with this. I suffered that man for two years after getting knocked up. Why are you trying to involve me with his problems again?"

I opened and closed my mouth. She'd always shut me

down in the past, and now wasn't any different. It should hurt, but I let the rejection bounce off me. Before, I'd pretended I was okay with this, now I knew I wasn't, but I'd survive it. "If you have any influence over him, now is a good time to help me out. I'm starting a new life with the man I love. In the UK, by the way. If you want anything to do with me, I need your help."

Silence held on the other end of the line. I checked the screen. *Call ended.*

"What happened?" My friend squeezed my arm.

"She just hung up on me." I stared at Ella. "All the times I thought we just needed an adult connection or some kind of common ground. And hating Dad couldn't be a better bonding place, right? But no. She didn't want anything to do with it."

"She's a bitch. And he's an asshole. When you were born, I think the best of them got sucked out and put into you. There is just no other explanation."

I sighed and commenced our walk. "What a fuck-up. Promise me we'll never screw over our kids like that."

Ella's sympathetic expression lifted into a more cheerful one. "Then you are planning babies! Hurry up so ours will be the same age."

I gave her a non-committal head shake, and we made our way over the pretty hillside to the castle.

At the heavy wooden door, my phone rang. I stopped, catching a glimpse of William inside with Callum, the two men deep in conversation.

"Go on in," I said to Ella. "Maybe Mom had a change of heart."

She left, and I retrieved my phone. The screen read *International*, and my pulse sped up.

My next move had been to call Dad. I wasn't running

scared. But if this was him, then he'd beaten me to the punch.

"Hello?" I answered.

"Taylor, it's Stefan. I'm afraid I'm calling with some worrying news. Overnight, your aunt's health has deteriorated further. I know you wanted any updates so I've just left her with her doctor to call you."

No. No way. My hand shook; my stomach instantly cramped.

"What happened? Has she had any visitors?" If Dad had been near her...

"Visitors? No, the illness can take this course. Her pneumonia weakened her significantly. If you can, I think is prudent if you return for a final visit as soon as possible." His gentle voice was weighted with meaning.

Final?

I couldn't have heard that right.

"A final visit?" I choked on the words and sank hard to sit on the cold stone steps. The little pebble I'd carried down the hill dropped from my hand. "She just had a cold! She was recovering. I just saw her a few days ago. You can't tell me that she's got worse. She's meant to be getting better. Please."

Warm hands landed on my shoulders, and William dropped onto the step behind me, bundling me in a hug.

"I'm so sorry to bear bad news," Stefan continued. "I know how much your aunt loves you."

Aghast, I thanked him in a strained, barely audible voice, then hung up. If I'd thought the call to my mother hard, this took first place.

"They think Charity's really sick. That she won't make it." I twisted and stared into William's eyes.

For a second, he closed his eyes, then he leaned in and

pressed his forehead to mine. "I'm with ye, whatever ye need."

"We need to go to see her."

He stood, taking me with him. Inside the castle, he explained the situation to his family, and I roused myself from my stupor to make an apology to Mathilda for having to go.

She waved me off. "I'm feeling ten times better today."

I wasn't sure that was true, but we had to leave.

Callum pulled something from his pocket and moved to stand in front of William. He pressed the item into his hand.

"What do ye need?" Ally—who I didn't even know was there—emerged from the den, his expression concerned.

"I'll look at flights," Ella said from behind me.

"Thank you," I whispered to all of them.

Then, in a few short hours, we'd packed, got back on the road, and were at the airport once more. Only this time, it truly felt like I was facing the music.

29

UNSLEEPING WATCH

*W*asp
Using my brother's credit card for money,
we returned to New York. Taylor gripped my hand the
whole way, and I'd never felt so useless in my entire life. All
I could do was get her to where she needed to go.

At Charity's care home, we were met by a red-eyed
Stefan at the doors.

"God, no!" Taylor howled. "Don't say it's too late. Don't
you dare!"

The man took a deep breath. "She's still with us. I think
she's waiting for you."

Taylor made a noise of distress and dove inside the
building, stumbling to her aunt's side. I palmed Stefan's
shoulder in silent thanks then strode after her.

Outside Charity's darkened room, patients waited, sad
faces on all. Inside, her nurse stood at her bedside while
another woman adjusted a machine.

With her bed laid flat, the light had gone from Taylor's
aunt.

Taylor paused at the door. "I didn't expect this," she whispered into the heavy air. "I thought she'd get better."

All I could do was hug her.

Together, we sat at the woman's bedside.

Overnight, under her beloved niece's unsleeping watch, Charity passed away.

* * *

Six days later, on a blowy but sunny morning, my brother and his wife arrived at the care home. Dressed in a black suit I figured he'd bought for the occasion, Gordain pulled me into a hug. At my side, Ella wrapped Taylor into her arms.

Her sobs broke my heart.

"The cars are outside." Gordain eyed me then mouthed, "Hearse, too."

I lifted my chin in acknowledgement. We'd stayed in a guest room at the care home for days, making arrangements to lay Charity to rest. Taylor had faced the press whose interest had been piqued, and she'd deflected questions on her father, keeping herself together despite her world falling apart.

She'd whispered to me that it felt like she'd made this happen. Trading one life for another, as crazy as that sounded. She'd cried, and I'd held her, and my eyes had leaked, too. I'd hated fate for fucking her over. But last night, we'd read sections of Charity's diary and, for the first time in a week, she hadn't cried herself to sleep.

I knew she had the strength to get through this.

"We need to go, love," I told her gently.

Taylor straightened up and composed herself, drying her eyes.

With her hand gripping mine, she led the way to the waiting transport. The care home staff turned out in force, their minibus bringing up the rear. On convoy, we drove to the cemetery on a low hillside above the sea.

After meeting in the little chapel, the minister brought the mourners to attention and led us to the grave site.

There, Taylor's father waited, a minder wearing dark glasses on one side of him and another person, lawyerly-looking in a sharp suit on the other.

"Oh my goodness. He came? How could he!" Ella snapped her hand to her mouth.

"It's for the press," Taylor replied, clipped. "We expected this. If you can, ignore him. I intend to. For now, anyway. We're here for her."

Turning a blind eye to the man, we listened to the eulogy. Taylor's eyes shone when the minister recounted Charity's happy life before her illness, and she took to the stand to read an excerpt from her aunt's diary.

"June fifth sum up. In the past two weeks, I've driven an open-top sports car with my niece, drank wine with and then kissed a hot Greek waiter despite neither of us being able to speak a single word of the other's language. I took a chair lift up then down a mountainside, and tomorrow, I start all over again." Taylor closed the book and swung her gaze over the audience. "As you can see, my aunt loved travelling, but she also loved good company and home comforts. Despite living in a care home for several years, she'd become beloved to so many. Her filthy sense of humour scandalised some and pleased others. I wish I'd had more time with her; I wanted her to get to know William, my fiancé, better, but some lives are short, and they blaze and burn out before their time."

She faced the white coffin on its green cushion. "I can't

tell you how much I'll miss you. But you should know that I learned from you how to be happy and make the most of my life. How to love hard and be a good person. I'll follow your footsteps and I'll never forget you."

Her voice cracked and, around the grave, people wiped their eyes or openly sobbed.

Taylor approached the coffin and lay her hand on it. "I love you," she whispered.

Then she was back in my arms, her muscles tight with holding herself up. I took her weight. I always would.

Others spoke. The minister concluded the service. Then the coffin was lowered. We each threw a flower into the grave, then the funeral was over.

People left, but Taylor and I stayed on the hillside.

Her father and his minions did, too.

At my side, Taylor's hackles rose. "Don't judge me for what I'm about to do."

"Never," I growled. "Make it good."

"I intend to." She marched across the grass, not taking her eyes off him for a second.

"Irene," her father started.

"It's Taylor," she snapped. "The cameras have gone, so let's make this brief. You saw what happened today? How many people showed up here?"

He cocked his head to one side as if curious.

"This is what happens when you're loved. You die surrounded by those who care about you. You are laid to rest and mourned. Charity might be gone, but we'll all remember her. Now? We're going home. I never want to see or hear from you again. Whatever happens to you." Her eyes sparkled with her speech, and her meaning was clear. She wouldn't be there for him. As far as she was concerned, he was going to die alone.

"Wait." He took a step.

I was in front of Taylor and glaring at him before he blinked. Then his minder was in my face. I stared right past the man, straight into her father's eyes.

"Stop." Taylor slipped under my arm and pressed her hands to my chest. "He isn't worth it. Whatever he tries to do to us, we're better than him."

I let her push me away—it wasn't as if I'd fight the man, but my blood was up all the same. With our backs turned, we left the grave and her father behind.

A rapid discussion followed, then someone hustled after us, their clothes swishing. I glanced back. It was the lawyerly-looking woman.

"Miss Vandenberg?" The woman hurried, rounding us.

We stopped.

"On behalf of your father, and your aunt, I need to talk to you." She peered at us over her glasses. Behind her, the governor watched but didn't approach.

"I think I made myself perfectly clear when it comes to my father. I don't want to hear—"

"For your aunt's sake, you should." The lawyer took a sheaf of papers from a folder in her satchel. "It's regarding Charity's will. Give me five minutes. Believe me, you'll want to hear this."

Taylor's eyes narrowed, but she gave a short nod. "Fine. We'll go into the chapel."

I gazed at her in silent question to see if she needed me there, but she shook her head then strode away, the woman at her heels.

Gordain met me halfway back to the car. "We're keeping watch on him, aye?" He indicated to Taylor's father, a mean expression on his face.

God, I loved my family.

"That's the one." We stood shoulder to shoulder, our arms folded, keeping Taylor safe.

The governor crossed the cemetery and returned to his car, sparing more than one glance for me. The driver who opened and closed the door for him wasn't Terence. Poor guy if he'd lost his job.

After a minute, the minder, with his sunglasses still firmly in place, exited the car and moved in on us. "Governor Vandenberg asked me to pass on a message."

"What are ye, an answering machine?" Gordain said with a scowl, and I grinned at him.

"He would like it known that he regrets his previous offer to you and wants to make it clear that his words at the time—"

"His threats," I helpfully clarified.

"His *words* at the time will not be acted on."

In the past week and a half, I'd heard nothing from Reportage One. But my focus had been on Taylor, so I hadn't chased it up. But I'd figured they'd been scared off from hiring me.

"I'm not going to talk to her on his behalf."

The minder shrugged. "I think he knows that." Then the big man walked away.

"What was his threat?" Gordain asked.

"He told Taylor he'd destroy my career. On that note..." I found my phone and placed a call to the agency.

"Reportage One, Claire speaking."

"It's Wasp McRae—" I started.

"Wasp, ah, I've been meaning to call you but I was waiting on a confirmation message. Firstly, I'll be forwarding you details of a new job. Closer to home this time. Four days covering a conference in Edinburgh. Now, there is a band performing on the final evening for the attendees, so fair warning not to hit anyone this time." She laughed at herself.

I blinked hard. "Did you talk to Rex?"

"Uh-huh. A couple of times since your family emergency. Oh, is everything all right?" she added rapidly, like she didn't really care and was only just remembering to ask.

Rex had called her. What the hell?

"We're good now." I wasn't about to explain the details. "What happened with the tour?"

"We sent a replacement. It's all been taken care of."

I clamped down on the next question, because it was obvious I still had a job. The governor had done what he'd said.

"Send the details. I'll be there," I said then, after Claire hung up, I fist-pumped the air. "I still have work!"

I shook my head in disbelief and resisted the urge to celebrate further. This wasn't the time or the place, but still, a huge weight lifted from me. I needed this, the ability to care for my own family in a career I loved.

Just like that, it had been restored.

Gordain's careful gaze settled on the car. "He's sick, and he regrets it, I'd say. His sister dying might've been the reality check he needed."

I pulled a face. "I'm not sure I even care. I'm considering myself lucky now." And I couldn't wait to tell Taylor.

But when she emerged from the chapel, shaking hands with the lawyer before returning to me, something haunted her. She stared after her father's car as they drove away.

"See ye at the airport for the flight home, aye?" Gordain murmured then left us.

I brought Taylor under my arm then guided her to our car. We needed to go back to the care home, change, then get onto a plane. "Talk to me."

"I'm so mad I can barely breathe." She drew a shuddering breath despite her words, then climbed into the back seat.

The driver took us out of the cemetery and onto the wide road.

I waited on Taylor's words. She didn't take long.

"I've been left money." Her wide-eyed gaze sought mine. "A huge sum. Charity inherited money from my grandfather when he died. She's given it all to me."

She named a figure, and I choked on air.

Then Taylor gave an outraged howl. "He knew! All that time, Dad knew she could afford to pay for her own care. And he still used me."

"Why would he keep paying when she had money?"

"Maybe because my grandfather made him? Or maybe just for his reputation? All bases covered, no skeletons in his closet. But to use that against your own daughter? Ella said I should tell her what was going on, but I couldn't. It was all for nothing. I can't even start to process that."

"Not for nothing. We wouldnae be together now."

She blinked at me. A laugh broke from her throat. "True. Then I don't know if I'm the least fortunate or the luckiest woman around. I lived a nothing life but now I have everything."

"Nope, I'm the one who has everything. Come here." I pulled her in for a single, chaste kiss.

"We can buy furniture!" Taylor squeaked. "You don't have to worry about finding work urgently."

"I don't, but for another reason."

I filled her in on my news, and we got back to the home then were away to the airport. In our bags, we had items from Charity's room—pictures, a few souvenirs—that would have pride of place in the crofthouse, and we returned to the Highlands far stronger than when we'd left.

"This past week has been the worst." Taylor snuggled closer, and the aircraft descended, circling Inverness. "One thing it taught me was to live life to the fullest. I will never keep a secret from you. I will never lie to you."

"Ye ken, it sounds like you're making vows." I grinned at her.

"Still waiting on that proposal, huh?"

A ripple of pleasure ran through me, potent and consuming. We considered ourselves engaged, but I kept up the tease. "Aye. I am. It's up to you to do it right."

Taylor smiled a secret smile and tucked her head down.

I'd wait until the ends of the earth, but that I guessed she already knew.

30

AT LAST

Taylor

How did one propose to the man of her dreams? Over the past six weeks, since Charity had died, it had been my constant preoccupation. Along with grieving, getting my head around a new job, and learning how to live in the Highlands.

I bumped closed the door to mine and William's very own car—bought with the proceeds of his first photography job—and crossed Castle McRae's car park. I came here most days to work with Mathilda, and today was no different.

Except it was—I'd had the best idea, and I'd had excellent news this morning. The inheritance I'd been gifted had been cleared for payment. It would be in my account any minute.

There was so much I planned to do with it.

First, I sought Mathilda in her office. I tapped on the open door to find another person inside. With long, burnished red hair and pert features, the woman was utterly gorgeous. And I recognised her from family photos.

"Taylor, you're here. I don't think you've met Scarlet,

have you? My baby sister." Mathilda beamed from her office chair. "She hasn't been here in forever since university and her exciting social life took her away."

I grinned at the newcomer. "No! But I've heard all about you."

"You have?" She offered a neatly manicured hand, and I shook it.

"Ally was over a couple of weeks ago, and he saw something you posted. You were on a beach somewhere."

A flush stole over her cheeks, fast, highlighting freckles and making her instantly appear younger. How annoying for her. No secret would be safe with such pale skin.

"How did I not know that Ally followed me?" She dug out her phone from her jeans pocket. "I was in Belize with Dad. Hell, I would've posted a bikini shot if I knew Ally would see it." Her eyes lit in wicked delight. "That would freak him out. What's his account? Did he take the old ones down?"

I gave her the name. "He did. There was something about an old fan of his he regretted. I don't know the details." I guessed William knew what had been bothering Ally. He'd asked about Ally's problem with the fan, and they'd had a short conversation mostly made up of shrugs and a silent twin exchange. I hadn't pried.

Scarlet's red eyebrows drew in. "Huh. He doesn't follow me, which means he's stalking me. I'm going to bombard him with nudes."

Mathilda clapped her hands to her cheeks. "You will not!"

Her sister laughed and made for the door. "Are you for real? Like I would. Dad would fry Alasdair for the crime of even looking. On that note, I'm going to leave you to work. Nice to meet you, Taylor."

She breezed away, and I switched my gaze to Mathilda. "Wow."

Mathilda blew out a breath. "I know. Scarlet plagues Ally. He treats her like an annoying little sister, which drives her nuts and makes her mess with him all the more. That's why she hasn't been here—Dad keeps her away because he thinks Ally will take advantage of her."

I wrinkled my nose. "Ally isn't like that."

"No! But Ally plays up to it and acts the idiot when Dad's here. He even flirted with my sister once, and it drove Dad insane. Dad has high hopes for Scarlet. He plans to put her in control of his empire one day. She's meant to be focusing all her time on her education, so no boyfriend has ever met his approval."

"Talking of empires, how are you fixed up for a chat? I have a proposal for you."

"I'm at your disposal. With you working here, I have more free time than ever before." She blinked. "Wait. You're not breaking up with me, are you? You can't go! I'll pay more!"

Snorting a laugh, I waved her off. "Stop! I actually want to give you money."

"Ooh! I'm listening."

"We've been working well together, right? And since I'm staying, I've been thinking seriously about what I want to do." Excitement rose in a champagne fizz. "I'd like to buy into the wedding business. Become an equal partner with you. You'd keep your role, but I'd take ownership of the new catering function. Plus, I'll be better placed to act for you on your maternity leave."

My nerves got to me, all of a sudden. I realised how I sounded. This business was Mathilda's baby. She'd created it from nothing, and it was thriving because of her and her alone. "I mean, it's just an idea. I'd need to learn a lot and fast, and I'll carry on working for you either way. I don't mean to step on toes..."

Intelligent eyes watched me. "That's a lot to think about." A smile of consideration lit her face. "Do you have this written up?"

"I'll email it now." I grinned back. She hadn't said no outright, so this was a huge step forward.

I made a little noise of glee and switched my gaze to my phone to send the outline over. A message from William arrived as the email sent.

I love you, lass, it read. *Ye better be waiting for me when I get in. And by waiting, I mean naked.*

My glee turned to instant lust. A week without his hands on me had been almost too much to bear.

How long are you going to keep me waiting? It would be a pity if I started by myself, I typed back.

His reply made me laugh out loud. *I'll walk in the door at seven. And now I have a hard-on. Awkward since I'm in a room full of elderly professors. One is giving me the weirdest look right now. Gotta go, beautiful.*

I returned my phone to my bag and then thought about my more exciting plan for the day. My other proposal. Lifting my gaze to Mathilda, I brought her into my planning.

"If you're available after work, I need a little help. But it's a secret."

She lifted one nicely shaped eyebrow. "Intriguing. I'm in."

And now onto the next part of my idea.

How do you make a grand gesture to a Highlander who didn't enjoy being the centre of attention? Luckily, the woman who wanted to marry the Scot knew her man well.

* * *

*W*asp

We approached the crofthouse, and my hurry to get home went on pause as I took in the dark windows.

The castle had been the same: no lights on, and no one home.

"Do ye think they all went somewhere?" Ally asked me.

I'd driven us home after the longest week of work, and though it had been fun catching up, I needed Taylor more than anything.

Then food.

Then her again. All night.

As Taylor and I shared a car, I'd used Ally's, and now he was going to leave me here and drive himself home.

"Your car's not even here. Something's definitely up." He took out his phone and made a call. "Mathilda? Where—?" Ally listened for a moment. Then he laughed and killed the call.

I brought the car to a halt halfway down the track to my house. "Want to fill me in?" I asked.

"Nope. Keep going."

Muttering, I drove us the final hundred feet and parked. Before I could get out, Ally placed a hand on my arm. "Good luck, bro."

"Why do I need good luck?" Then it twigged. "Oh Christ. This is it, isn't it?"

"No idea what you're talking about."

"Aye, ye do. She's going to propose!"

Ally shrugged and pretend-examined his nails. "Get out of my car."

I punched his arm then jumped down, grabbing my

bags from the back. Earlier, on the drive home, Ally had asked why I wasn't the one doing the proposing. The answer was simple: Taylor needed this. I'd already told her I wanted to marry her, and I had a ring just waiting for this moment, but also, I liked it. She was mine and she was making me hers. How perfect was that?

I approached the crofthouse's door. It opened, and Scarlet, Mathilda's wee sister stepped out.

"Hi—" I started, but she raised a finger.

"Put this on," she demanded and held up a strip of cloth. "It's a blindfold. It goes over your eyes," she added when all I did was stare.

"Right!" I dropped my bags at my feet and took the cloth, covering my eyes. "Now what?"

No additional instruction came.

But then a hand landed on my shoulder, pushing me into my house.

"Over the step. There you go," the voice said. My sister-in-law's.

"Thanks, Mathilda," I answered. "Is everyone else here as well?"

"Nope. And now you're on your own." The door closed behind me with a *snick*.

The next person who neared, I knew from her scent alone. "Taylor," I breathed.

The smell of burning also tickled my nose.

Careful fingers found the blindfold and removed it, then I blinked to see my lass in front of me. Her blue eyes took me in, and all I could see was her.

Makeup I needed to smudge. Her golden dress—Christ, what a knockout.

Flickering lights at the edge of my vision had me

glancing up to see candles all around the lounge. "What's this?" I asked, knowing exactly what it was.

Taylor took my hand, entwining our fingers. "God, I've missed you," she whispered. "I have so much to say to you, but it comes down to this: You are without a doubt the very best person who ever lived. You're gorgeous, funny, and so kind. You loved me when I thought I was unlovable, stayed with me when I was making all the wrong choices, and you gave me a home."

"Worth every minute of the wait," I added, emotion flickering like the candles.

"You're everything to me, so I want to be everything to you. I made dinner, with help. I borrowed a rug, a TV, and *Casablanca's* lined up ready to watch."

I could tear my gaze away, follow her gesture at the lounge at our left, but I wanted to just stare at her. She'd basically described my perfect evening. With one extra thing...

"Marry me, will you?" she asked, so soft and sweet.

Ah Christ, no way could I be manly right now. Fucking shaking, I reached into my pocket and took out the box I'd picked up in Edinburgh.

Then I dropped to one knee.

"Aye, lass. I will. But only if ye marry me, too."

Her eyes rounded. "Oh my God! Yes!"

Standing, I plucked the ring from the box and placed it on her finger. It fitted perfectly.

"Now for the next part." Taylor gazed at the ring for a moment then reached back and found the zip of her dress. She pulled. The gold material fell from her body in a silky slide.

I made a sound of pure need. "I get a present, too? I'm going away more often."

After that, there was no more time to speak. With urgency, I leaned in and took her mouth, our kiss fast, passion escalating. I'd had the dream to take her in the entryway, but we'd done that once or twice already, and tonight called for gentler care. I lifted her in my arms and headed for the stairs.

"You're going to be my wife," I told her, placing her on the bed and stripping as quickly as humanly possible. My shirt hit the lamp and my jeans the floor, right over my shoes.

"You know it. Can we get married next month?"

"As soon as possible."

She leaned to the bedside table and picked up her packet of pills. "I want to ditch these. I want to fill this place with babies that look just like you."

"Deal."

Boxers off, I knelt on the bed and dragged apart her thighs, a new force driving me to get inside her rather than play first. Luckily, she had the same idea. She wrapped her legs around my waist, lining me up and arching up to meet my thrusts.

We kissed, made love, many times, laughed about making a baby, then snuggled down with dinner and a movie.

In all my life, I couldn't have pictured anything more perfect.

EPILOGUE

*W*asp A little over three weeks later, in the white chapel across the loch, Taylor entered through the heavy doors. Holding my breath so I wouldn't quake, I stood with my brothers and James at the top of the church, our family tartan worn with pride.

I gazed at Taylor as she approached.

Ah Christ, she was beautiful.

Her off-white dress hugged her form, and if I'd ever thought her a Hollywood pinup, she'd long blown them all out of the water. Blue and white flowers made a crown in her blonde hair. Heather adorned her bouquet. She glowed.

In front of her, the wee lasses scattered petals. Behind, Sebastian and Lennox jostled each other before remembering their role as her guardsmen.

At her side, my twin held her arm.

Around us all, a small gathering of family and friends attended. With my mother and her family, Taylor's mother sat on the edge of the pew. She'd made the journey, a new boyfriend in tow, but only after being convinced Taylor's father had declined the invitation. No loss from our point of view. We'd send him an announcement when our firstborn arrived, whenever that might be, but otherwise he could stay an ocean away.

In one corner of the church, Theo, the man Taylor was supposed to marry, held hands with his fiancée, Karen. She and Taylor had spoken on the phone a few times and had become friends.

Strange how things worked out.

Then Taylor was at my side, and all other thoughts left my head.

"You're a picture," I whispered. "So beautiful I can barely take ye in."

Happy tears welled in her eyes. "Look at you in a kilt! And you're all mine? I can't even think straight."

A laugh left my lips, but then the pastor called our attention.

We made our vows, promising each other our worlds. We exchanged rings, kissed, with maybe a little too much passion from the catcalls, then we led the way to Castle McRae and the party of my lifetime.

It was perfect, every bit. Nothing could ruin our happiness.

* * *

*M*arried life was bliss.

Our stay-home honeymoon had us working on the crofthouse, and we'd finally reached the stage where we could buy furniture. In Inverness, outside a home interiors place in Queensgate where we'd just spent a small fortune, I bundled Taylor into a hug and kissed her hair. "Mrs McRae. Have ye any idea what you've done? You're a dream come true."

She pulled away, and a smile lit her face. "Mr McRae, that's all you."

A passing shopper stopped in her tracks, her sharp inhale drawing my attention.

I glanced at the middle-aged woman, ready with a grin. Taylor and I were cute, for sure. Newlyweds, brimming over with joy.

But a strange expression met my gaze.

"McRae?" the small woman asked. The expression morphed to pure anger. "I know that name. I know your face now I look at ye! How dare ye?"

"I'm sorry?"

"So ye should be!" the woman squeaked.

Taylor tilted her head, the confusion on her face echoing mine. "How do you know my husband?" she asked.

I was glad she'd asked, as I was taken aback by the bad vibes coming my way.

"Your husband?" The woman shifted her shopping bags from one hand to another, her fingers tight on the handles. Bags from a baby shop, stuffed with clothes. "Ye poor lass. Well, at least he married ye first. Watch out that he doesn't leave ye in the lurch, too."

Then the woman lifted her chin and marched away.

I gaped, still dumbstruck.

No, I wasn't having this. I strode after her. "Hang on. Ye say you know me? How? And who did I leave in the lurch?"

"My great niece!" The woman spun around and glared. "Kathleen Reid. Ring any bells?"

Kathleen? "None." I reached back to take Taylor's hand. "I've never heard of her. I'm sorry, but you've got the wrong man."

"I've seen your picture! Ye can't lie. Kathleen died taking her secrets to the grave, but that bairn looks just like you, Alasdair McRae."

My stomach flipped.

Taylor's hands flew to her mouth. "Baby?"

"Bairn?" I said simultaneously.

"Try telling me that we'en isn't yours." The woman snatched her phone from the depths of her bag and held it up. A tiny bairn's scrunched-up face appeared. Eyes closed. A thatch of blond hair.

The absolute spitting image of us as newborns.

Too much information at once. I forced my mouth to move. "I'm not Alasdair, I'm William. He's my twin." I ran my hand over my still-short hair, a memory triggering. "Ah God, did Kathleen go by Kaylee?"

The woman ran her gaze down me, her untrusting expression settling to something pained. Even desperate. "Aye, she did. Then I'm right."

Fuck.

"Did you said she died?" Taylor stared at the child.

Now, the woman crumpled. Her hostility melted, and her gaze dropped to the pavement. "She did! She had a weak heart, and it gave out after the birth. She was twenty-two years old, and now her poor bairn is motherless." She drew in a shuddering breath.

But maybe not fatherless.

"Give me your name and number," I said.

Ally was away, but he needed to hear this. Now.

The woman reared back an inch, suddenly appearing doubtful. "I'm nae sure. What kind of man is he if he left her to go through all that alone? Why wasn't he with her?"

"I guarantee he didn't know." I pressed my hands together. "Please. Your number."

Hesitantly, she searched her bag. "I'll find a pen. Is your twin here?"

"Not right now. He'll be home in a few days or sooner if he can."

Taylor turned her big blue eyes on me. "Can this be true? Is Ally...?"

"A da," I completed for her, the incredible revelation sending me spinning.

Of all the paths my brother's life could take, with his career flourishing, his chilled-out, love-one-love-all attitude, now he could be a single parent.

"Ally's a father," I repeated.

The End.

* * *

Thank you so much for reading Wasp and Taylor's story! Do you want a wee glimpse at how their story continues? Download their bonus epilogue here BookHip.com/RKGGJR (in doing so, you'll add yourself to my reader newsletter.)

The next in the series, Oh Baby (Marry the Scot, #5), Ally's story, is available now: mybook.to/OhBaby

. . .

*R*ead on for a sneak peek at Race You, my standalone office-based enemies-to-lovers romance.

*T*o be the first to hear about my publishing news, access giveaways, and receive bonus content, be sure to add yourself to my newsletter list here: https://www.jolievines.com/newsletter

ACKNOWLEDGMENTS

Dear Reader,

I'm so sorry. I know you are all cross with me and aghast at the way Picture This ended. Poor Ally, what a cliff hanger of a predicament. But fear not! You don't have to wait for his book - it's live now. I wouldn't do that to you.

Wasp and Taylor's story felt like it was a very long time in the coming. The twins have been beloved pests since the start of this series, first featuring in Storm the Castle as wily sixteen-year-olds taking a joy ride in a stolen car. Now, they are men grown, and having romances of their own.

Taylor also featured throughout the series, first appearing as James's alternate bride in Love Most, Say Least. She had one heck of a journey to believe in herself, and in love. Wasp, of course, was way ahead of her. I honestly think he's my favourite of all the McRae brothers. What a gentleman. (Important note: Each of my heroes is my favourite when I'm writing his tale. There's no true favouritism here.)

Thank you to everyone who reads my stories and gets lost in my worlds. I adore knowing my books are out there and being loved. Thanks also go to my wonderful bloggers, ARC readers, my beta readers Annalise, Tara and Katie, all my lovely social media friends, and my critique partners.

The gorgeous cover is by the talented Natasha Snow, line editing by the fabulous Emmy Ellis from Studio ENP, proofreading by my writing bestie Zoe Ashwood, and teaser graphics by my other bestie Elle Thorpe at Images for Authors. You all rock.

Go ahead and get on with Ally's story now!

Jolie x

ALSO BY JOLIE VINES

Marry the Scot reading order

1) Storm the Castle

2) Love Most, Say Least

3) Hero

4) Picture This

5) Oh Baby

Standalones:

Race You: An Office-Based Enemies-to-Lovers Romance

Visit and follow my Amazon page for all new releases amazon.
com/author/jolievines

Add yourself to my insider list to make sure you don't miss my
publishing news https://www.jolievines.com/newsletter

SNEAK PEEK - RACE YOU: AN OFFICE-BASED ENEMIES-TO-LOVERS ROMANCE

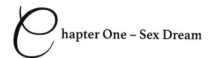

*C*hapter One – Sex Dream

*E*mma

Last night, I had a sex dream about Arnie. Again.

For the whole of the Tube journey into work, my cheeks burned, the memories fresh, *hot,* and traumatising, and I slunk into the office like all my tech worker colleagues could tell my dirty secret. At my desk, I kept my head down, setting up to start the day. Absolutely not glancing to the right where the blond devil lurked behind aisle dividers and computer screens.

Across the floor, Mr Sweeny, the boss, approached the avocado-shaped swing chairs, deep in conversation with someone I couldn't see. He wasn't looking my way, so I screwed my eyes closed.

My body was tight with need, and I had a ten-hour shift ahead of me, same as Arnie did. No let up from the smirking, lounging idiot whom, for some bizarre reason, my subconscious had picked as the object of all its sexual fantasies.

I was hard up—that was obvious. But Arnie?

Behind my closed lids, the dream replayed. His bold hands had been all over me. Our bodies clashing, kisses raining down hard as we'd tried to best the other in giving and seeking pleasure. Chasing good feelings, gripping, sliding. *Laughing.*

I'd never laughed with anyone during sex.

A fresh wave of heat flooded me, and my jagged sigh became lost in the busy background chatter of my colleagues at Frugal Enterprises. Phones rang, messages bleeped, keys tapped, and my case queue was only getting bigger. I needed to get it together. Keeping this job was vital, and I wasn't about to let a stupid dream derail my performance. I had to find my way back into Mr Sweeny's good books.

"Sweetie? Are you hyperventilating?"

I raised my hot head at Lily's voice.

She peered at me from her desk, her kohl-rimmed eyes concerned through her glasses. Then her lips curled. "Oh, Emma. Not another one?"

"Maybe?" I'd confided in Lily last week after the same dream had haunted me two blistering nights in a row. My friend thought it hilarious. "Is that weird?"

"Totally." She exhaled happily. "Once is enough to tell you what you really want, but three times is practically an intervention."

"That's ridiculous."

"Nuh-uh. Your body has a message for you, and you ought to pay attention."

Lily folded her tattoo-sleeved arms, and I absently

rubbed my own bare wrist. Against my friend, I was plain. Or maybe that was the case against most people. Neat, smartly dressed, hard-working Emma; nothing more, and hopefully nothing less.

"There is only one way to stop having sex dreams about a person," Lily continued. "Grab the bull by the horns and bone them."

"Who's having sex dreams?"

The low, masculine, and humorous voice at my back had me snapping upright, my stomach dropping like a stone. No. Oh god, no.

"Hey, Arnie." Lily grinned and tilted her head, focusing over my shoulder.

I didn't need my friend to ID our visitor. I could sense the man like my spine had an idiot-detector installed.

Okay, damage control. He had no idea what we were talking about. I tiptoed my office chair around. Slowly. Putting on my game face.

"Can I help you?" I faked a polite smile. I might not be able to help my thumping heart or my burning cheeks, but Arnie Montrose could never find out about my dreams. Not if they were the last words my lips could utter to save my life. Not if I was on a sinking ship and that phrase was the password to launch the lifeboat.

"Sure, you can." He rested his forearms on the sturdy green panel that divided my office space from the aisle, then looked me over, a typical cocksure expression plastered all over his handsome face.

Yeah, handsome. I had standards, but I wasn't blind.

"I sent a job through to your queue, but it's one of my favourite customers, so can you bump her up the priority?"

"You couldn't Ping me?" Ping was our office messaging

system. I'd set up a tone especially for Arnie so I could ignore his messages first.

"I could, but then I wouldn't get to hear all the exciting news from the bug fix team."

His brown eyes left me and sought Lily. She was as bad a gossip as him, but she'd never—

"Emma dreamt about you," Lily chirped.

What?

I spun in my seat, catching the delighted look developing on Arnie's face.

Lily's grin was the size of the M25 motorway that circled London.

"What?" she mouthed at me. "Bull. Horns."

"Fix it," I mouthed back, pleading her with my eyes. Arnie's scent crept under my nose. God, he smelled good— manly and mouth-watering and *sickening*.

Lily huffed in defeat then smiled again at Arnie. "Kidding. It was my dream. I was dreaming about you all night, baby. The things you can do. So talented."

"Aw, that's sweet. Is the whole of the bug fix team wild for me? I need to buy more of this aftershave."

I squeezed my eyes tight shut then opened them again. "It was a film," I spluttered, twisting back. I was the worst liar. Well, maybe not as bad as Lily.

"A film?"

"We were talking about a movie. If you stop distracting me, I'll find that case. I'll Ping when it's done. No need to come back." I gave him a smart, professional smile, at odds with the way my toes curled in my sandals.

Arnie pushed his long body upright, his fingertips braced on the divider. His quizzical gaze darkened and he pursed his lips. There was a pause, and my brain cells scattered. I couldn't read his expression at all, though magnetism came off the guy in waves.

Like a small boat in the wake of a destroyer, I bobbed nearer.

"Well, you owe me one, so we'll call it quits," Arnie said.

"Since when do I owe you anything?"

He shook his head, then turned and walked away, calling over his shoulder, "After everything we did last night? I'm exhausted. You're so demanding in the sack, Worthington."

My mouth gaped open fish-style as he vaulted the divide to his own desk. If I tried that, I'd fall flat on my face over the flimsy board. Then he dropped into his chair and nestled his headset among his thick blond curls. He greeted his next caller with his arms behind his neck. The pose, coupled with his rolled-up shirt sleeves, showed a hint of defined biceps I didn't know he had, and I let my gaze relax and blur.

In my dreams he had a great body, but I couldn't picture Arnie going to a gym. He was laziness personified. What was it about him that pushed my buttons so badly? He made me bristle, and I wanted to prove how I was better than him at everything we could possibly compete at. My competitive streak became a hyperactive kid in the playground where that man was concerned.

"You're drooling."

"Bad friend." I twisted back and gave Lily my best frown.

She beamed, undaunted. "No, I'm a good friend. You need to get laid, and he'd be great at it. Why don't you give him a go?"

"Him?" I scrunched up my nose. "But he's so..."

"He's good-looking, for a guy, and I know someone he's slept with who said he's a rock star in bed. She's still talking to him after. Plus, he's into you, no doubt."

I'd heard the rumours, too. Arnie left a trail of ex-*friends* behind him like well-serviced happy customers. Five-star ratings and glowing reviews.

Not that I was paying attention to who he slept with.

"Nuh-uh, no way. We hate each other."

"Why?"

So many reasons, but I could never tell her the main one. The event that ruined my first day in the office and set up me up to fail in this job before I'd even started.

I counted the lesser crimes off on my fingers, my silver ring glinting in the office lights. "He's irritating. The boss loves him, though he flaunts all the company policies. The rest of us work our backsides off for zero recognition. He has everyone eating out of the palm of his hand—"

"And you'd rather have him eating out something else?"

"Lily! Would you keep your voice down?"

Lily's loud snort-snicker had heads turning, and Mr Sweeney squinted our way, adjusting his inelegant position in the swing chair. I ducked my head and got to work, finding Arnie's case midway through my list of unchallenging work. It was an easy coding fix the customer probably could've done themselves, but that was why we were here. To provide and support websites for our clients. With my degree in Computing for Industry, this was a cakewalk.

It was also impossible to find a way to shine in this job. And I needed to. Badly.

"This conversation is over," I hissed to a still grinning Lily, and I worked through the broken website to make my repairs.

Finished, I checked the client, curious about who Arnie's favourite customer was. 'Doris Banks' the field read, and the site was a knitting blog, an older lady smiling cheerily from her profile picture.

I blinked. Arnie had a sweet side? There I was, thinking he was all trust fund and dirty-blond hair.

I fired off the case-closed prompt so Arnie would know the work was done. His Ping tone sounded as he sent me back a thumbs-up emoji, and I hid the chat box then selected my next job to work on. But halfway through reading the customer's complaint, I stalled, waiting on something. The thumbs-up bugged me. Too easy?

Once, when I'd spilled coffee all over my desk, a roll of paper towels had magically appeared, taunting me for my clumsiness. Another time, when Mr Sweeny made a speech at the front of the room about juice diets being great for weight loss, I'd snorted at Lily mime-eating a range of invisible foods. The boss had fixed his gaze on red-faced me, lecturing about the perils of sugar for a solid five minutes after.

Arnie left me a KitKat, square in the middle of my keyboard. No one saw him do it, but I knew it was him.

He took every opportunity to make me feel stupid. But so far, on today's mishap...nothing. Maybe he wouldn't tease me on this. What would he get—

Ping! The tone sounded again, and I unhid the chat with a wince. A picture of the moon appeared in the chat window, along with a winking face. *The moon?* I tapped my lip with my pen, staring at the screen.

Oh, bedtime? I slammed the mouse button to exit the chat and sat up in my chair, my stomach performing a funny sort of twist. Ready with a visual takedown, I glared across the aisle, but Arnie wasn't looking. Still, a smirk pulled at his lips, and I wanted to throttle both him and Lily.

At the top of the room, Mr Sweeny clambered out of the swinging chair, finishing his meeting. The woman with him hadn't sat down and, as she turned, her heavily pregnant belly strained at her floral dress. I frowned at the poor choice of meeting location—had he expected her to climb on the swing?—and tried to place her.

Ah, Henrietta Blume. She worked in Frugal's sister office the other side of London. I hadn't heard she was expecting. A fizz of excitement on her behalf went through me, though you could fit what I knew about babies and pregnancy in a single Twitter update.

Except...

My mind whirred, and my interest stepped up a level. She'd have to give up work soon, wouldn't she? That meant she'd need maternity cover.

Opportunity flashed in bright lights in front of my eyes.

When I'd joined Frugal, almost six months ago, it was on a risk-filled temporary contract. I'd broken my heart leaving Litmus Holdings—the company I'd joined from university. I'd loved it there, and Chelsea, the operations manager, became my closest friend and the sister I'd never had.

Litmus couldn't offer me the Digital Designer job I wanted, and Frugal had hinted they'd be hiring that exact role soon after, so I'd taken the risk and jumped ship. Plus, they offered plenty of overtime so I could earn enough for the crazy rental prices in London.

It was probably a good thing my dream job hadn't arisen yet. After the incident on my first day, I needed to score some serious points if I was ever going to get back into the boss's favour. I squirmed in my seat, recalling the mortification.

The broken lock on the bathroom. The method to unstick it given to me by a certain blond trickster. The door sliding open, Mr Sweeny, on the toilet, his eyes wide in horror...

The boss had never raised it, but he also never spoke to me if he could avoid it.

Nor had he mentioned extending my temporary contract past my end date of just over a month's time. As things stood, I'd be unemployed after the summer.

Glancing away from Henrietta, who was pressing both hands to her lower back as Mr Sweeny talked at her, I carried out a quick search on her job title. My heart sped up. She *was* a designer.

A designer who was about to leave her job to have her baby.

Our basement office received no natural light on the fake brick pillars and trendy blown-up celebrity photography, but I swore a beam shone down on me. That job was mine. It had to be. I'd earned it with all the long shifts I pulled and the way I diligently supported the company, even if their policies were weird.

It would mean compromises, working in the sister office, near one person in particular I never wanted to see again, but I wanted this promotion. Needed it.

I hugged myself. There would be competition, but I was the most experienced person here. I had this. All I needed to do was be ready for the announcement and look smart and promotion-worthy before then.

I tracked the boss and Henrietta as they started down the aisle that separated my team from Arnie's. My shoulders back, I struck at my keyboard like I was saving the world with my coding fixes.

They both waved, passing Arnie at his desk, and I allowed a slight turn of my head to watch better. Arnie saluted and continued with his telephone call, his stupid, sexy grin never leaving his face.

Then Mr Sweeny leaned in and *patted Arnie Montrose on the shoulder.*

My breath caught in my lungs, and in a rush, I saw my problem. Arnie wasn't qualified, but with his popularity he could steal the opportunity right out from under me.

The one guy who hated me, who teased and tormented me, held the power of my future in his casual grip, and I knew without a shadow of a doubt he'd steal my dreams from under me. Just like on my first day, he'd laugh as he walked away.

*C*hapter Two – Cake Crumbs

*A*rnie

Big Ed shoved his phone in my face, separating my mouth from the blueberry and dark chocolate muffin I'd liberated from the secret stash. Whoever snuck cakes in the kitchen each day at five was my hero. It was a kick in the nuts to the company's stupid healthy-food-healthy-worker policy, but the baker only enacted their sugary protest after Sweeny went home, showing it was for their colleagues alone.

If I ever caught them at it, I'd kiss them right on their sweet lips.

"Read the messages and tell me where I'm messing up," Big Ed insisted and stuck out his bottom lip in a peculiar sort of sad face.

I took the phone gingerly—who knew when he'd last cleaned the thing—and scanned the dating app messages between him and Kaylie_97.

Pure car-crash reading scrolled before my eyes. I liked Big Ed, but he was clueless when it came to the opposite sex. The messages he sent me throughout the day were perverted enough, and entirely not safe for work. I'd get a picture of a cute dog with the line *Open for a surprise!* When I'd open it, there'd be some guy's penis and hairy balls pasted in the frame.

Every. Time.

What he'd written to his online matches wasn't much better. "For a start, you mentioned your dick in the first conversation, then you called her 'girl' when she's a woman."

"That's a rule?"

I slid the phone back and rubbed my fingers on my jeans under the cover of my desk. I wasn't a germaphobe, but a guy had to have standards.

"Dude, she tells you that right there on the screen. It's disrespectful."

Big Ed's thick black eyebrows merged as he reread the lines. "Oh. Right. No calling chicks girls, and lead in slowly to the dong chat. That sucks as it's pretty much my only asset." He gestured up and down his enormous body. "Anything else?"

"You're really going with 'chicks' instead?"

"Bitches?" He winked, and I let out a long sigh.

How had the late shift turned into me giving Ed Sully a dating lesson? I pushed my half-eaten cake back and planted my elbows on the table, rubbing my eyes. It was quiet on the phones now. Most people called us in the morning or over lunch when our US customers woke and found their sites down.

Emma wasn't in her seat, so there was nothing for me to do.

I humoured him. "Be a normal human. Women aren't a separate species. Someone will want what you want if you're honest about it."

He leaned in, his gaze earnest. "Yeah, fine. I *want* a girlfriend, but I *need* to get laid. You get sex all the time. Help me."

I cringed and took a quick glance over my shoulder. Big Ed made me sound like a player, and that was the last thing I wanted anyone to think. Well, it was the last thing I wanted one person in particular to think.

"I don't get sex all the time," I hissed.

"You nailed that girl, I mean woman, at the office drinks party the other month. What was her name? The sales rep with the blonde hair to her arse? You tapping that on the regular?"

"Would you keep your voice down? Her name's Diana." I liked Diana. As a rule, my hook-ups followed an upfront, honest exchange. Just me and them blowing off steam. That was all I could offer, and it worked just fine. All the fun with no one getting hurt. That last part was important to me.

Crucial, in fact.

"Bummer. Did you keep it quiet because she ditched you?" He scanned the open-plan office, taking in the scattered late shift workers in their little pools of light. "Or is it because you've got your eye on someone here? Maybe I do, too."

I pressed my lips firmly closed, but Big Ed's eyes turned evil. He grinned and bared his teeth, looking less wolf-like than I guessed he imagined, and more like Donkey from *Shrek*. "Scared of a little competition?"

My shrug only sharpened his gaze. I wasn't about to tell him my deepest, most concealed thoughts, even if they'd never come true. My phone warbled, and I hit the grace-saving button to answer the call, relieved to turn away from offensively large, waggling eyebrows. As I gave my standard greeting, Emma returned to her seat across the aisle, and something inside me settled.

"Oh, Arnie dear, it's Doll. I'm so glad I got you. I did it again," a trilling voice hailed me, interrupting my opening spiel.

"Doll? Didn't we just fix your site this morning? How did it break itself this time?"

Doris, or Doll, as she'd asked me to call her, my favourite customer, chatted away in my ear, and I smiled, reclining back in my chair. If I had a soft spot, and I had a few, it was for sweet, older ladies. Grandmotherly types, though nothing like my grandmother. I shuddered at the thought and clicked through to the website where Doris ran her knitting group. Her friends met at seven in her forum, and it was six-thirty now.

"Give me a second and I'll get this done for you," I promised, scanning the mess on the screen. Her home page had vanished, and her forum was locked.

Usually, I'd send the job Emma's way, just for the pleasure of getting one of her glares. Well, not only that. It was company policy for the customer contact team to only handle the calls, then pass the jobs on, so it looked like what we did was complex and worth the money customers paid for their support plan. But even I could fix this.

Besides, Emma looked stressed tonight. She tapped her pen against her mouth in that maddening way which had me wishing I'd been born a piece of stationery.

I wanted her back in the mood where I could mess with her. The only way I got to see the real Emma was to antagonise the shit out of her. When we argued, the mask she wore at work came down and I saw the real heart of the woman.

Over the months, I'd become addicted to that sight.

My basic repair to Doris's site paused as the system froze up and did its thing, so my mind drifted to Lily's words from earlier. The images they'd created went straight to my dick. If Emma really had a sex dream about me, which is what I'd concluded, I'd never get away from the thought of her writhing in her bed, thinking about me.

Fuuuck. That image carried a maximum heat level warning.

Had she touched herself? Made herself come? What had she imagined us doing? The screen blinked in front of me, unfreezing, and I swallowed hard and forced myself to focus, taking a deep breath before I clicked back into my call.

"Hey, Doll? It's done. You went into edit mode again and moved the pages around, that's all. Tell you what, next time you want to change something, give me a call, and I'll talk you through it."

My pulse calmed, and I listened to Doris's thanks and promises not to mess her site up again. I mean, it was her site, but the company configured things strangely, so no wonder our customers got confused.

I hung up the call and stole another peek at Emma. She'd fetched herself one of the muffins our office mutineer had left us. So, Emma was a rebel, too. Eating the poisonous sugar Sweeny lectured us about.

"You totally could've upsold that caller."

Big Ed kicked my chair, and I spun around.

"Why would I want to?"

"To make money, of course. That's your job, lover man."

"See." I grabbed my cake and took a bite. It was the nicest muffin I'd ever eaten. Tasty to the moon and back, and the blueberries were little bursts of flavour. "That isn't how I view it. If I make customers happy, that's got to be good for everyone."

Doris didn't need a more expensive service, and I'd have felt bad if I'd wasted her money. She sold pieces of knitting on the side, so I doubted she had the cash to spare.

"You could sell that old bird the premium package without breaking a sweat. How is it you're so popular with the boss? I make a bundle every month, and he never pats me on the back."

Ed threw his massive hands up, but his own phone rang, and he turned away with a grumble. I pulled a face at his back. I was popular because I was a nice guy. Everyone liked a nice guy, and Sweeny loved me, proving the point that sales weren't everything.

My mind returned to Big Ed's tease from a minute ago. Did he really have his eye on someone in the office? If so, who? And would they like him?

Ed had five or six inches of height on me. He wasn't bad-looking, and the Lurch thing worked for some people. At five-eleven, I wasn't the tallest guy in the world, but I wasn't short either. I liked my proportions. When I'd stood next to Emma in the hall last week, her head would've rested perfectly against my chest, right under my shoulder, had she chosen to lay it on me.

I mean, she hadn't, and she never would, but a guy could imagine.

Picking at the last few crumbs of my cake, I let myself drift. Would things be different if I didn't have a plane ticket burning a hole in my pocket? If the end of my time in London, at this job, wasn't approaching fast?

I squinted at the calendar on my screen and counted the weeks left until the end of the summer. So soon? In my distraction, I inhaled the cake crumbs.

My throat seized up from more than the shock of the date.

"Shit." I choked and pitched forward, thrusting my chair back on its wheels as I bent over my knees. I coughed and hacked, trying to breathe while my throat spasmed.

At the next desk, Big Ed glared at me, pressing his headset harder against his ear.

"Sorry," I wheezed and stifled my barking cough with my hand against my mouth. Bracing myself, I turned to hang over the aisle divider.

"Are you okay?" Emma peered at me from the aisle. She had her bag over her shoulder and a floaty blue scarf thing wrapped around her neck.

I froze. This was breaking protocol. We didn't talk nice.

I scrambled upright and wiped my eyes. Of course, she had to come over when I was a mess from my coughing fit. Whoever made those damn cakes had something to answer for.

Maybe I wouldn't kiss them after all.

"Fine," I rasped. "I'm good. Cake tried to kill me."

"Right." With a look I could almost mistake as concern, if Emma hadn't made it clear she hated my guts, she turned on the heel of her sandal and took off towards the exit.

My cue to leave.

In ten seconds flat, I logged off, powered down my machine, and flicked my screens to black. Then I grabbed my phone and wallet from my desk.

"See ya, don't be a douchebag," I called to Big Ed and took off after Emma.

***

I caught up with her at the entrance to the Tube station. She glanced over her shoulder as she bounced down the concrete steps and then pointedly looked away. At the platform, I kept my distance, but every time her gaze found mine, I awarded myself a point.

Honestly? It was my favourite part of the day. Just the two of us, in the middle of a crowd of bustling strangers, sharing our unspoken routine.

I mean, Emma had no idea why I was here. At least I didn't think she did. As far as she knew, I happened to get the same train. But that had never been true.

The 19:12 slid to a whining halt in front of us, bringing a hot breeze that had the ends of Emma's wavy auburn hair dancing, and we climbed on board. Via different doors, naturally.

At Emma's stop, I exited then strolled ahead along the warm city streets, checking every now and again in the shop window reflections that she hadn't lost sight of me. By the time we reached the delight that was Brixton's Penholme Street, with its boarded-up block of murder flats at one end and the halfway house for drug addicts at the other, Emma was right behind me.

"Stalking me again, Worthington?" I swung around and walked a few steps backward. My CrapMobile was where I'd left it this morning, demanding that I acknowledged the gods for another day of it not being jacked. Like anyone would want that heap of junk.

"In your dreams, Montrose," she retorted, looking both ways before she stepped into the road.

"Don't you mean in *your* dreams?" I quipped back, and my heart slammed into my chest. Normally she walked away without a word.

Tease me. Take me on.

Emma paused mid-step, and her mouth dropped open as if she wanted to deny or hopefully explain more about this new element to our interactions. The prettiest shade of pink flooded her cheeks before she put her head down and darted away.

I waited, tracking her while she made her way up the incline of the road to the front door of the old chapel building. As always, I made sure to watch the big wooden door close tight behind her, then I climbed into my car and took off.

Emma was safe, and my evening waited. Her alleged sex dream had me thinking far too much about her in ways she wouldn't appreciate, and Ed talking about me getting laid had highlighted how it'd been a while. Maybe I needed a night out.

Ugh. I squirmed in my seat. No, I didn't fancy it for some reason.

At the junction with the high street, a guy lurched into the road, and I jammed on the brakes. The car shuddered around me, a screech marking our halt. The man glared, and I made a sarcastic *after you* hand gesture, my other hand clutched to my chest over my speeding heart.

The man slammed both hands on my bonnet, his face twisted in a snarl. "Fuck you," he mouthed, his lips slack in his slur. Under his jacket, the hilt of a knife stuck out. My blood froze as he glanced in the direction of it and grinned, half his teeth missing. Then he swayed back upright, flipped me off, and continued on his merry way.

Fucking hell. This was why I did what I did. Right there. That dude. The area was a shitty place to walk alone at night. Or in the summer in broad daylight. Not for me, I didn't care about myself.

Come autumn, Emma would be walking home alone from the late shift in the dark.

I hated that.

My road ahead now clear of local junkie vagrants, I

squared my shoulders against my seat and accelerated away through the narrow streets. The same argument batted back and forth in my mind. *But you won't be here. And she isn't yours to protect anyway.*

Even so, a small piece of me sat wrong with the whole plan.

A buzzing in my pocket pulled me out of my thoughts, and I grabbed my hands-free and took the call. "Hello?"

"Hey!"

"Frankie?" I frowned, changing gears and merging onto the dual carriageway that took me home to Knightsbridge.

"You're still living in the same place in London, the one that Dad found for you, right?"

"Yeah, why?"

My sister's sigh was heavier than the London buses that menaced the drivers in this city. I knew that sigh. Our family had caused me to make it many times when I was a teenager. Before I learned the importance of responsibility.

"Uh-oh," I said. "What did they do this time?"

"If I had a Euro to tell you every little thing they did that drove me bonkers, I'd be a rich girl."

"You are a rich girl."

"A richer girl, then. Whatever."

I grimaced, checking my mirrors before I overtook a couple of slower cars. "Did Mum send you to Nonna Bianca?"

The name of our maternal grandmother had my tongue wanting to curl up and die. I pictured my little sister with her messy mop of blonde hair being sent *there* and I shuddered. Frankie wasn't a kid anymore, but I couldn't quite see her as an adult yet. Even if she waffled on about boyfriends and her plans for university on our fortnightly phone calls.

"No. I haven't done anything wrong. Not yet anyway..."

"Spill. If you need my help, I can get a plane and be there tonight. Just say the word."

A tad dramatic, I knew that, but I'd been worrying about Emma, and I really would go to the ends of the earth for my sister. I owed her. Our family's home in Italy was only a few hours away by plane and taxi. Not that I'd been there in a while.

"No, no, Arnie. Don't go nutso. I'm just checking in. Look, I'm fine, and I've got to go. We'll speak again soon, all right?" With that, my sister hung up on me.

I ground my teeth as I settled in for the thirty-minute drive. Everything I was doing was for a good reason, and Frankie's weird phone call only cemented that further in my head.

And yet...

Glimpses of the burnished evening sun sparkling off the Thames had my fingers itching for the paints and canvases I'd put into storage. Or a set of watercolour pencils. Spray paint cans. Anything to capture the colour that so closely matched the highlights that shone bright in Emma's hair. But I'd set aside that part of me, the skills I'd perfected at art college, and it was out of the question releasing it again.

In that second, I knew which part of sticking to my plan I'd regret the most.

I'd just driven away from walking her home.

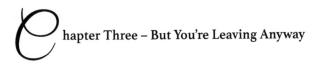

hapter Three – But You're Leaving Anyway

. . .

*A*rnie

My tenth caller of the morning had chewed my ear off for fifteen minutes straight already, and to be fair, I didn't blame him. His online t-shirt printing shop had gone wonky, and his orders were missing.

Rant o'clock.

We had every ilk of caller on Frugal's customer services line. Most were factual and friendly, but some, like Mr Hemmingway, were angry jerks. Or in Frugal's terms, *needing extra special care.*

I had my own reasons for enjoying the call. Mr Hemmingway's rant gave me the perfect opportunity to play my favourite pastime with Emma. I called it Race You. Whether she considered it a sport or not I had no clue, but she joined in the fun all the same.

In Race You, I'd write up the case while talking to the customer, issue it to Emma's queue, then watch her ears prick up as it *bing-bonged* onto her machine. She'd slide me a look to see if I was still on the call, then her gaze pixel-fixed and her fingers flew as she raced to fix the problem before I hung up.

Beautifully simple. Who could finish first: me pacifying a difficult caller, or Emma with her lightning-fast coding skills.

As Mr Hemmingway appeared in no way done with describing Frugal's vast incompetence, Emma would nail this one.

I sent the case and snuck a surreptitious look. Her head snapped up. We locked gazes across the aisle, and I cocked an eyebrow. Emma's stormy grey eyes darkened: game on.

"You're absolutely right, sir," I mollified, stretching my

legs out under my desk. "Now if you'll let me get started on the repair…"

Not that I would ever attempt to fix this mess—it was way above my abilities, I was an artist, *no*, not anymore. Now, I was a lawyer in the making, not a techie—but I said it for Emma's benefit and just loud enough for her to hear. From where I sat, I couldn't see her screen, but I could see her expression and the rapid movements of her hands.

She was delightfully on form today.

"If there was any way I could've done this myself without involving you bunch of muppets," Mr H continued, "I would have. But you don't make it easy, do you? Oh no, the code is hidden, and it's non-standard, so it forces me to have to waste my time and money—"

I zoned out and settled into making automatic *uh-huh* and *hmm* sounds while I watched Emma work. I had absolute, if slightly bored, sympathy for my customer, but he couldn't compete with a hot woman doing something she was great at.

With her mouth slightly open, Emma scanned her screen like she was interpreting the Matrix. She was the smartest woman I'd ever met, and it turned me on like a neon sign over my head screamed *hot for you*. Since she'd joined Frugal, I'd watched her perform fixes Sweeny had previously hired expensive contractors to do, and I had no idea why she hadn't been promoted yet. She should be running the bug fix team. In fact, she could be running the whole development section.

Her trusty pen—which she had no real use for that I could tell—was tucked in behind her ear, holding back her hair. Hair I'd imagined time and time again tangling in my fingers. It was the prettiest colour, like the English autumn I wouldn't see after I left this country's shores. It fell to her shoulders in waves.

I liked that she left it natural. Or maybe it took her hours to perfect each morning—I was a guy, what the hell did I know? My gaze continued to wander. Today she'd tucked her deep yellow blouse into a flowing skirt. The colour was a rich cadmium—shit, why couldn't I get away from thinking in paint colours? I blinked the thought away and refocused on Emma. Occasionally she'd choose shirts that exposed a small sliver of skin at her belly when she took off her outer layers, or if she threw her arms back in a yawn.

Those were the days my concentration slipped the most.

Every day, Emma knocked me out.

She also drove me nuts in ways that had me grinding my teeth until my jaw ached. Like how much she respected Frugal's dumb rules. I once overheard her admiring the office chairs that hung on chains from the ceiling. They turned adults into overgrown children.

Have you ever seen an executive in a five hundred quid suit swinging her legs out mid-conversation like she's in a playground? Stupidest thing I ever saw. And don't get me started on the ethical workplace claims the company made. It was a trendy front designed to impress. The super low carbon footprint? Sweeny had flown to Florida three times already this year to play golf at the same resorts my dad visited, and no doubt racking up the same air miles. The recycled rainwater from the roof used to flush the toilets? Yeah, great, but what about the mountain spring water they imported by the crate for shareholder meetings?

It bugged me that Emma bought into it, and I wanted to argue about that with her, too. Bait her. Let her convince me, or the other way around, preferably with us getting into a big argument that led to us kissing to make up after.

Oh hell, kissing Emma... I could not think about that. Nope. Imagining her red lips on mine was banned unless I was in the safety of my apartment with my door lock firmly engaged.

Not that I'd let myself go *there* too often.

That slippery slope only led to pining for something I could never have.

Emma slid the pen free and tapped it on her lip, then sat up. My time had run out. She was working through the last part of the problem. I had to hustle for this to look like a genuine competition.

"Mr Hemmingway," I quietly interjected into the ongoing tirade in my ear. I had five, four, three... "I'd like to apologise again for the inconvenience you've experienced, but if you'd care to refresh your browser, I think you'll find—"

Emma punched the air.

"It's back!" my caller exclaimed. "My orders...they're all here."

I ended the call with my usual courtesy, all the while taking in Emma's triumphant expression. My chest expanded as she high-fived Lily, and I exhaled as she fell back in her seat and swung her limbs out. Then she rolled a heavy-lidded victory gaze my way. I dropped my own grin before she noticed and absorbed the loss with a shrug. *Look at me over here, so rueful and beaten.*

I let her win just over half the time. And I knew she kept score.

Emma kept the staring match going for a second longer than usual, and my hidden glee flipped to something else. Warmer. Darker. She rolled her pen between two fingers, bit her lip, then turned back to her work.

She had to feel the spark. The tension between us couldn't be completely one-sided.

I knew she didn't have a boyfriend; she'd told Lily when she'd joined Frugal about being dumped by her ex shortly before. What a jerk-off he must be.

Sweeny swaggered his way into the office, Henri at his side. She was here to discuss her maternity leave and fit to pop with her baby. I'd seen her in the hall yesterday and told her she looked gorgeous and glowing, and the woman had clutched me to her side in an awkward squeeze and started to cry.

I'd returned her hug, and she'd called me a sweet boy—accurate—then she'd taken my hand and placed it on her belly. The baby did something, and it was the weirdest, squiggliest feeling. Like a writhing, cute little alien.

I guessed at some point in the future I wanted kids, but in my mid-twenties, that was far from my reality. Besides, who the hell was I to consider looking after another human being? I was a long way from earning that right, whatever steps I was taking now to redeem myself.

The good feeling I'd got from Race You left me in a rush as the gut-wrenching terror of my mistake loomed large in my brain. *Lost. Panicked. Dark night and headlights on the side of the road.*

The words that condemned me.

I gripped the edge of my desk and, with force, willed the memories away.

"Great job you're doing today, Arnie." Sweeny paused in the aisle next to me, his booming voice carrying and pulling my attention back to the present. "Pop your phone offline for a moment now, Ms Blume has an announcement I hope you'll find interesting."

Sweeny strolled around the juice detox bar and on to the

centre of the floor. Henri waddled after him. Across the way, Emma sat bolt upright like she knew what was going on.

Henri clapped, and the office fell silent. "As some of you might know, I'm due to leave in a month, and the company needs cover for my job. I'll be taking a full year out…"

Emma leaned in, rapt. Why was she so interested? My brain supplied the answer slowly, and I sucked in my stomach. She wanted Henri's job?

An uncomfortable sensation curled in my chest. Of course she did, and she'd be amazing at it. But if Emma got that job, she'd have to move office. Our location in Soho was great, but Henri worked at the ass end of Woking—over an hour away. Other than Henri, I didn't know anyone from that office and I had no reason to go there.

But you're leaving anyway.

My logic dried up, and I tried out the image of Emma's seat being occupied by someone else. I'd taken the job in Frugal because I'd had something to prove, but I'd done that and had no real reason to stay anymore. My time was almost up, and I needed to set a date for that flight home. Put stage two of my plan into play.

Except it was still a vague notion, not yet a reality.

I had to give Emma up.

The thought was as pleasant as an electric shock to my balls. Henri talked, describing her job, and Emma nodded along enthusiastically, but I slowly went to pieces.

With weekend overtime, I saw her every day, except Sundays, which sucked as they were no-Emma days. It had come over me slowly, my misplaced addiction to her, but I'd acknowledged it the half-week she'd taken off sick with the flu.

I'd missed her. Horribly. When she'd returned, the relief had legit bulldozer-flattened me, and it forced me to confront my behaviour. I'd been using Emma as a distraction; I was good at that. But knowing it didn't stop my gut from wrenching.

Sweeny's baritone pierced my thoughts and he took over the announcement. "Ms Blume's maternity cover will be offered via a competition. Teams of three people will compete to bring the best innovation idea to the end of summer party. I will judge the competition entries and I'll select the winner from among the team members."

"I fancy that." Big Ed flailed an arm my way, hitting my chair.

"You want the job?" My voice hitched with surprise. Big Ed wasn't a designer; the most he knew about developing websites was choosing his favourite naked selfie for his dating profile.

"No, that girl. I mean woman. Emma Whatsherface. Look at her over there, all perky and excited at this shit. Tits bouncing every time Boss Man says 'promotion'. She's up for it. Chick never leaves this place, and I bet she hasn't been laid in months. This is my in." He snickered and hit my chair again. "What's the odds the red is a dye job? Bet collar and cuffs don't match."

If it had been possible, my entire body would've morphed into a fist.

Was it a crime to involuntarily punch someone? If your mind had no part of it, and it was an instinctual response to extreme provocation? No court in the land would convict me of smacking Big Ed in the face for talking about Emma like that. Even him *thinking* of her like that had me—

"Choose your teammates wisely," Sweeny continued, his eyes focusing on me before moving on. "You'll be reliant on one another to make your idea shine. Remember, you can't enter the competition on your own, and the winner will receive full training. This is a once-in-your-career opportunity."

Emma's gaze darted over the room, and she drummed her fingers like she was considering the possibilities.

People shifted, and small groups formed under the aisle's ludicrous decorative miners' lamps.

"I'm with Emma," Georgie Henley called out.

Sweeny made a note on his iPad. He'd moved to stand near my desk, his back against a pillar.

"You'll need a third," Sweeny commented to the petite blonde who I'd heard compliment Emma's work before. Wise woman.

Big Ed rubbed his hands together. "I'm going for it. If she's on my team we'll have to work late together. Which will involve alcohol. I'll give her a week to get used to me before I mention the big gun, and she won't be able to resist."

A joke. He was joking, right?

He nudged me out of the way and strode his long legs to the end of our divided space. As he rotated the corner, his lust-hungry, skyscraper-high gaze fixed on Emma.

My Emma.

"I'm in." Shit, was that my voice? It was, and I'd stood up abruptly. Faces in the aisle snapped my way. "The third in Emma and Georgie's team. Put my name down."

Sweeny beamed, babbling something and jabbing his finger at the screen. Then he turned to take down the names of the next team shouting for his attention.

"Dude, what the fuck? You cock blocked me," Ed gritted out, returning. He barged my shoulder then stalked away, muttering.

Georgie crossed the aisle wearing a cheerful grin. "This is just super! Marvellous! You know all about the customers,

I know about the staff costs, and Emma knows the techie computery bits. We're going to rock!"

She fist-bumped me. I responded automatically but barely heard her words, Sweeny's praise, or Big Ed's commandeering of another poor soul's team.

I only saw Emma's face. It wasn't the look she'd given me earlier, with victory and glee and her chin held high. No. Now, annoyance crinkled her brow. She tilted her head to one side, and the look that blazed between us lit me up just the same as it burned.

Emma wasn't happy with me. Not one bit. But I'd saved her from a fate as bad as Ed, and she'd thank me if she knew.

 uy Race You now!

ABOUT THE AUTHOR

JOLIE VINES is a romance novelist who lives in the South West of England with her husband and toddler son.

From an early age, Jolie lived in a fantasy world and is never happier than when plot dreaming. Jolie loves her heroes to be one-woman guys. Whether they are a huge Highlander, a touch starved earl, or a brooding pilot, they will adore their loved one until the end of time.

Her favourite pastime is wrecking emotions then making up for it by giving her characters deep and meaningful happy ever afters.

Want to contact Jolie? She loves hearing from her readers. Drop her a line at jolie@jolievines.com, find her on Instagram, and join her Fall Hard Facebook group

Made in the USA
Columbia, SC
06 October 2023